Also By Francine du Plessix Gray:

WORLD WITHOUT END

LOVERS AND TYRANTS

HAWAII: THE SUGAR-COATED FORTRESS

DIVINE DISOBEDIENCE

OCTOBER BLOOD

FRANCINE DU PLESSIX GRAY

BALLANTINE BOOKS • NEW YORK

Library of Congress Catalog Card Number: 85-10885

ISBN 0-345-33683-6

This edition published by arrangement with Simon & Schuster, Inc.

Manufactured in the United States of America

First Ballantine Books Edition: November 1986

For Alice Mayhew

PART I

1958

How could you find me elegant,
if you have noticed me?

—BEAU BRUMMELL

AT HOME

MANY IMPORTANT PEOPLE WERE EXPECTED AT Mother's party on that particular February evening, I was excited. Mother had announced the guest list to me on the telephone a few days before: it would be Coco Chanel's first appearance in New York since she'd gone into exile after the war (well-deserved, I'd quipped, since she'd shacked up with the biggest Nazi kraut in Paris during the occupation). Mother had coolly let that remark slip by, adding that Jacques Fath and Jean Dessés would also be there, and Hubert de Givenchy, all the other bigwigs to whom I'd passed canapés since I was old enough to say *Bonjour*. And I had rushed downtown toward the party from my college room, filled with an immense sense of power, ready to convert assemblies of hundreds to my new vocation as a seer—teaching others how to read the future and work for a better deal in the next life. Mother had asked for my attendance at her gala, I quote, "in whatever adequate mode of dress, Paula dear, your curious new state of mind can summon." So I had devised a turban with several shades of purple gauze and glued a large fake ruby in the middle of my forehead, hardly the getup to thrill my mother's gang.

To say that Mother was fussy about clothes is like saying that Queen Victoria was conscious of etiquette. Mother was editor-in-chief of *Best*, the most influential fashion magazine in America, perhaps in the world. And she looked on this gathering as particularly important because her assistant editor, Babs Hollins, was returning to New York that very day to report on the Paris spring collections. Their future had been made chancy by the recent death of Christian Dior. (He'd died of overeating the previous fall, during a trip that his private fortune-teller—yes!—had warned him not to take.)

My own decision concerning the central role of clairvoyance in human affairs had been made the night before, when I'd lain in bed in my college room, limbs shaking and head pounding with my newfound knowledge—return to the world's most ancient science, explore the truest path of self-knowledge, save yourself by unlocking the secrets of your future in this life and the ones to come! I had raced all the way to the Bronx to share the message with Sala, the Haitian maid who'd brought me up since infancy, who'd trained me early in the wisdoms of palmistry and astrology, who'd taken care of me during the long weeks and months in which Mother was away from home deciding the fate of hems in the Western world. It was to tell Sala about my new calling that I'd run to her the night before Mother's important party. To let her know how much I loved her, I'd put on the heart-shaped diamond locket she'd spent most of her savings on two years earlier for my high school graduation . . .

But as I stood at midnight before the stoop of Sala's walkup flat on 137th Street, I realized that I'd run up there to commune with Sala in spirit only. Sala had died the previous month; I'd read it correctly in her palm since I'd been twelve. So Sala was dead and gone, and Paula had sat down on the stoop of a decrepit Harlem house, crying and singing some songs from Shakespeare plays that Sala had particularly enjoyed: "Tell me where is fancy bred,/ Or in the heart or in the head? . . . With gazing fed; and fancy dies/ In the cradle where it lies. . . ." Due to her arduous training in the dramatic arts, Paula had developed a fine singing voice, strong and clear. Paula's mother had destined her daughter for the stage from an early age, and since she'd been eight Paula had recited bits of Ophelia's, Joan of Arc's, Portia's lines to the clamorous applause of the dressed-up nitwits who attended her mother's parties. And that evening, sitting on the stoop, Paula had used her voice to its utmost lyric power, enjoying the feeling of singing to no one on this earth, singing to a memory, singing only to the dead who were off on their long journeys through millennia of becoming fountains, mountains, giraffes, linden trees . . . "Let us all ring fancy's knell:/ I'll begin it—Ding, dong, bell. . . ."

A few windows opened on Sala's street, a few voices mumbling or shouting obscenities to shut me up. A policeman drove down from his beat on Morningside Heights, and Paula gently spoke the lines from her recently performed Saint Joan: "It's no use, Charlie, thou must face what God put on thee; come, let me see thee sitting on the throne. . . ." But a police car screamed out a block away, and the cop sped off before Paula had finished her message; so far this hadn't been a productive day. I went on singing, more softly this time, offering Sala some very special perfection in my tones. No question of going back to my college room at Barnard that night, there was too much urgent business at hand. I was obsessed with the sheer amount of work that had to be done before the morning was over. The city was asleep, the waiting for dawn most painful, so

I started to walk the hundred blocks from Sala's house to the parlor of Mr. Ashok Modi, the one decent seer I had met since Sala's death. It was just dawn when I arrived. There was a lovely glowing purple globe in the window of his shop on Ninth Avenue which said "Palmistry, Advice, Necromancy." February, but the air so gentle I lay down in a doorway a half block from Mr. Modi's and slept so soundly that by the time I woke up there were already seven customers sitting in Mr. Modi's shop and I had to wait my turn.

The very first time I had gone to see him, Mr. Modi had told me that in my former life I had been a tree. That was just what Sala had always said, so I knew he was my man all right. I had found him one afternoon shortly after Sala's funeral when I'd walked all the way from 125th Street to Times Square, stopping to see every diviner on the way. Most of them were wacky Hispanics who received you in their digs amid unmade beds and dying plants. And after asking five dollars for reading two palms, three dollars for just one, they said things like, "I'll tell you, sweetheart, you've got a beautiful smile but inside it's all solitude, solitude and *mucho* unhappiness, too many people are bad-mouthing you behind your back because they're jealous of you, if you let me be your friend I'll help you, I'll give you a special candle you can light to keep the evil thoughts away. You don't think twenty-five dollars is worth saving your life with my special candle? You're *loca* in the head, sweetheart, *loca*. . . ." I'd seen dozens of those fakes, I was a seer junkie, I knew they were all quacks.

But Mr. Ashok Modi was something else. He was a calm, plump, orderly Hindu who wore a faded blue turban and a false ruby on his forehead and had very smelly feet. He had no interest in becoming anyone's friend, he was solely concerned with the ancient science of the past and the future. The people waiting for him in his parlor weren't so dumb, they knew the real goods, the wisdom of the ages had prevailed. Seven middle-aged citizens with shopping bags impatiently waiting their turn to save their lives. The sheer number of Mr. Modi's clientele pleased me. I had come to help out the master seer, I was ready to read their palms free, *gratis*, to take some of this terrible load of work off his hands. Mr. Modi made his consultations behind a Chagall-blue curtain embroidered with a bright half moon of silver sequins. His voice lilted softly, sibilantly behind the curtain and I longed to set my eyes on him again and tell him my plan.

While waiting my turn I took up a magazine left behind by a previous client and ruffled through it. It was a recent issue of *Best*. "Style has nothing to do with being well-dressed," Mother was saying in her lead editorial. "It is something possessed by certain thoughts and certain animals. Look at gazelles, look at Oscar Wilde." Style, rile, guile, for the past year Mother had told me that I was beginning to dress sloppily and "totally lose my former style." "Nothing more polished, freshly scrubbed than a gazelle," her copy continued, "nothing more honed than one of Wilde's sayings . . ."

An advisee with a large Gimbel's bag came out of Mr. Modi's booth, looking pleased. I had an urge to run in the streets again, preparing for an important afternoon, but I was afraid of losing my place. So I started carefully tearing up each page of *Best* as I waited my turn, glancing to see what words of wisdom Babs Hollins, Mother's assistant editor, was offering in her famous column "Why Not." "Why not just *decide* to be sexually active forever," she'd written this month. "It clears your sinuses and makes you feel so alive." "Why not check yourself out by taking all your clothes off twice a day and staring at yourself in the mirror to see how your body is changing . . ."

I stood up and looked at myself in the mirror of Mr.

Modi's waiting room. I looked just fine. I was wearing torn blue jeans and knee-high cowboy boots and a ten-gallon hat and had a superb grin on my face. I sat down again and tore at the magazine very methodically, folding each page into fourths and eighths, tearing neatly down the crease of an article on Jamaica written by the travel editor of *Best*: "In the hilly cockpit country the night-blooming cereus throws out its thick vanilla perfume and voodoo tom-toms still throb on moonless nights. . . ." I had fun folding some pages into sixteenths so I could scatter about me the individual mouths, eyes, nostrils of Mother's and Babs Hollins' pals. My colleagues in the search for wisdom sat calmly through my performance, absorbed in their salvation; time went by seamlessly as I continued shredding Cee Cee Guest's pleated Grès chiffon, Babe Paley's mutton-sleeved Balenciaga. When Mr. Modi finally let me into his parlor he made a discreet bow over his folded palms which intimated genuine, collegial respect. Sala had been a great teacher; the one time we'd met before I'd read his hand with such accuracy that he'd slumped into his chair murmuring "Stop, miss, stop, my heart is pounding." And after I'd revived him with a glass of water he'd hiccuped softly and had taken me to the door with a whispered plea, "Do not come back again this month, do not come back."

This particular morning, however, the day of Mother's Chanel gala, Mr. Modi seemed delighted to receive me. I could see that he was vastly overworked. There were dark circles around his eyes, the ruby lay half unglued on his sweating forehead. "I am exhausted by this litany of clients," he whispered. "Humanity is growing in its understanding of the ancient wisdoms, but I am bearing the brunt of its infinite enthusiasm. . . ." I promised never to read his hand again, and he looked increasingly pleased as I talked eloquently for a few minutes about how I could ease the brunt of his success. We struck a bargain. I would take two or three advisees an hour—whatever overflow he had—and only receive one-fourth of the regular fee; he would pocket the rest. "My heart cracks with joy, Miss Fitzsimmons." Our pact was sealed over a glass of the sweet tea he kept constantly boiling in a corner of his booth, and I promised to return the following day, properly attired for working in his parlor.

It was twelve noon when I left Mr. Modi, and there were only a few hours left to prepare a revolutionary toilette for the afternoon gathering, at which I'd decided to rehearse a costume fitting to my new vocation. I hastened to the Village and shopped all day to find an orange blouse and wide white skirt, made in India of course, exuberantly embroidered with the many kinds of merry beasts—elephants, monkeys swinging from trees—which Mother's guests might turn into in their next life. I decided that red was the only right hair color for seers. Not having the time for a professional change, I returned to my college room and rinsed my hair with several bottles of mouthwash, which left a curious streaked pattern of bright orange stripes. I looked at myself in the mirror and still found myself too conventional. I subwayed back to Times Square to find interesting colors with which to paint my bodily surface— bright emerald green for nails, dark brown pancake for cheeks, red dye for the large red spot that was essential to my forehead. I devised a turban with several shades of purple gauze that emulated the melancholy sweep of Mr. Modi's headdress. Into my school bag I stuffed sheaves of stationery on which I planned to entice Mother's acquaintances to Mr. Modi's parlor; and thus attired I went uptown to attend that important party.

I NEEDED TO SURVEY THE SCENE CAREFULLY BEFORE I made my appearance, in order to time my entrance with the greatest possible effect. Mother's living room—walls and ceilings of lacquered black, all furniture custom-de-signed in white lacquer—was on the ground floor of a townhouse in the East Sixties. I stood outside the front door at an angle to the window to study the company. Mother—the famous Nada Fitzsimmons—was wearing the same Balenciaga model she'd worn throughout her decade as arbiter of Western fashion. It was a straight, monastic chemise, '49 vintage or so (collarless cardigan neckline, false double hem, single-breasted buttoning down the side). Her hair had turned to silver by the time I was born and tonight it looked particularly crimped and abundant, rising with the authority of a mother superior's over her regal face. Chanel was by her side all right, sharp little hips thrust forward flapper style, her arm nonchalantly slung over Mother's shoulder, the way I'd seen them in photographs of the 1920s. (When Mother worked at *Best*'s office in London, where she was born and brought up, she had played an important role in making Chanel famous; Chanel riding to the hounds wearing all her pearls on a jersey vest, now that is *thrilling*, Nada Fitzsimmons had written in an early edition of *Best*; jewels are only elegant if they're treated as junk . . .)

Anyhow, today Coco the witch wore a straw boater on her head and a navy blue suit with lots of white braiding on it, like an eighteen-year-old apprentice sailor's; her get-up was considerably queerer than mine. A cigarette hung from the corner of her mouth, her mean, wrinkled little face was thrust forward like an old bull about to charge. "France should have a monarchy again," Coco was saying. "We haven't been right since it's been abolished . . . the Jews and the Socialist swine in the thirties, then that brigand de Gaulle allowing Communists and Jews into his government again. . . ." Mother hovered ecstatically over her. The great Chanel is back, Paula darling, and she's certain to recapture center stage in couture since poor

Christian's death, there's no one else who knows so well how to suppress, suppress . . .

Suppress. Oppress. Impress. Finesse. Noblesse. Confess. Loch Ness. Undress. Since I didn't see Babs Hollins in the room yet—she always waited until the last third of the party to make her entrances more theatrical—I decided I'd charge in pretty soon to greet our guests. Sala's nephew, wearing the red turban he reserved to help out at parties, was busy mixing drinks, and I let myself into the house with my key. I straightened my own turban, which tended to fall off to one side, and stood for a moment in the hall to take in the familiar scene. Salvador Dali was spiraling his mustache and only eating caviar canapés. His crystal cane had always been one of my favorite sights at these events. Today he was saying, "I am eating the plump thighs of Napoleon, fifty small goblets filled with lukewarm milk hung on a rocking chair these are my images of the plump thighs of Napoleon, at the age of seven I wanted to be Napoleon and thus I am devouring the past image of myself . . ." Next to him stood Valentina, the dressmaker who drank her vodka straight up and said "Meenk is for football" and used to twitch my chin: "Nada, usually I theenk cheeldren are only for suburbs but thees one ees divine." And of course there was always Elsie Mendl ("She was utterly plain when she was thirty," Mother used to tell me, "but what with long bouts of standing on her head and her devotion to cosmetic surgery she's come into her own as a great beauty at the age of eighty-two . . .").

One of my favorite guests was Elsa Maxwell, who always wore a hat with a veil down to the chin and carried on, saying how she would write about me when I made my debut. She used to scrutinize me with such attention that she often lifted a canapé to her mouth and chewed at it right through the veiling of her hat; the hat slowly descended, smearing her face with cream cheese and sardines, it fell over her eyes and she'd rush to the bathroom, moaning, to wipe the gook off her cheeks. . . . I listened to them all making the familiar din: "Is it true about the Aga Khan?" "Yes, yes, absolutely, he's left his redhead contessa and taken up with a Swedish cabaret girl, the Begum is livid . . ." "How was Gstaad this winter . . . ?" "Don't even mention that word, only place to be seen this year is Courchevel. . . ." "Nada darling, is it really true about Saint-Laurent simply sweeping Paris yesterday?" "Well there are rumors that it was an absolute triumph, Babs is coming any minute to tell us all about it . . ." "I hear he's raised hems to an inch below the knee!" "Could he really be Dior's successor . . ."

What happened in Paris yesterday when Saint-Laurent showed the first collection he'd designed for the hallowed Maison Dior? For a while little else was talked about. "A child of twenty-three ordering us to bare our knees!" Elsa Maxwell thundered. "Dictating tripe to sensible women!" agreed Baron Vincent Von Bulow, *Best*'s travel editor. "That urchin will bring back Dior's boned and corseted dresses," Chanel wheezed, "good for nouveau riche whores . . . let him turn a few hundred women into overstuffed armchairs and I'll dress them decently by the tens of thousands. Vodka, *ma belle*"—she passed her glass to Mother—"your best Stolichnaya—none of that swill you offer to journalists." She flicked her ashes onto Mother's black carpet. "Those pinched-in waists of Dior's, all for titled whores who never pay their bills, that poor boy won't last a season."

"You're quite right, Coco, he mightn't go over, he mightn't sell at all . . ."

Paula standing at the door, a little meditation on selling and success. How many times had I heard it since I'd been toilet-trained. Is the line successful? How's the new line selling? Each issue of Mother's that sold less well than the last would bring thunder from the cold-cereal conglomerate that had recently bought out *Best*. And each of the Seventh Avenue or Paris duds she gave space to in her pages had to sell mighty well in order for the issue to be considered a success. Mother herself was the most monumental success in the world of fashion journalism. Even the *Kansas City* Star admitted that she expressed "the quintessential elegance of our time." There were thousands of beauties all over the United States trying to imitate her style, bleaching their hair platinum, finding little dressmakers to copy her timeless Balenciaga chemise. For years as I'd walked home from school, I'd waved and called out to women walking down Madison Avenue in coiffures and snakeskin shoes and loden coats identical to hers, only to see a total stranger's face peer out at me from under a dome of dyed lunar hair. Mother had generated more successful sales of handbags, hair dyes, cars, china, towels, sheets, mascara, wrinkle creams, resort hotels, than anyone else of her generation. She had created a style that sold. And Paula had to be her best-selling daughter. Slaughter on Seventh Avenue. Daughter for Slaughter. My wares, my bares, my cares, my prayers, my maidenhairs, my *croix de guerres*, my étagères. Am I ever going to sell, I'd asked when I was five. Selling hot, selling short, selling long, selling out, an hourly Dow Jones of the human surface. I wanted out. I wanted to live the slow patience of the turtles, the tree I'd once been. The reason I was about to cop out of being an actress was that it would be too much like Seventh Avenue or avenue Montaigne. On stage I'd be like the newest peplum waist in Paris or this season's Catalina beachwear line. Up for hailing or helling the very night you'd step on the boards. The show would close if you didn't seduce the customers in that one split evening of sales. How did the show go over, sell overnight or you'll be buried forever, Paula thrown in the garbage can at six A.M. after her first Broadway opening. One more point. I wanted to be loved for what I was, for the very small and precious kernel that was myself. I didn't want to be loved for my talent, beauty, manners, anything that had made me charming and irresistible to the jerks and perverts I'd passed canapés to for a decade. I wanted to play a no part they'd never predicted for me, be a no-woman, a nobody. I would strip myself of all my adorable junk and dare my mother to love me in all my new ugliness; she'd worn me like a piece of jewelry for eighteen years and I wanted to see how fast she'd discard me, clink, I was testing the love of the love of my life. This would be the ultimate test, will she still love me now that I've become a howling green-nailed hobo-dy in delirious gypsy's clothes . . .

Enter Paula. Silence. Beautiful, frozen silence. I was so happy I didn't know how long the silence lasted. I was ecstatically enjoying the weight of human eyes upon me, the delicate horror in Mother's gaze.

The veil of Elsa Maxwell's hat was slowly being drawn into her mouth as she continued to chew on her sardine and cream cheese canapé. Dali's glass cane suspended in midair, mustaches thrusting upward like antennae. Vincent Von Bulow had laid one palm dolorously onto his cheek, as if stricken with a terrific toothache. Chanel was the first to break the silence.

"Qui est cette gitane?"

"It's my daughter," Mother whispered.

"Merde alors," Chanel said, "who did you ever fuck to come up with that?"

"It's not our little Paula Pumpkin," Baron Von Bulow whispered. "It's not she, it's something . . ."

"It's the miracle of reincarnation," Dali said with great excitement. "For eleven and half years I have been predicting a miracle of reincarnation in this house and now I have it before me. She is sublime. She is reborn from Queen Mefista the Seventh of the thirteenth century, I have been waiting with impatience . . .''

I wanted to start my new career right then and there. I threw my satchel on top of the bowl of caviar and headed for Coco Chanel and grasped her hand. "You," I said, "I'll start with you. Long lifeline curving down to the base of your thumb, a monumental lifeline. You'll live at least until the age of ninety, you lousy collaborationist. And in perfect health, the health of a perfectly bred bull, which is what you were in your last life.'' Her veined, shaking hand was feeling hot in my palm, a sign of the most accurate readings. "Look at that line running up toward the third finger, line of Apollo, of vocation, success. Don't you dare put down the art of divination, you witch, you were made a millionaire by the fortune-teller who told you that number five was your lucky number. Ever since then you've had everything you've ever wanted, British dukes, Russian emeralds, Jew-hating millionaires, Nazi generals . . .'' I patted the turban firmly onto my head.

" . . . Six months ago," I continued, "a great king passed away and you will become queen in his place. You will remain a ruler until your dying day. You are still to conquer continents. . . . You will conquer Scandinavia, Latin America, Japan . . .''

"Merde alors," Coco croaked through her cigarette ashes. "That kid has something after all."

A circle had gathered about us, Dali's antennae were trembling with excitement, his crystal cane pounded swiftly on the floor. Elsa Maxwell's veil had become a gooey mess of sardines through which she weakly tried to stare. Mother had straightened herself to her fullest height, looking like the lead in *The Dialogue of the Carmelites.* I was about to grab Dali's hand and read it next but damn it, that was the moment Babs Hollins chose to make her entrance.

She was a meticulously underfed woman whose fine-boned little face was plastered with a thick curtain of white powder. Her mouth was a gash of electric pink, her sleek cap of brown hair was touched up with a *soupçon* of boot polish to give it extra sheen and tightness. ("Small heads are *in* this year," she'd written for a recent issue of *Best*.) Along with Baron Von Bulow (Uncle Vincent), Aunt Babs Hollins was part of that triad which Mother had referred to for years as "our Little Family." Babs' son, Nicolas, had been my best friend throughout my early adolescence and had wisely run away from the rest of us when he was sixteen, to join the navy. Babs was known as the most amusing woman in town; only I knew that she was just another of those New York freaks who realized that they were nobodies and feared that they might disappear altogether if they weren't constantly stared at. Her natural manner was to jostle, strut, clatter amid admiring crowds, but this evening she came in very slowly and stood at the entrance of the living room, raising her arm in an oracular gesture; even the little pug dogs she always dragged along with her were quiet for once—she may have drugged them to dramatize her message. She wore a flounce-skirted black taffeta whose hem barely grazed the knee. She didn't even see me in my own new marvelous outfit. She raised her arm very high and proclaimed very slowly: "France . . . is . . . saved . . ."

Brouhaha. Whispers, groans, what *is* she saying.

"Please, Babs darling," Mother said, "make yourself clear."

"I am just . . . off the plane," Babs announced slowly. "Do you realize what happened in Paris yesterday?"

I plunked myself down on Mother's couch. The room was in a state of unprecedented confusion. Stunned guests were leaning against walls, eyes darting from my green and turbaned face to Babs' Delphic gesture, not sure which was the greatest show in town. A triad called the Lopez-Will-shires ("I must take you to the seventeenth-century man-sion of the Baron de Rastignac, Mr. Lopez-Willshire's lover—no, Pumpkin, *his* lover, not hers") were tenderly clutching on to each other in a corner of the room. One of Mother's favorite Rothschilds ("The walls of his Paris drawing room are hung with a silk originally woven for Marie Antoinette, he's busy adding a Gothic chapel to his chateau in Normandy to perform the operas he's commis-sioned") was holding on to two doorknobs for support. The mayhem gave me time to catch my breath and perfect my next few acts.

So I sat there looking at the many photographs of Grand-mother Fitzsimmons which stood in silver frames on the mantelpiece. The life of fashion was not one to which we were newcomers. I had been instructed since infancy about Grandmother's "passionate devotion to the art of cos-tume." When Georgia Fitzsimmons ordered new clothes, one of Worth's or Patou's assistants came to her house in London for fittings—Mother remembered bevies of thim-ble-fingered women hovering about the tall, silver-haired beauty, their mouths full of pins, whispering *"Comme c'est ravissant!"* Grandmother's generosity was legendary, and led to a reputation of great eccentricity: after couture fit-tings her seamstresses received port and cake; sometimes Grandmother put her hand in her pocket and handed them loose amethysts and topazes. . . . Georgia Fitzsimmons had been particularly fussy about her footwear. She owned some two hundred pairs of shoes fashioned of leathers as flexible as silk that were custom-made for her by a curator of the Cluny Museum. And she collected dozens of violins so that her cobbler could turn their light, thin wood into shoetrees for his creations; even with its tree, each shoe weighed no more than an ostrich feather . . .

"Can you understand what happened in *Paris* yesterday?'' Babs was asking, impatiently waving her hand. "Saint-Laurent has saved the French economy . . . our dear France is saved!''

Murmurs of excitement, disapproval, relief. I was quite forgotten.

"How did he pull it off?''

"Is it the Trapeze?''

"Vive la France!"

"Won't sell,'' Chanel muttered.

Babs burst into tears. She stood bawling in the middle of the room, the pugs yapping at her feet again, mascara streaking her cheeks.

"Yves!'' she wept. "Saint-Laurent, a child of twenty-three, a prophet . . . the child in the Temple . . . has been chosen . . . as if by divine election . . . to continue the tradition of our great Christian!''

Most had sat down out of shock. Chanel still slouched disdainfully over her vodka.

"The king's mantle fallen on a child so young . . .'' Babs continued, sobbing, "the beauty of that collection . . . the delicacy, the surprises . . . the Trapeze, *le* look of our time . . . and all black, very black, endless black, like a beautiful mourning . . .''

She wiped her tears, took a swig of the vodka Uncle Vincent had handed her.

"Our dauphin, the Dauphin Saint-Laurent . . . crowds of French citizens gathered beneath the windows of avenue Montaigne . . . ordinary citizens, bakers, plumbers, all shouting for the Dauphin to appear . . . then this ethereal young man coming to the balcony like a king, a king! And the crowds shouting, 'Yves has saved France, Yves has saved us . . .' ''

She finished her vodka in one draught, weeping uncontrollably. And as she drained her glass her eyes rested on me. I was quietly sitting on Mother's black-upholstered

Louis XV chair, missing the signs of Sala, the smells of Sala's cooking. She'd made the world's best meat loaf and given it to me raw off her warm hand, seasoned with onions and green pepper. . . . I stood up and moved toward Mother's black coromandel screen, hoping I could next read Dali's palm.

"Who in the world . . ." Babs stuttered. "Oh, my God, it's our Pumpkin . . ."

"Next thing we know her hands will bleed on Fridays," Chanel quipped, "and swarms of fakirs will be bringing in their burning coals."

"You look like Port Authority Terminal," Babs moaned.

Babs had always been kind to me and lavished me with gifts. I looked at her terrified eyes and detected pain in them and felt a pang of guilt, but it went away very fast. I grabbed a plate of canapés and started passing them to the guests, with the fine little curtsy I'd once used as an exit for my Saint Joan. "We are all subjects of the King of Heaven," I said to Elsa Maxwell. "He gave us our costumes and our language and meant us to keep to them," I said to Chanel, "and you're in great danger of hellfire, so shape up, you lousy Nazi!"

During the fracas that followed I sensed the crowd's eyes riveted on me, their attention stretched like a dark taut line by the magic of my body, the attention I'd enjoyed since my early success on the stage, but this time there was no more love in that dark magic rope, only the great fright of those who dread anything, anyone, not certified as famous, lovely or powerful, only a mayhem of eyes and voices baying at me, pursuing me. . . . I was saying a last farewell to our photographs of Grandmother Fitzsimmons. Besides her interest in costume, horses and music, Grandmother was an authority on the literature of mysticism—she'd attended Annie Besant's meetings, she'd visited mediums about the nightmares that plagued her sleep.

Despite her great and famous beauty some had found her eyes terrifying. They were set above frail, high-pointed cheekbones and were almond-shaped, almost oriental in their slant. George Meredith referred to them as "questing panther eyes," others described them as the eyes of a gypsy, a seer; all that was understatement—staring at the kindly smiling mouth and London's most famous amethysts I saw the eyes of a creature in torment, of a caged tigress. . . . The crowd was clamoring, rushing toward me like a pack of hounds, hayooooombrabrayayashoooo-yashoooo their screams came toward me—Bye-bye Mama, Grandma, tribe, Paula's breaking out. I picked up my schoolbag and started running out of the party.

"Mefista the Seventh, Queen Mefista!" Dali shouted, his crystal cane beating the air.

"Les Américains sont tous fous!" the Rothschild was proclaiming.

"Catch her, catch her!" Chanel called out.

"Save her," Babs was shouting louder than anyone else, "call an ambulance!"

MOTHER

THE YEAR MY MOTHER WAS BORN OSCAR WILDE HAD just been buried at Père Lachaise; there would still be a decade of dazzling London seasons before the outbreak of the Great War. Grandmother Fitzsimmons' hair was worn very high and wide, stuffed out with paddings and wire switches. Every few days, before a social gathering, a mustached man with wavy sepia hair strode into her room with a brown leather bag. Nada sat on her mother's lap and watched him ignite a spirit lamp and heat long metal tongs over a blue flame, an exciting odor of methylated alcohol and singed hair spread through the house. Later in the evening, hiding at the top of the stairs during her mother's parties, Nada studied the many glorious textures of guests' clothes, filigree-embroidered tulle, garlands of miniature roses on *diamanté* trellis, foot-high feathers plucked from egrets and birds of paradise. Throughout her life Nada Fitzsimmons would retain a passion for the texture and shape of human dress.

Nada Fitzsimmons' mother, Georgia, was known in

London society as the Virgin Queen because of her chaste and sumptuous life. When she traveled abroad she took along ten trunks, the size of hansom cabs, which carried her wardrobe and the many bibelots she collected on her trips. She ate seldom and sparsely, and like my mother her long slender limbs gave her the look of some graceful, benevolent spider. She had posed for Rodin, Bourdelle, Sargent; Boldini alone did three portraits of her. He referred to Grandmother as "art in its living form." At her luncheon parties on Grosvenor Square, a madeira 1873 might accompany the *filets de truites à la Russe*, a Moët-Imperial '92 followed with the *jambon d'Espagne*, the *ortolans Robinson* deserved a Château Langoa '74. Little Nada loved the odor of melon and cigar smoke that rose through the house at the end of a luncheon party, when she was allowed to come in to curtsy. After the guests had left, Georgia Fitzsimmons would often listen to operatic music with her daughter; her gramophone had a horn of crimson enamel like some immense tropical flower on which she played arias of Melba, Tetrazzini, Caruso. One of their favorites was an aria from *La Fanciulla del West, "Ah se una volta sola."*

The one day a month he came into town from his country estate Grandfather Fitzsimmons wore a black morning coat to lunch, striped trousers, and a pearl pin in his cravat. He still considered that the vicar of one's church could only be invited to light Sunday suppers; doctors and solicitors might be asked to garden parties but not to lunch or dinner; and those engaged in the stage, the arts or commerce should never be invited at any time. Yet between the years 1900 and 1915 Sarah Bernhardt, Réjane, Caruso, Paderewski, Cecile Sorel, Isadora Duncan, Mary Garden, Toscanini dined at Grandmother's house in Grosvenor Square—so Cedric Fitzsimmons had little place in his daughter's recollections. He had a complexion of brick hue and lived year round on his estate in Sussex, Barkham Hall, where he relished the company of men, the thrill of the fox hunt, blaze of horns fading into the mist of evening, blood-encrusted creatures lying in the great hall after a chase, ports and brandies shared with his fellow hunters over dinner.

Here's an interesting question about those days, Nada Fitzsimmons would say years later to her own daughter, were women more hysterical or were their tight vestments conducive to violent emotions? Shackled in corsets, stabbed with osprey feathers, tasseled trains sweeping for many yards on the floor, women were barely able to descend unaided from carriages—Nada had even seen a duchess faint at one of her mother's At Homes when another beauty entered wearing the same dress, there was romance in the air, there was terror. . . .

BY THE TIME I WAS BORN NADA FITZSIMMONS HAD MOVED to New York and become editor-in-chief of the American edition of *Best*. Her declarations were as widely quoted as Dale Carnegie's or Monsignor Sheen's.

"Beauty is the only promise of happiness we have."

"The most primitive tribes understand the spirituality of costume."

"All that is profound needs a mask."

The first two she got from Baudelaire, the last one from Nietzsche. I often caught her in the act; she could get a lot of quotes out of a book by flipping through its pages for five minutes, that's how the best journalists work. More from the oracle, perhaps originals:

"Our love for vestments is a sign of our immortal appetite for beauty."

"Let's not be harsh on vanity. Vanity gives you discipline, Vanity Fair mirrors society in all its foibles and splendors."

Observations doled out to colleagues at "21," on the

phone to foreign journalists, during interviews in her black and white office. She sat up much of the night before interviews, rehearsing her sentences until they came out like some perfect paragraph of her magazine. When offering a particularly pithy saying ("The essence of elegance is to suppress," "Elegance is refusal"), she'd point one foot toward the camera, thrusting out a tapered snakeskin shoe (she only wore snakeskin shoes). She knew precisely the angle at which she wanted to be photographed: standing in profile as erect as a cavalry officer by her lacquered desk, blowing a plume of smoke from her long white cigarette holder.

There was little sense wasting color film on Mother. Her perennial Balenciaga chemise was made of black serge in winter, beige linen in summer; its colors were changed as punctually as the vestments of the liturgical year—black to white around May 18, back to black September 25. The woman who dictated that "enchanting, this year, starts with a capital E for Empire," or "There's a lifted waistline this fall for every woman breathing," never followed the caprices of fashion. As high priestess she'd chosen to remain neutral. This was much admired and discussed.

Nada Fitzsimmons was known as a perfectionist, a tough editor. There was a lot of hiring and firing and terror at Mother's magazine. Vincent Von Bulow's predecessor in the travel department was said to have jumped off the terrace of his penthouse after he'd been dismissed for not finding new, amusing enough resorts to write about. When a set of photographs didn't put enough emphasis on the new trends of a Paris collection—flare of skirt or novel swell of sleeve—shootings were rescheduled for two, three, four A.M. Many photographers took a Benzedrine before each sitting to get that verve, that "zing" Mother required in each of *Best*'s fashion pages. "Don't be ridiculous," she'd say, when she was told that certain props she wanted in a picture were unobtainable. "Don't be ridiculous, we certainly *can* find a hundred yellow orchids for that color shot, we certainly *can* find six white swans for that Patou ballgown." Upon request her cohorts fanned out through the zoos and streets and botanical gardens of the city to bring back live panthers, human dwarfs, thirty varieties of cyclamens.

Mother didn't like having to leave me to go to all the parties she had to attend, there was a sad longing gleam in her eye when she kissed me good night on those evenings. But to miss one important event could be disastrous to the magazine, moguls might think that *Best* was falling into bad times and cancel their advertising space. So within one season it was vital for Mother to attend the United Cerebral Palsy Drive Ball, the Cystic Fibrosis Foundation Benefit, the Supporters of Vacations for the Blind Ball, the Juvenile Diabetic Foundations Benefit, the National Foundation for Ileitis and Colitis Ball, the Damon Runyon Memorial Cancer Fund Ball. Almost every form of disease and crippledness brought out New York's most fashionable women. These benefactresses had to be closely observed to know the month's trends in coiffure, jewelry, shoewear, hemline.

Mother also had to travel to maintain *Best*'s prestige in what she called "the provinces"; she couldn't afford not to be seen at the yearly Benefit Ball for the San Francisco Opera Company, the Friends of the Corcoran Ball in Washington, D.C., the Rhino Benefit Ball in Houston, Texas (organized by Helena Rubinstein, who bought massive advertising space in the magazine, to purchase two baby rhinos for the Houston Zoo). Being Seen Everywhere was a standard of Bestness.

Now a few words about myself:

I had taken early to the stage, I suppose, because I wished to conquer people's affections in a manner as swift and total as possible. From infancy on I had a violent and sincere desire to please. I could not stand the notion that someone, somewhere in the world harbored feelings of ill will against me; at that very thought I was ready to fly across the globe and conquer such persons with the most winsome ways available. By the time I was six, when I'd learned to read, I would take down volumes of Shakespeare from our bookshelves and memorize six or eight lines to impress Mother. This seemed to delight her; after offering me some most interesting coaching she would have me do my act at one of her parties. There was nothing sweeter to me than the surge of praise that followed such performances. In order to keep admiration flowing I changed the repertory often; in one season I'd memorized dozens of Juliet's, Rosalind's, Portia's lines.

It was Uncle Vincent Von Bulow who first suggested that I should be enrolled in drama classes in order to nurture my talent properly. He had been a poet in his youth and wept fluently at my salon performances, proclaiming my gifts. So from the time I was nine I was excused from the Brearley School at lunchtime several times a week and taken by Sala to the American Academy of Performing Arts. I was thorough and industrious. My preparations were fastidious. I often rose in the middle of the night to rehearse my gestures in front of the mirror, striving for my teachers' total approbation. And by the age of ten I was acting in one or two Academy performances a year. On weekends Mother and I might ride out to some isolated part of Manhattan—the Battery, the upper reaches of Central Park—where I would shout out my lines with all the power in my lungs to test the variety of pitch and volume I could get into my voice. I loved the way Mother ruffled her hand through my hair and hugged me tight when I'd done my lines well. She gave me much courage, she said I had terrific flashes of imagination in my acting.

Once, while playing Puck in *A Midsummer Night's*

Dream, I decided at the last minute to make my first stage entrance turning cartwheels. The audience's tumultuous satisfaction delighted everyone concerned.

I loved any role in which I could wear men's clothes— Viola, Rosalind, Portia—and of those my favorite part of all was Portia. I admired her shrewdness, her dedication to terribly important issues of mercy and justice, her modesty. When I rehearsed her lines about mercy ("twice bless'd; It blesseth him that gives and him that takes . . . an attribute to God himself") Sala used to do the sign of the cross and say that came straight out of the New Testament.

Ah, the applause, the delirious, intoxicating applause! Green baize flooring of the stage seeming to rise against my feet, luminous attention of the crowd stretched taut by the magic of my voice across the darkened hall, the sense I could have held their love indefinitely!

I'd occasionally receive notes from a member of the Academy's audience. "Dear Miss Fitzsimmons: Your expert handling of the trial scene reveals a lady gracious, witty and wise, you are our poet's Portia to the life. . . ."

Mother used to frame all such notes and hang them on the walls of her bedroom. Mother's pride in me was touching and remarkable, she was always trying to improve me. She'd have me standing on a stool in the dentist's office declaiming Rosalind. I'd do Juliet's balcony scene seated on the banquette of Le Pavillon in front of admiring *maîtres d'hôtels*. "Shakespeare must be kept up"—one of her dictums—"or we shall become a third-rate nation."

Mother would often read aloud to me from the memoirs of Ellen Terry, one of whose last performances she'd seen on the London stage when she was a small child: "The actress must cultivate a vigilant presence of mind which constantly deters the petty obstacles which might intrude upon her imagination and remind her that she is not *really* Juliet or Belvedera.''

That was no problem. In those days there was not much of me to remind me I was not really Juliet or Portia. I was never self-conscious (the beginner's curse) because I had so little self to be conscious of. I always felt part of a much bigger person called Mother whom I found very wise and beautiful, everything I did was to please and make happier that person inside whom I resided.

Off the stage I was impassive, reserved, smiling often but quietly, conscious that every turn of an actress's eye, every move of her hand could speak a world. And throughout my school years I had precious little contact with my classmates at the Brearley School. Sala had whisked me off to the Academy of Dramatic Arts by the time the other girls were yelling around the basketball court and hockey field, ganging up at Longchamps over ice cream sodas. I never felt lonely; there was so much to do in life I barely knew how to apportion my time. Anyhow I rarely invited other girls to our house because I was terrified of how they'd react to Mother's decor. My classmates lived with Georgian highboys and grandfather clocks and Queen Anne chairs upholstered in needlework of simpering shepherd girls. I was afraid they'd scream with laughter at Mother's black walls and stark white plastic furniture. And I was particularly terrified by the possibility that they might drop in on us at Christmastime and see our tree.

The tree. I came home every third week of December my arms laden with the normal merry ornaments I loved— tinsel, angels, shiny baubles. "But that's everybody's gaudy kitsch," Mother exclaimed. She'd relieve me of the ornaments and take them to the kitchen so Sala could give them to her relatives. She'd bring out a big striped box labeled "Bendel's" and I'd ruefully watch her do up the tree with her idea of Christmas—one year with nothing but stuffed white doves and pink roses, another year with a hundred black velvet ribbons, anything to be new and original I guess.

And in the summers I never saw my classmates because I accompanied Mother to the year's most important event—the fashion collections shown every July in Paris.

MOTHER IN THE SUMMER WEEKS OF THE PARIS COLLECTIONS—ah, that was a remarkable spectacle, a memorable performance. Few duties were more important in Mother's life than to meet the deadline for *Best*'s crucial October issue, which brought to tens of thousands of impatient American women the latest news from the capital of Western fashion. Ever since I'd been seven, when the couture world was fully recuperated from the German occupation, we'd spent the last two weeks of July in a suite at the Crillon Hotel. On collection days the frenzy began at dawn and lasted until after midnight. Mother ran a very tight ship, attended by many acolytes who rushed in and out of our hotel suite to send cables to her New York office. She often dictated the messages from her bath, which was doused with quantities of jasmine oil to allay the drying effect of Paris water. "Dior's tulip silhouette is the newest, most exciting in Paris, gives new emphasis to the bosom— Dior's wiring throws breasts forward, broadens them in a rounded, widely separated line, flattens the diaphragm into stem slimness. Balenciaga's collection: sleeves shorter, uncuffed, set at a dropped shoulder level on straighter jackets—nothing more mysterious than Balenciaga's simplicity . . ."

In the depths of her tub she also studied mail, talked on the phone with the London, New York, Rome branches of her magazine, chose photographs from contacts made the night before, sent out assistants into the city to pick up the clothes for that day's sittings. Every couture house in Paris had sent her flowers, the beige-brocaded fake Louis Seize of our Crillon suite was smothered in a hothouse of tuberose and peonies. Early in the morning or late at night a mannequin was modeling a dress in our living room for Eric, a fashion artist famous for the speed with which he drew and the loud, deep animal grunts he emitted as he struggled to render the folds of a garment. Several messengers fidgeted by the door, waiting to rush back the models to Fath, Givenchy, Dessés, Patou. Uncle Vincent Von Bulow sat in a corner of the room working on some travel memo, proclaiming his text out loud whenever a paragraph particularly pleased him. ''Was it Landor's cook or his wife whom he threw out of the window on his last trip to Italy, realizing just too late that the violets below the window would be crushed? The cook? The wife? Whichever, the incident occurred in the delicious village of Saturnia, where one can still taste any one of thirty-six different recipes for trout and listen to Wagner on an ancient gramophone. . . .'' In the center of the living room there sometimes sat Cristobal Balenciaga, Mother's best friend in Paris, dolorously sipping camomile tea. Infrequently exposed to clothes other than his own, he mostly came to curse at the vulgarity of the costumes being paraded in Mother's suite. He was a thin, depressed, nomadic Spaniard with perennial dark glasses and some twelve houses spread over the map of Europe, all of which he hated. He would spend a few days at his hacienda in Seville and leave it, complaining of the noise, go to his chalet in Switzerland to cure his sinuses and sell it the following morning, complaining of the insects. His only passion besides his work was looking for antiques, and he could spend a month piling up Renaissance tables and Persian rugs to furnish a flat in Barcelona which he'd leave after a night because he disliked the Gaudi building across the street. He traveled everywhere with a long-haired dachshund called Zurbarán and carried in his pocket several immaculate linen hand-kerchiefs with which he wiped the dog's bottom after each sidewalk performance. When he and my mother greeted each other every summer he would scrutinize her dress with a tragic air, hands on her shoulders, to be sure that she was wearing one of his originals, and then tug at different parts of her collar, sleeves, waistline to show that she was not wearing it properly. Uncle Cristo loathed children and seldom addressed a word to me, spending his time in our rooms cursing at the dresses Eric was drawing and staring disdainfully at Mother's distilled mayhem. The three telephone lines of our suite never stopped ringing, buyers from Neiman-Marcus, Hattie Carnegie, Bergdorf's were trying to discover which models from which houses Mother was having photographed, what "direction" she was taking in *Best*'s October issue, whether she was stressing the A-Line, the H-line, the Y-line, the Eiffel Tower line. Mother refused all such calls. She continued calmly dictating her cables over the ringing of phones: "Balenciaga's big news for daytime, wide buckled belts slung around the hips of bloused suits . . . Patou's ballooning tops for evening, many printed silks and chiffons like English party dresses . . . Let's not forget Dior's many greens, field greens, bronze greens, courageous greens. . . ."

I hovered by Uncle Vincent's side, quietly rehearsing some Shakespeare lines to myself—July in Paris was one month when no one had time to listen to me perform. Or else I tried to decipher the unintelligible scrawl in which Uncle Vincent wrote his travel notes. "What do you think, my little Muse? Shall I say *delicious* for the way Mrs. Bandit Potter arranges her immense collection of articulated silver fish? Would *delectable* be better?" He always made me feel wise. He was the only very close friend Mother had and I loved her for that choice. "How I admire your ferocious discipline and studiousness, *chère petite*,'' Uncle Vincent would whisper, "quite like your dear mother, whose innermost self remains unsullied by our world's frivolity and who I hope will allow me to adore her at a distance for the rest of my life . . . ah, chaste pleasures, more voluptuous than the grosser deliriums.''

Then at about nine-thirty it was time to assist Mother as she emerged from her bath. "Paula angel . . . my robe.'' I jumped up and ran to the bathroom and held out her terrycloth robe. l loved to see her emerging from the water, lissome and tiny-breasted, skinny boyish arms locking around me after she'd been wrapped in the white toweling. The jasmine smell of that pristine body which I'd never associated with any man, never associated with any body but my own. The jasmine of Mother's bath, this is the scent that would assail me much later when she began having to fish me out of closets during my periods of looniness, her cool efficient arms, the clink of her single bracelet against my darkness, the calm efficient voice saying, Paula dearest, we must pull ourselves together and go to the hospital now. . . .

I patted Mother all over, drying her. "I had always cherished the idea that a country must be filthy to be romantic until I went to Portugal,'' the baron declaimed. "Amidst pale pink, pale green houses tumbling toward the sea like a box of spilled fondants, the enchanting eighteenth-century town of Larego bubbles with baroque. . . .'' I rubbed Mother with her towel robe, she complained I was rubbing too hard, she pummeled at my own back, briefly we laughed, we played. She changed into a black dashiki and went to hold court in the living room for another hour, watching the parade of accessories. A procession of bag merchants, shoe designers, jewelry manufacturers who'd been waiting outside the door of our suite had burst into the salon to exhibit their inventions. Cristobal's dog yapped hysterically as the tradesmen spread their wares on couches and tables, unfurled their scarves and shawls with the flourish of merchants in a *souk*. "Odious, intolerable," Cristobal muttered, curtly kissing Mother goodbye to attend to his dog's bowels. Mother was careful never to hurt feelings. She said, "Interesting, interesting" as she scrutinized each item, kept a dozen samples of accessories for the day's sittings, sent the artisans home after offering them tea and croissants. For the next few minutes she was getting dressed to leave for the ten-thirty collection at Dessés, Patou, Lanvin, whoever was scheduled that morning to show his creations to several hundred fashion journalists from around the globe. And after quickly robing into her white Balenciaga, she dedicated the half hour before departure to perfecting my own appearance.

However neatly I'd tried to do it by myself, each braid was carefully redone and tied with a fresh ribbon, my knee-high white socks were straightened so as not to show a fold. I missed Sala's soft black hands; I whimpered as Mother crisply tugged at every part of me. Stay still for a minute, rabbit—my hem was checked for evenness, my sweater was changed for a more harmonious color scheme, she had my shoes repolished to a gleam, I was the diadem of her exhibit-studded life—ah, now you're perfect. . . .

EVERY JULY MORNING DURING THE PARIS COLLECTIONS WE left the hotel too late for comfort because Mother wished to be the very last to arrive. Her lateness in leaving was purposeful, craftily planned. Austerely adorned as she was, she depended on me, and on precise timing, to produce the desired spectacle. She enjoyed the war of nerves she ran with herself before every major collection; rushing out of the hotel at 10:19 to make the 10:30 opening at Fath or Givenchy was part of the game. She'd kept the same chauf-

feur she had before the war, a wily Norman with a white
Mercedes whom she rewarded generously for burning all
the red lights between the Crillon and our destination. Our
rides would be studded with a barrage of talk which I always took to be a mask for her tensions. "Look at the
hideous satchels women are carrying for pocketbooks these
days, veritable feed bags; the curse of modern times, no
sense of scale; and the mass of costume jewelry these girls
clank around, when they want to undress all they need do
is stand in the middle of a room and shake . . . indifference, indifference to details. . . ." We sped through the
Paris streets with the authority of a President of the Republic or a state hearse. We'd arrive at a couture house
between 10:33 and 10:36, just as the first mannequin was
about to start the show. And as she entered a salon, amid
the whispers of "adorable" that greeted her exquisitely
spruced child, waving to her acquaintances as grandly as
royalty from a passing carriage, she'd thrust me ahead of
her with a gentle little shove on the nape of my neck, as if
it was I, not she, whom she meant to be the center of her
spectacle.

DURING HER CHILDHOOD IN LONDON, NADA PREFERRED
those days when there were no guests about and she went
riding with her mother in Richmond Park. From the age of
ten she had to be ready to follow her mother on horseback
all day, worried that she would be frowned upon if she did
not perform "like a little soldier," trying to keep up with
her mother's frenetic pace as she galloped her horse to the
limit of endurance. . . . When they stayed home they
played many games together: merry chases of hide-and-
seek up the stairways walled in beige moiré, through the
drawing rooms filled with Adam chairs upholstered in magenta velvet. Grandmother had great patience, she was ca-
pable of hiding behind a stairwell for an hour while Nada

pretended she could not find her, delaying the cries and embraces, the exciting shock of encounter. . . .

During the Great War Georgia Fitzsimmons began gradually to change her life. "She started to see the inappropriateness of displaying luxury," in Mother's words, "and devoted herself to causes of reform." She worked at the hospital several hours a day rolling bandages; she became an ardent champion of women's suffrage. One day, when Grandmother was calling on Lord Asquith to press for a law that would increase wages for women who worked in factories, news came that much of the British Second Army was decimated in battle. Shortly afterward Grandmother dismantled her house in Grosvenor Square and moved to a small flat in St. John's Wood. She put up most of her belongings for auction, keeping only a small Velasquez and one Flemish tapestry.

Aged nineteen, a year after the war's end, Nada went to work at the London office of a new fashion magazine, *Best.* Grandmother Fitzsimmons traveled with increasing frequency now that her daughter was launched in a career. In the mid-twenties she seemed sated by Europe and began her first journeys in North Africa. One spring she hired a native guide and spent a month traveling on horseback to visit ancient mosques south of the Atlas Mountains. "I find in the desert a clearness of belief that I have sought for much of my life," she wrote her daughter. "Barren landscapes, renunciation, peace. . . ."

In London Nada was documenting for *Best* the newest whims of European fashion. The words "cocktails" and "nightclub" had spring up in the early twenties. . . . Fashionable hostesses had started to serve breakfast foods for dinner; haddock, kippers, scrambled eggs were superseding vol-au-vents and stuffed ortolans. . . . Mrs. Corrigan of Cleveland, Ohio, had conquered London society by standing on her head, entire hotels were being taken for a night and decorated to resemble circuses. . . . In Paris Chanel was launching the little black dress; Poiret complained that Chanel's slouching flat-chested women looked like starved Western Union messengers, but no one listened to him anymore. . . . In the mid-1920s Nada Fitzsimmons, ravishing fashion editor of London's *Best*, was often photographed with Coco Chanel in Biarritz or St. Paul de Vence, their arms wrapped about each other's shoulders. . . .

But Grandmother Fitzsimmons could not observe with her usual care Nada's marvelous career, her increasingly influential essays and collection reports. In 1926, Grandmother disappeared into North Africa. One day, when Nada was twenty-six, Georgia Fitzsimmons left her flat before dawn, leaving a brief letter for her husband and a voluminous one for her daughter.

Perhaps she just couldn't stand it anymore. Stand what, you ask? The pomp. The illusions. Those artifices that my female forebears considered to be the mainstay of civilization, at which they'd been so skilled. . . .

NADA FITZSIMMONS HAD CONCEIVED ME AT THE AGE OF thirty-nine with the same calculation and prescience she exhibited in every detail of her career: in the fall of 1939, making it just under the line, biologically, politically. She'd foreseen the events that might make it impossible for her to report on Paris collections the following summer, if the war was to continue. So in 1940 she'd had me instead of a collection. She was a follower of Isadora Duncan's, she believed in genetic mating, my father's identity (I think he died before I was born) was never talked about. She invented me with the same independence and rehearsed precision with which she laid out her pages and wrote her famous memos:

"Taste is the only education."

"To have no mirrors, no self-image, that is my definition of hell. There are no mirrors in Sartre's *No Exit*."

Nada had a chartreuse pen which zigzagged over the pages of her colleagues' texts in an oblique, monumental hand. She had a strong aversion to all conventional language. In her pages dreams could never be golden, subservience total, appeals desperate or the state of the world chaotic, browns could not be rich or blues celestial, needs could not be dire or interests keen or sources vital or relationships unique. She had metaphors of her own which might have been better or worse, I wasn't sure. "Fashion makes the frivolous moral." "Fashion is the aperitif, the prelude to the divine cake."

At the office Mother was surrounded by a regiment of young acolytes who faithfully copied every detail of her style—Balenciaga chemise, jasmine bath oil, Black Sobranie cigarettes. She disdained her imitators. Whenever any of the assistants swarming about her made a particularly silly comment, she'd give them a haughty sideways glance that seemed to say I need you around to tell me what's in the air, you idiot, but do shut up. That conference which took place in her office, for instance, to find a headline for the appearance of the bikini. "Here's how *Yes!* has it," one of the pale, chemised priestesses commented. " 'The bikini is the greatest thing since the atom bomb.' " "Abominable, as usual," Nada snapped. "Next?" "Bikini—nothing more beautiful since Versailles," another silver-haired acolyte offered. "Better, but hardly the best," Nada said.

Mother had a contemplative streak I admired which may have come from Grandmother Fitzsimmons. There were often books by her bedside with titles like *The Real St. Francis*, or *Immortality and Reincarnation*, which she seemed to read with great attentiveness. We frequently went to mass (High Church Anglican). She looked sad during some of the services, and held my hand as if I offered her protection. Occasionally, she'd take out the same little sketchbooks she carried to Paris openings and draw the fold of a surplice, the curve of an alb.

NICOLAS

EVER SINCE JULY 1947, WHEN WORLD EVENTS AL-lowed the Paris couturiers to resume their yearly fashion showings, I'd sat next to Mother in the front row of Givenchy's, Dior's, Patou's salons, loathing each dress she took her damn notes on. Even then I chose to hide my disgust, aping the exalted sighs of the sadists and flagellants seated around me, muttering *"divin,"* *"ravissant"* as each model swept by. Mother thought I was constantly delighted. There was never a time when I was totally sure I was alive. Sometimes when I excused myself to go to the bathroom during a showing it would be to hide in a dark corner whispering my name, Paula, Paula, to make sure that I existed. The collection I hated the most was Balenciaga's, Mother's favorite. "Someday you'll understand, darling, that he is the Michelangelo of couture, whereas Dior is merely its Watteau."

Balenciaga's salon was as bare and sparse as the crypt of some Spanish church and was directed by a dour chignoned lieutenant who allowed almost no one in the press

except Nada Fitzsimmons to photograph the emperor's
clothes. I'd see them groveling in the *directrice*'s office
right after the showing—the *New York Globe, Le Monde*
clamoring and begging for *numéro trente-six*, and seconds
later Mother had already arranged to have *trente-six* deliv-
ered to our hotel room that evening. Balenciaga took pride
in having the ugliest, scariest mannequins in town. They
were Draculan creatures with big square heads who walked
with their eyes fixed on the ground, not allowed to smile
at anyone, arms swinging out like orangutans. Balenciaga's
was the only couture house in town where no one was
permitted to clap or talk or even whisper. I'd look up and
see the circle of dotards whom Mother referred to as "my
dear intimates"—Bébé Bérard, whose fingers twitched in
his filthy beard because Balenciaga's was the only salon he
wasn't allowed to doodle in; Daisy Fellowes, who always
wore identical bracelets of diamonds and rubies on each
wrist (she ordered two of each because she loathed asym-
metry).

At the age of ten I decided that Balenciaga's would be
by far the smartest place in Paris to faint in. My drama
coaches had taught me spectacular ways. Toward the end
of the collection I stole one last glance at Mother, who
became increasingly inscrutable as the spectacle pro-
gressed, so that no one could predict which models she
was choosing for the October *Best*. I rose a few feet off
my chair; clutched at my throat like Hamlet's mother right
after she's swallowed the poison; bent my knees in that
special way I'd learned in class, and passed out into the
runway. Mother rushing out of the room to fetch me a glass
of water, a reporter from *Der Sturm* kneeling at my feet with
a flask of brandy, even our principal competitor, the editor
of *Yes!*, sending around her lavender smelling salts. Cristobal peeked out from behind his red velvet curtain hoarsely
calling out to his mannequin, "Dominique, Dominique!"

Dracula had stopped in her tracks, face iced in disdain, and strutted back to the *cabine* with a military stride.

Let me add that the second and last time I fainted I waited politely until the end of the collection, when the wedding dress came out. My Paula wouldn't have missed the wedding dress for the world, Mother would say to her colleagues, there's an individualist for you, where did she get an obsession for marriage in this family of single women! Meanwhile, I was lying on the soft blue backseat of our Mercedes, daydreaming about the country parson I wanted to marry. I, Paula Mary Fitzsimmons, had decided that I wished to marry a country parson who would liberate me from all this shit. After a glorious but brief career on the stage, I desired a husband like those in the photographs of *Country Life* magazine which say the Reverend and Mrs. Cyril Bottomsley are shown here with their purebred Airedales and their six delightful children. I yearned for hollyhocked gardens, blooded horses, rabbit hutches, I wanted to compete in flower shows at which I would receive prizes for developing special strains of violet hybrid roses. No more of our nomadic existence I'd decided early on, no more crazed women leaving their daughters to roam the desert, no more of these ghastly Paris summers filled with groaning artists and cadaverous women parading their tulle and sequins and spooky Spaniards whose dogs poo-pooed all over our rugs. I wanted to live in a parsonage because those were the places best suited to my intimate sense of scale; I liked tiny dark rooms. Later on when I'd go balmy I'd hide a lot in closets; when Mother and I played hide-and-seek she knew she could go off and finish a slew of fashion notes during the game because I was happy to sit in a small dark place for hours, just thinking. So when I lay in the back of our Mercedes outside of Dior's or Balenciaga's salons, I dreamed of tiny dark Tudor parsonages and of putting up blackberry jam much of the summer and

of the Sunday sermons Reverend Bottomsley might preach
on the Joys of Country Life. "In our days of vanity and
caprice a simple pastoral existence, enriched with the joys
of the Creation and filled with punctual observance of His
gifts, will bring us closer to . . ." Well, at least that's one
good thing my beloved Nicolas would do for me, he'd get
me out of going to the Paris collections.

THIS IS MY FIRST MEMORY OF BABS HOLLINS' SON, NICO-
las:

I hadn't been introduced to Nicolas yet, but I'd stared
hard at him as we sat across from each other one afternoon
on a Madison Avenue bus. It was the fall I was eleven.
There's no way I could have overlooked him, he was by
far the most interesting-looking person my age I'd ever
seen. He had a prominent, determined chin and very long
pale lashes and continually darting, bright blue eyes. A
copy of *Midsummer Night's Dream* was sticking out of his
pocket. He was very large for his age, he wore a blue St.
Bernard's blazer and clutched in his palm a small toy which
he didn't want anyone to see. Other kids from his school
sat around him with their baseball mitts and hockey sticks
whispering what are you hiding there, what have you got.
A tall mustached man stood over Nicolas, one of his so-
called stepfathers I guess, saying show your nice friends
what we bought today. But Nicolas didn't want to share,
he seemed adamant about keeping that toy hidden. The first
thing that struck me about him that day was the animal
defensiveness in his blue eyes, as if he felt surrounded by
a pack of predators and was preparing a counterattack.
There's a nice boy, the mustached man said, show your
friends the toy. . . . But Nicolas didn't open his hand, he
continued staring furtively at all of us, hovering over his
clutched palm; and when he finally spoke up I knew why
he hadn't talked earlier. He fixed his eyes on me, perhaps

because I was the shyest-looking person on the bus, and said, "All it is is a tt—tt—tiny bb—bb—blue chair."

Some two weeks later I saw Nicolas again, at one of Mother's first-of-the fall, back-to-black parties. This particular gathering was in honor of Nicolas' mother, Babs Hollins, who had just been promoted from *Best*'s Paris bureau to be second in command of the New York office. Babs had swept into the room with magnificent brutality, jostling, kissing, shimmering. Rose gash of a smile, news of all Europe on her lips, opinions on hems, sculptures, novels, perfumes, cars. She wore sequin-encrusted satin pants modeled on a toreador's fighting costume that evening, her two pug dogs were yapping on their leashes. She was trailed by the same blond eleven-year-old I'd admired on the bus the previous month, who today was desperately tugging at one of his mother's jeweled fingers, and by a yawning new lover a decade younger than she. The finger had soon let go of Nicolas as Babs rushed across the room and, cling clang, her show commenced.

"Bonjour, trésor, comment vas-tu? Yes, yes, Hubert did lower waists by a whole three inches, *quel toupet!* He just took me to lunch at a horrid little bistro too near First Avenue, East River typhoid best, he swore he'd lower his waists again next year. . . . Elsie, that blouse is divine on you, it makes you look positively drowned. Vincent, *come sta Sua Maestà?* Are you still recommending visits to those desolate Third World countries of yours? I just received the most divine post card from Molyneux dated Calcutta saying delicious day, perfect weather and not a dead person in sight. . . . Nonsense, Evelyn, don't worry about the French going communist, it might be the best thing for them, they'd finally have superb gardens again, the gardens in Russia are the world's prettiest . . ."

Her strong, deep laugh was that of a very large woman, it came from within her bowels; one could barely imagine such a raucous fat sound emerging from that filigreed androgynous body. "How is Jacqueline? Back in pastels again. Jean-Francois? His paintings are going to the Biennale this year, he married his rich boyfriend's sister, the plain one with the tic, and took on a very beautiful young man as studio assistant who squeezes his tubes I suppose. . . . Ah, who do I see across the room who-do-I-see. . . . Marie Hélène! *Raconte moi tout!* Have you heard about Patricia? A disaster! She ran away with a dancer while writing her biography of Diaghilev, she's left Patou, she's left her husband, she's left everything!"

Pugs yapping, frenzied on their leashes, *ciao tesoro, come stai!* Splendid teeth bared, alabaster feet exquisitely sandaled, Bulgari jewels gleaming at ears, neck, wrists amid bouts of deliberate, appalling laughter. And within five minutes of his mother's entrance Nicolas was huddled alone in a corner of the living room floor, hugging his knees, looking pensively and warily at the crowd. An occasional guest bent down to Nicolas to say well hello, darling, how are you? Would you like a sandwich? *Quel enfant exquis!* Aren't you going to talk to me? And though a charming, knowing smile seldom left his face, Nicolas' eyes had darted from one adult to another with suspicion and terror.

But as soon as Nicolas saw me across the room all fear left him. With me he would never be timid or wary, he would be shrewd, wily, dictatorial. If anything I was the shy one, my acting and my summers in couture had kept me apart from other children for years before I even met Nicolas. When my classmates at Brearley visited each other in Greenwich or Oyster Bay, talking about dancing class or the rumors they'd heard about the Period, all I'd have to talk about was how to play Portia, Dior's sleeves or Balenciaga's false double hems. I'd have sounded pretty batty to them . . . but with Nicolas I felt immediately at home. He was the first person of my age I'd met with whom I could share my solitude. He beckoned me that day and grabbed a pillow from the couch so I could sit on the floor next to him. And from then on, for many years, we talked our own private language, spun out our own private worlds.

I LOVED SPENDING SATURDAYS AT NICOLAS' HOUSE. BABS' decor was nothing very special (as Mother said, Babs was "a superb workhorse but not totally original"; with a few variations she copied Mother's style, bare white walls and stark black lacquered furniture instead of the reverse color scheme). But Nicolas' own room was unlike any other I'd ever seen.

Instead of the puzzles, roller skates, ship models, soccer balls, baseball bats I'd imagined to find in a boy's room, or telescopes and microscopes, or toy soldiers, water guns and electric trains, Nicolas' den was filled with a variety of objects that had to do with domestic life. There were tiny china tea sets complete with strainers, tea cozies, sugar tongs, three sizes of plates and spoons and pitchers. There were five-inch-high replicas of the kind of furniture both our mothers would have banned as disastrously bourgeois—cozily tufted Victorian sofas and ottomans and armchairs, double beds with baldachins of rich blue velvet. There were also illustrations of extremely normal interiors similar to those I'd admired in the pages of *Country Life*— dark, snug Tudor cottages with diamond-lozenged windows and dark wood paneling, chintz curtains, many fireplaces; and several miniature sets of kitchen equipment in beautifully polished copper—pots and pans, double boilers, whisks, frying pans; next to his set of Shakespeare, a variety of books on cooking, on Mediterranean cuisine, on how to make many kinds of veal and chicken dishes.

And then his obsession—the children. On Nicolas' walls

there hung photographs of children from every corner of the world: emaciated, curly-headed Haitian children playing half-naked in the dust of some hovel; joyous, plump, tow-haired Scandinavian children lined up for gymnastics class on a beach; mysterious, seductive Arab children, clutching the hands of their veiled mothers; wealthy Western children in Little Lord Fauntleroys or ruffled dresses, walking stately behind their uniformed nannies.

So Nicolas had surrounded himself with these imaginary friends and homes, imaginary shreds of the family life he'd never known. His mother had been a famous fashion model before she had joined *Best*. After a brief, early marriage to the French car racer with whom she'd allegedly conceived Nicolas, she'd gone on to enjoy a regiment of other husbands and lovers from several countries of Western Europe. She'd thrown so many tantrums during their presences and disappearances, led such a nomadic existence, that no one had been willing to remain in her employ for more than a few months. So by the time Nicolas was eight Babs had given up on nurses and took him with her everywhere—collections, fashion sittings, sometimes chattering so heatedly with colleagues to glean the information she needed for her career that she forgot him like a stray package at some couturier's or countess' salon.

MY SATURDAYS AT NICOLAS' WERE SPENT SOMEWHAT IN this manner:

I was greeted at the door by Babs, who after offering me her thickly powdered cheek would thrust into my hand some expensive present I seldom knew what to do with—a huge panda bear, a two-inch-high replica of the Eiffel Tower with fake snow that fell on it when you shook it. And after a few exclamations (''*Quel trésor* you are for coming, darling . . . Nicolas can't do without you anymore'') she'd be off to the Lighthouse for the Blind Benefit Ball, the Aga

Khan's surprise birthday party at "21," Mainbocher's little dinner for Wally and David.

The apartment was already suffused with the smells of Nicolas' own little party. He would greet me at the kitchen door (there'd often be a grumbling maid in the kitchen waiting to clean up after him, but they changed so often we never paid any attention to them) and soon thereafter our feast would commence. His favorite menu consisted of cream of spinach soup, filets of sole with mushrooms and seedless grapes, and apricot mousse. He sat me at his candlelit table with a little bow and within a few minutes reappeared with the first course. He watched me carefully as I ate, studying the pleasure I received from his food, concentrating so intensely on my appreciation that he ate very little himself. In the company of others he tended to cover up his stuttering by remaining very silent, expressing himself by a variety of gracious smiles, nods, gestures. But within a few weeks of our meeting we'd perfected a language of ornate words (often culled from my constant rehearsal of Shakespeare) in which he could speak as fluently as I.

"Sweet Paula, tell me full opinion of my fare."

To reassure Nicolas I ate with considerable gusto, hamming it up, rolling my eyes and smacking my lips in appreciation. He was never satisfied with his accomplishments. "A touch more salt perhaps, less paprika!" No no, I said, it was perfect. I had started dedicating myself to the goal of making Nicolas feel indispensable.

After dinner he would offer to listen to me rehearse lines for whatever role I was learning that term.

"The attribute to awe and majesty," I'd recite, "wherein doth sit the dread and fear of kings . . ."

"Perhaps a little more stress on the word *majesty* . . ."

So I'd do the line again, wanting above all to impress and please Nicolas.

Before Sala came to take me home we sat in Babs' black and white living room, talking about events in school or the next weekend's menu. Nicolas was four inches taller than I and because of his love for food tended slightly to plumpness. He had a way of lounging on a sofa, his long legs perched on a floor cushion, which I found very seductive. I was struck by the ease of his beautifully groomed body, the animal naturalness of all its functions. Occasionally he'd break wind after one of his decorous dinners, as softly and casually as one might exhale a sigh of comfort. Perhaps because of his own fears, his stutter, his shyness, he managed to infuse me with a sense of great power and self-confidence. He seemed ever so kind and wise, and he had given me a new life.

FOR BY THE TIME I WAS TWELVE, NICOLAS HAD MERCI-fully spared me from ever having to sit through a Paris collection again. Mother had rented a house for us to summer in. ("That boy's childhood has been *ridiculous*," she'd said, "we must give him a *home*.") The summer house was two miles from the nearest village, far from the company of other children. In July and part of August Mother and Aunt Babs and Uncle Vincent went to Paris to cover the collections. Except for the times we went to shop for groceries, Nicolas and Sala and I saw no one but each other for many weeks at a time. There were lots of activities at our house that Nicolas relished. And few did he enjoy as much as having our palms read by Sala. She was descended from generations of Haitian fortune-tellers who excelled at reading the course of previous and present existences in the lines of the hand.

"Look, Nicolas baby, see the fine line right beside Paula's pinky here, it means that in her past time on earth she was a tree. Now tree's even higher than human being because it's source of life, tree lasts hundreds of years and watches humanity be foolish under its leaves and knows more wisdom than you or me and nourishes birds and many animals, and for this she rewarded to be *ma belle fillette* and she continue having all good thing if she take care and not fall sick. . . ."

Sala always concentrated on my previous existence; the few times she'd studied my palm for my present life her face had tightened early in the reading and she'd stopped. I knew something bad would happen to me at about the time I should be getting married, and I'd told her to go on to Nicolas' hand.

"Hoho, Monsieur Nicky, look at this hill beside your thumb, mountain of Venus. In your last life I see too many marriages . . ."

"How mmm-mm-many?"

" . . . one hundred and thirty-seven. Now, baby, what this mean, it mean you chased and chased so much after those girls you had little time to do any other work, not even plumber butcher baker . . ."

Turban of red silk twisted about her wiry hair, pupils rolling like berries in the milk-white of her eyes.

" . . . oooh *quel homme tu étais*, you were hunter all right and you're going to be big man again in this life, no animal chase so well as you . . ."

"What about our next lives," we both wanted to know.

"Only Him above can tell."

Early on in our friendship Nicolas and I became interested in reincarnation. I figured that it was because we'd had no fathers and were determined to get a better deal next time around. At the age of twelve we'd devised a theory that our galaxy was being dreamed by an immense white bull whose sleep and wakings dictated our future fates.

"We're living at the very end of Great Bull's dream," Nicolas would elaborate. "When his present dream stops, all that's around us will melt away and we'll be assigned fresh, powerful, new bodies for our next life. . . ."

We considered becoming vegetarians in order not to consume someone who'd been a relative in a former life, we huddled together on the living room floor discussing which sacred animal would be the next to assign us our new forms, what lives we most desired in our next incarnations.

And for the next few years winters also became much more fun because I had someone to help me with Mother's canapés. Nicolas and I smiled together now, passing canapés at least once a fortnight, from October to May, during Mother's Black period.

We passed salmon to Uncle Vincent, who said, "Beautiful children! Did I tell you that I discovered a marvelous new resort south of the Atlas last spring? A five-room hotel in the middle of the desert, lunch with a Berber sheik who fed me pigeon and honey pie on a terrace overlooking the most ravishing valley in Morocco . . ."

We passed caviar to Fulco Verdura, who designed Babs' favorite jewelry and said, "I've just returned from Madeira, *che maledizione*, not a decent duchess in sight!"

We passed watercress to Elsa Maxwell, who'd just caused a furor by giving a dinner in Paris at which guests were asked to knock down statuettes of Italian, French and British statesmen with rubber balls, prizes from Cartier awarded to whoever had scored the most hits.

"Délicieux, adorables enfants," a chorus of Paris visitors rose at our sight, Jacques Fath, with the bleached blond pompadour, who walked as if he had a drum majorette's baton stuck up his behind, Jean Dessés, swarthy and bald, looking like a Syrian rug merchant who'd just spent a week unwashed on the Orient Express.

Christian Dior came to Mother's parties every time he

was in town and inspired us with much confidence because he looked even more terrified than we really were. He was bald and shining and his ears stuck out extravagantly on each side of his pink cheeks. Even if standing in the middle of the room he kept his plump hands folded docilely on his belly, like a neurotically obedient Benedictine monk. He'd stare at us with dolorous eyes and softly deliver a discourse which went something like this:

"Chers enfants, how happy I am to see you again! You know New York is nothing but a tiny village, much tinier than Paris. It consists of twenty streets and five hotels and three restaurants in which you will meet anyone you'd ever want to meet. There on these blocks you see the fifty people who *are* New York, strolling on the sidewalk. I find Americans the least hurried people in the world . . ."

Uncle Christian had a terrier called Bobby and made Framboise liqueur out of his own raspberry canes (so I'd heard from Nicolas, who'd attended the February collections all the years I'd attended the July ones and was a walking repository of Dior lore). Uncle Christian's favorite hobbies were playing canasta and doing needlework tapestry. When flower arrangers came to his apartment twice a week they were ordered to move about in soft felt slippers so as not to scratch his eighteenth-century parquet floors.

"There are few women alive who can give parties like your mothers. Great parties are genuine works of art; we in Europe are tired of bombs dropping, we wish for fireworks. I have no words to say how pleased I am to see your dear little faces on avenue Montaigne every year, and to note the deep emotion my work seems to offer you. . . ."

When Uncle Christian was fourteen a gypsy fortune-teller wandering through Normandy helped to shape his destiny by predicting that he would rise to wealth and fame by adorning women. Uncle Christian loved his mother more than anyone else (Nicolas particularly enjoyed this detail); it was the memories of Madame Dior *mère* with her tiny, corseted waist and the rustling full skirts of the 1910s coming in to kiss Uncle Christian good night that had inspired the New Look . . .

". . . I am nothing but a merchant of happiness, dear children, women have rewarded me with their patronage because they realize that I make them not only more beautiful but happier. I believe that costume is one of the few last repositories of the magic, the marvelous, the sacramental. That is why I wish my mannequins to be priestlike, mysterious. You should see my young women preparing for the sacred moment of displaying clothes; my little Victoire gets ready for the ceremony with all the gravity of Iphigenia before the sacrifice. . . . From my childhood on I was only moved by that which was most sparkling, most frivolous. When someone objects to the fact that my clothes are ill-suited to our times I reply that the times will change, a great period of happiness is on the way which will make my creations come truly into their own. . . ."

IN BETWEEN MOTHER'S COCKTAIL PARTIES, NICOLAS AND I immensely looked forward to Aunt Babs' many trips—Japan's Inland Sea to photograph sables, Chicago to show Dior's A-line against the newest skyscraper. When Babs traveled Nicolas would come to spend a few weeks with me in the middle of the winter; and at nights when Mother went out to her own round of events we'd sit in the middle of the living room floor perfecting my current stage roles, arguing in a euphoria of private language, carefully studying Sala's way of making creole gumbo and apple fritters. But Babs always came back quickly. She came back to write her unique copy. As Uncle Vincent put it, Babs did not have the "style" Mother had—that was the ability to invent and sustain a "line." But she had plenty of "flair"—

the instinct to detect style in others. Babs knew which duchess's garden in Wales should be photographed for the next spring issue, which couturier would be the first to use snakeskin in evening wear, which ski resort would be in fashion two winters ahead. Mother had hired her from the European bureau of *Best* to compete more aggressively with the outrageous chic of *Yes!*, and as usual Mother's gambit had succeeded. In just one year Babs' hard work and flamboyant style had considerably boosted *Best*'s sales, and her column "Why Not" had become the magazine's most popular item. ("Why not throw out all your furniture on New Year's Day for a fresh start, like the Romans do?" "Why not wash yourself with ripe avocadoes instead of soap to give your skin a silken sheen, the way they do in Athens?") By the time we were twelve Nicolas and I could easily tell the difference between Mother's sentences and Babs' in the pages of their magazine; Babs was always sent out to meet the press when something truly newsworthy, controversial was needed.

"Fashion is the only thing that's always with us," Babs would tell the *Boston Courier*. "Only fashion survives wars, pestilence, economic crises."

"I believe in *waste*. After a golf game Tallulah Bankhead would smash a whole bottle of Lanvin perfume on the edge of her tub—now there's a glorious gesture! Not a middle-class bone in *that* body."

"Dinner wear shouldn't be *extraordinaire* when you're the hostess . . . a cardigan, a pair of silk pants and a few sapphires, right?"

"All that is important is that a great, great prettiness go on."

THE LITTLE FAMILY

As far back as I can remember there was always someone on the staff of *Best* talking about getting away from It All. There was always some editor leaving the magazine to build a house in a godforsaken Mexican village, a lingerie specialist threatening to retire to a little chalet in Bavaria. Uncle Vincent was particularly fervent about his craving for the simple, the primitive. So this was a frequent subject of conversation during those summers he and Mother rented a house on Long Island to give Nicolas and me what they called "a wholesome seaside vacation."

It was a typical late June afternoon on a weekend when we were thirteen, shortly before the family went off to Paris for the collection frenzy. We were gathered on the terrace. Mother sat very upright in her wicker chair. The baron reclined in a chaise longue. And Aunt Babs paced up and down the lawn, contradicting much of what the baron was saying.

"I've finally found the place in which I wish to retire,"

the baron announced. "Nothing as pure, as austere as northwestern Spain. Amid craggy landscapes, great monasteries rising on the edge of precipices . . ."

"Vincent, an idea!" Mother exclaimed. "Why not do a story on the Duchess of Lerma! She's given her entire castle to an order of Franciscan nuns and kept two rooms in it, one for herself and one for her maid."

"What bliss, two little chalk-white cells in a desolate corner of Extremadura, the plainest bread . . ."

"Do get off that purity kick, Vincent," Babs exclaimed. "You aren't even a valid Bohemian yet."

"At the age of fifty-two," the baron said, "I might finally have the pleasure of finding myself."

"Sleeping ecstatically in hammocks, in some outpost inhabited by unwashed *campesinos*!"

"I want to end my days in some simple Mediterranean setting," Uncle Vincent insisted. "I'm fed up with the triteness and frivolity . . ."

Mother leaned toward her friend with an affectionate smile. "Austerity does not become you, Vincent."

The baron sighed and threw his head back on his chaise longue, staring at the sky. "Can't you see that world of ours is dying, my darlings? Mere caprice and illusion! Leave the sinking ship!"

"No one's going to spoil my summer evening being monastic," Babs said.

Babs paced ceaselessly on the terrace; she had merely come for the day to see Nicolas and she showed impatience with the isolation of our summer house. She kept looking down at her watch and up again at the driveway, in hopes that the lover and the car that were to take her back to New York might arrive ahead of schedule.

"It used to be that one error in a dish or a domestic ruined my day," Uncle Vincent continued, "but no more. Now I only wish to reduce, pare down."

"You've made a charming reputation as our travel editor," Babs said.

" . . . and I wish you to remain our travel editor until the day you die," Mother said firmly. "Your great gift is to observe oddity, which requires precisely the kind of frivolity in which we live."

"Who else has discovered places as amusing as you have when they were still dreary villages?" Babs exclaimed. "Acapulco! Hammamet!"

"Yes," Nada agreed. "You've always had an eye for style, and after all these years it would be a dreadful mistake for you to become an earnest man."

"Yet look how happy I've been since I fired my cook!" the baron insisted. "How exhausting always having to decide in the morning what you're going to eat that night; there are days when I don't know, others when I want porridge, others when I want . . . nothing. I've been a happier man dining in tiny restaurants, my first step toward the natural."

"Nature?" Mother interrupted. "Nature can be very violent. We must protect ourselves from it by every means at hand."

"If you're going to go back to nature you might as well go to Holland," Babs added. "There's money there and where there's money there's life."

We'd just unwrapped the armful of presents Babs always brought us from F. A. O. Schwarz—a huge map of the world for Nicolas, roller skates for me. I'd always figured that presents were the easiest way she had of showing she loved anyone. It was 1953. Babs had adorned her flat-chested, carefully starved body with white harem pants gathered at the ankles, a white criss-cross brassiere, numerous gold coin chains about her neck and waist. ("White now!" she'd written in the June issue of *Best*. "Little white

drifting pants, the salt of the earth wherever you go . . .
give it bezzazz with tribal gold . . .'')

"As I advance inexorably toward old age . . ." the baron
tried.

"Nothing advances inexorably," Babs interrupted.
"That is bad *copy*."

"As I inexorably advance in age," the baron persisted,
"I'm increasingly depressed by your giddy innovations . . ."

"You're *très sympathique* but full of shit," Babs said.

"Our very living is earned through that class of society
which is still able to create luxury," Mother remarked
softly.

"Baudelaire!" Babs shot out. *"L'inutile, ce luxe nécessaire!"*

I could tell that the baron, who tired easily, would soon
capitulate.

"We tell the world where the most exciting jewelry,
cars, food, hotels, interiors are found," Babs added. "We
tell them where the *aura* is."

"Ah well," Uncle Vincent sighed, "it *is* style that makes
us believe."

"That's why I still welcome a good church service,"
Mother said.

"I could use one," Babs said, as she stared anxiously
toward the driveway. "Kneeling is so good for the thighs."

"Paula, that is *my* shell!" Nicolas cried out.

All three adults sprang to their feet. We were each the
center of their lives. The wind stirred in the birches. I
thought of Grandmother Fitzsimmons in the North African
desert. I slid the shell back into the back of my shirt.

"That shell is m-m-m-mine!" Nicolas cried out again.

We'd been sitting in a corner of the lawn, arguing about
our collection of seashells. By the time we'd spent a few
years together, Nicolas and I were trying to outdo each
other at whatever activity we engaged in. If I'd spent a

week learning a monologue from *The Tempest*, he'd manage to learn three monologues overnight. The summer Aunt Babs had given him his first set of water colors I'd devoted the vacation to painting many exquisite still lifes twice the size of his. Nicolas became an expert at philately, Uncle Vincent's favorite hobby, and upstaged me by finding collections of rare nineteenth-century Venetian stamps. So I tried to surpass him in marine science, identifying every sea creature we found on the beach. . . . I clutched at the shell behind my back, I'd found it by myself that morning. Nicolas had his arm around me, trying to grab it. We fell on each other, rolling on the grass, our bodies hot. Sala stood behind us muttering now don't hurt my Paula, Nicolas, you bigger than her. "A ninny thou art, my faithful Sal . . ." The family had sat down. They were used to our arguments. But Babs did cry out, "Nicolas darling! Do share that shell with Paula!"

"Look at them in the grass," the baron said. "They are our only hope."

"Monsieur Nicolas, I'll skin your rintrum." Sala's voice rose. "What you do on top of her like that!"

"I adore Paula's hair that length," Mother said.

"I miss her braids," Uncle Vincent said. "I miss my little *Mädchen* with the long brown braids."

"Remember the time she cut them off herself to play Portia!"

"She looked appalling," Babs said. "She looked like an Arab urchin."

ALL THROUGH MY CHILDHOOD I HAD FELT LIKE ALICE IN Wonderland, dressed in her finery, running down the tunnel, being observed by my mother and her friends through long powerful telescopes, running, running away from their lens. It had begun in first grade. That tear in the sleeve of your uniform, Pumpkin, the pleats of that gym skirt are awkward, only the French can still do proper pleats. Your hem is rising to the left, your bangs are getting too thick, why hide your eyebrows darling! When I was eleven and Babs came into our lives the observations doubled. What huge feet she's going to have, throw away those governessy shoes dear, pull your belt down over your sweater or you'll look golf linksy. Only Sala and Uncle Vincent never looked at me but smelled me, knew me. He often recited to me the lovelorn verses he'd written as a student in Budapest. Throughout a childhood of Mother's parties I would only wait for one person, I'd wait like one in love for the appearance of Uncle Vincent. If he came early enough, before the room was filled with guests, he put on the gramophone and seized me by the waist, and I put my patent leather pumps on top of his big black leather shoes and off I went, three inches taller, hugging Uncle Vincent's waist and dancing along with his large lyric legs, *"Ah ma chère petite beauté!"* Let my Paula be, Vincent always said, her shoes are just fine, her bangs are perfect.

Nicolas, who was barely ever observed, was just now standing in his bathing trunks, shouting into the sunlight.

"Will everyone ss-ss-stop tt-tt-telling Paula how she looks?"

"Nicolas," Aunt Babs ordered. "I can't abide it when you're not amusing."

"Always babbling like a group of snobs!" Nicolas continued.

"Ah, dear boy, do not dismiss snobs," Uncle Vincent interrupted. "Snobbism is a form of despair."

"Please be original, Nicolas!"

"I shall be aboriginal!"

"Ah, that's better," Aunt Babs said.

We went into the house to clean up and came out again like good children, scrubbed for tea. Mother. Tea. She insisted on tea every day, had kept many of the habits of her youth. There was a book by her elbow titled *The Way of the Pilgrim*. The summer house stretched behind us, white and laundered, acres of thick woods and a lawn sloping toward a little inlet of Long Island Sound. Mother loved its isolation. It was "an escape from the hell of the office," where she was always pursued by dumb reporters wanting to know what she thought of the New Look, plastic surgery, the future of knitwear.

Mother poured tea.

"Delicious children!" Uncle Vincent said. "What kind of an afternoon are you planning?"

Nicolas leaned down to my small height and whispered something to me. When a practical demand had to be made I often spoke it for Nicolas to spare him embarrassment.

"After tea Nicolas and I would like to walk to town."

"Paula dear," Babs said, "not with *that* belt on."

"Let her be," the baron ordered.

It smelled like rain. The baron sighed. The wind stirred in the birches. Nicolas took my hand. We started walking.

"I LOVE PAULA'S WHOLE *aura*," AUNT BABS USED TO SAY when she paid her monthly visit to us. "She's going to be one of the divine creatures of our time."

"I am preparing a poisoned ring, like the Borgias," Nicolas spoke softly.

"Très drôle," Babs said, and I'd see her look up at Nicolas with anxious, perplexed eyes. Only I could tell that she was pretending not to notice him because she couldn't cope with him. She feigned to be absorbed in her work and calmly continued writing her fashion notes. "Needed immediately for evening! Banana velvet, fabulous wrapped in sables and dazzled with many rubies . . ." "In this fall! The ravishing artistry of the Bolshoi Ballet . . ."

After Babs had visited a few hours some very beautiful young man would come to pick her up in a swank convertible. They changed every few weeks, like Bonwit Teller's windows. She liked artists—it was beginning to be in at *Best* to name-drop paintings or books. There was one beau of Babs' called Sebastian who spoke with a thick lisp in five languages and painted melancholy still lifes of eggplants and guitars. Another called Jean-François about whom Babs said "He is a cross of Matisse and Dali!" and who brought us beautifully wrapped sets of watercolor brushes for our own masterpieces. *"Trésor, comment vas-tu!"* Babs would exult at the end of a visit, falling into Sebastian's, Jean-François', Benvenuto's arms. She'd get into a car and we wouldn't see her again for several weeks. I liked Aunt Babs because she made me feel important; I figured she made all that noise because she was terrified of not living up to my amazing mother. I just found all those men around her confusing; I'd always had a frightful time imagining people in bed together, I'd never known anyone to be in Mother's bed.

Over the years I'd watch Nicolas be moody, ebullient, wily, grasping, magnanimous, seductive, spinning out various roles and destinies with which to baffle and annoy his mother. He denied that his father had been a brilliant French car racer, as Babs would have it, and claimed that he'd been a humble Parisian baker, the best in Montmartre. He described the heat and floured whiteness of the room in which the breads were baked, the supple way his father's hands molded dough into delectable brioches and croissants. Within the span of one year he'd threatened Babs with the prospects of his becoming a carpenter, a mortician, a seaman—the U.S. Navy somehow terrified Babs the most.

Nicolas particularly enjoyed relating the various tactics he'd invented to confuse his mother at the Paris collections. The exquisite new ploy he'd devised one spring, for instance, when he decided he'd give his mother a run for her

life. At the end of a Dior collection she'd stand around so
absorbed in the mysterious bargainings of the trade ("What
do you mean you're taking out 'Van Gogh' for a sketching
this evening, I already reserved it hours ago . . .") that if
he'd thrown himself into the Seine she wouldn't have
known it for six hours ("Well what nerve you have, *I* was
the first to ask for 'Gauguin,' I'll immediately talk to
Christian himself about it . . .").

In the midst of such exchanges little Nicolas cowered by
Mama's heels in a state of dreadful boredom and growing
hunger, trying to hang on to a corner of her garments to
be sure she wouldn't forget his lunch again—our mothers
were generous with all that money could buy, Paris dinners
were an endless feast of boeuf en daubes, poulets au Cal-
vados, tartes tatins, but lunch at Dior time was made dicey
by their loony ambitions. . . . Well, no more skipping
meals, Nicolas decided. One day he'd brought a long length
of string and kept it in his pocket throughout one of Uncle
Christian's parades; and right after "Wagner" (raspberry
taffeta ballgown flounced in tiered hems) he'd tied an end
of the string to a handle of Babs' Hermès handbag—he'd
unwound the twine as she launched into her usual bedlam
of greetings and demands, crawled through the crowd toward the inner sanctum where the dresses were kept—it
took Babs a good hour to realize Nicolas' absence, she
noticed it when one of the mannequins tripped over the far
end of his rope and fell to the ground with an electrifying
scream, grievously cutting her chin on a champagne glass—
"Christian, mon enfant, j'ai perdu mon enfant!"

In that ornate language I'd taught him to speak (as eloquently, I thought, as Laurence Olivier), Nicolas would
mime the scene with great brilliance, shifting his voice an
octave higher to imitate Babs. I often feard that Nicolas
was a more gifted actor than I could ever become, he could

burst into tears, shriek with laughter or fall dead with complete conviction.

". . . Uncle Christian hopping about his salon, not so much concerned with me as with his mannequin, who would remain disfigured for some months, and without whose ethereal physique—five feet eleven, nineteen-inch waist—a score of dresses had to be remade. . . ."

So Nicolas knew the year of the zigzag line, the H-line, as well as any of the hags from *Paris-Flair* or *London News* who'd haunted the Paris salons. Beyond excelling at culinary tasks the way I never could (chopping onions and peppers for Sala, baking birthday cakes) he hoarded much fashionable knowledge to charm the Little Family, making himself useful in all kinds of situations. "Let's see, Nicolas dear," Mother would ask, "what year was Christian's Eiffel Tower line, '49, '50?" "'Fifty-one," he'd answer with a winsome smile, blinking his blue eyes to reassure her that it was a minor lapse.

(I kept remembering Nicolas the first summer he'd shared with us, the way his hand had shaken as he held it out for another cup of tea. . . . Mother so generous, so gentle with both of us I was sometimes jealous, Mother buttering his second scone, spreading it amply with jam . . . Uncle Vincent hovering over his stamp collection, also smiling at Nicolas, ah, my little prince, what splendid manners, here's a lovely item from the Belgian Congo. . . . We'd all taken turns sculpting, rebuilding Nicolas from the shreds he'd brought us, I'd feared for his survival if I didn't give him everything he wanted. . . .)

WHEN WE'D BEEN YOUNGER ONE OF NICOLAS' FAVORITE games had been called "Let's Play Fathers." Nicolas was all set and ready to go with his Parisian baker, but that was one game I was rotten at. The way Mother had brought me up it was as gauche to ask about one's father as to put your

gloves on wrong side out or eat a salad with your spoon.
So I hadn't given much thought to the matter since I'd been
ten or so, all I could think of was that I might want a parent
who was a champion ice skater. That grew monotonous so
we'd start rehearsing *The Tempest* again. Miranda is a lousy
role, she keeps standing around like an idiot, looking gorgeous, while her own father keeps warning her not to lose
her virginity. And I'd rather have worked on the roles I
was preparing for the fall season at the Academy, Rosalind, Portia; but *The Tempest* was Nicolas' favorite play
for three whole summers and as usual I let him have his
way. He enjoyed taking turns playing Prospero, Sebastian,
Caliban.

"In a few years you're going to marry me," Nicolas
said. It was July 1955. We'd been sitting on the beach,
reading on a postcard from Mother and Babs that Dior's
show was too chichi this year, the smash hit of the season
was Chanel's collection, "buoyant, enduring, irresistible."
"If you don't marry me I really will join the navy." When
Nicolas had said that I'd giggled and poked at him a lot so
that he would continue pinning me down harder on the
warm white sand.

Mother had no idea what she was doing, leaving us alone
year after year, in that isolated house.

Much of the summer we'd have little to do but sit on
the lawn waiting for Sala's fragrant meals, arguing about
how to stage *The Tempest*, why I refused to read Nicolas'
hand. Sala had started me on her science when I was ten
and by the time I was twelve I'd become a fairly expert
palmist, but I was choosy about the hands I read. I refused
to read Mother's or Uncle Vincent's because I feared seeing
something threatening in them. I couldn't read Babs' because I didn't like holding her hand—it was so red-clawed
and fidgety it made me lose most of my art. The lifeline
of Sala's palm took a subtle break in its fifth decade and I

never looked at it again. As for Nicolas, his head line was long and sturdy but the first half of his lifeline was so disturbing that I also refused to tell him about it. It was striated and foliated like those of persons who can never finish any tasks they've begun, whose lives are all dispersion, there were twelve Nicolases there, so different one from the other they should each have had another name.

SALA SITTING ON THE ROCKER WATCHING US ARGUE ABOUT Prospero and tussle on the lawn, chuckling to herself as she got high on her beer in the late afternoon, wandering in and out of the house to look after her gumbo and apple fritters.

"Fair encounter of two most rare affections!"

Sala hovering over us on the beach: *"Levez-vous, enfants,* I reckon I saw you! You, Paula, get out from under that boy and put on a clean shirt for supper!"

Nicolas' obsession to be noticed and admired had led him to adopt a new hobby every summer. Aged fourteen he took up the cello. He played Haydn and Mozart with violence and some skill, leading Uncle Vincent to proclaim that this was his greatest gift. I loved to stare at Nicolas' large blond body as he hugged the instrument between long legs covered as with peach down, fingers fluttering with passion on the strings. At times I thought it was magic, his faculty to excel in all manner of things, at times he scared me. What would happen if he'd decide to control me the way he'd conquered our household, the family's attention. During the last summer I spent with Nicolas I often woke up crying in the middle of the night, wondering what I could do to protect myself from what I feared was his great power.

THE JAWS OF DARKNESS WILL DEVOUR YOU, FAIR MIranda, if you do not accept me as your lord.

* * *

AS WE GOT OLDER I'D MAKE UP FIGHTS WITH NICOLAS about everything under the sun so we could struggle on the lawn or the beach together, I'd invent fights about how he should speak Caliban's lines. I loved to feel the new pale blond fuzz on his chest and underarms when he was in his bathing trunks, trying to have his way.

CO-MATE IN EXILE, ISN'T THIS LIFE MORE SWEET THAN that of our mothers' painted pomp. The white cold virgin snow of Nicolas on mine. Mother always in her black and white office, her white Paris limousine. I kissed Nicolas deeply on the mouth.

"I'm going to tell on you two to *Maman* when she come back, you keep on like this and we're going to have you no birthday!"

"Good my nurse of virtue Sal, though dost babble like a thing most brutish. . . . Sweet Miranda, your tongue cannot conceive what is my dream of felicity. . . ."

WE LAY ON THE BEACH ONCE, CLEAN AND WHITE. NICO-las' eyes were soft and azure. As if his eyes were holding their breath. He stretched out my arms and held them pinned behind me, his shining hair wild and out of place. A mean snarl of his muzzle, tiger pouncing on his bone.

At first I hadn't wanted to.

At least that's the way I'd first remembered it.

"HER LITTLE BREASTS," I HEARD MOTHER WHISPER TO Uncle Vincent when the family came back in August. "It's so moving, a young girl's early breasts."

"She's growing up," Uncle Vincent said. "My little *Mädchen* is growing up."

* * *

WE WERE ALONE AND UNSEEN AS OUR MOTHERS HAD willed it. King and queen of our bodies, our domains. Loving and sipping each other dry like bones. All could have burned about us.

O FERDINAND, THOU ART THE SUM OF MY EARTHLY DESIRES . . ./
There's wildness in it when you start. Again and again and again.

THERE WAS LITTLE LEFT TO CALL MYSELF. LYING IN THE dark, searching for my limbs. Nicolas' legs and arms wrapped all about me, my body melting into his. He could destroy me, he could annihilate me.

COMMAND THESE ELEMENTS TO SILENCE . . . / OUR REvels now are ended . . .

IN THE SEPTEMBER OF MY SIXTEENTH YEAR I BEGAN TO lock myself in closets to get away from Nicolas.
Mother's faint jasmine smell as she stood at the door of the closet trying to make me come out: "Now, Pumpkin, when are we going to pull ourselves together?" And then Sala: "Come, Paula baby, what are you fussin' for in there, there's no one going to hurt you no more, I need my baby out so she can take care of old Sala . . ."
Cling clang, Babs' jeweled approach. The faster you get out of there, lovey, the sooner I can give you a nice silly lunch at Le Pavillon. Uncle Vincent's tender whispers, where is my dove, where is my little Duse.
It took Sala several tries to get me out and only she could do it: "Paula honey, come out of there, Nicolas is gone and there's no one going to hurt you no more. . . ."
Well, no one could have guessed that Nicolas' threats were so precisely carried out. During the weeks I was hav-

ing my first little "disruption," as Mother delicately put
it, Nicolas had celebrated his sixteenth birthday by running
away from what was left of our childhoods, joining the
navy.

AND SOME TWO AND A HALF YEARS LATER, THE DAY SAINT-
Laurent saved France and I ran away from Mother's de-
krauting party for Coco Chanel, I never did make it back
to Mr. Ashok Modi's fortune-telling parlor. I ended up
instead in the office of Dr. Sanford Kubie, a fashionable
psychiatrist who was flown to Texas in a private plane each
time someone at the King Ranch went off his rocker.

   *Paula Fitzsimmons first began to develop aberrant be-
havior at the age of fifteen, the classic age for the onset of
psychoses . . .*

   *The rebellious pattern exhibited by Paula is most often
latent in children who have shown a particularly docile,
loving behavior towards their mothers . . .*

   *Alternation of elated and catatonic moods . . . urgency
of message she must preach to redeem the world . . .*

   I enjoyed stealing glimpses at the notes lying on the
doctor's desk when he was off answering calls from a press
tycoon or the assistant secretary of state. I'd gotten the Best
in shrinks.

FAILING

ITHIN A WEEK OF MY DEBUT AT HER CHANEL party Mother had mastered the jargon of looniness as swiftly as she'd boned up on Nietzsche's aphorisms, Eliot's *Waste Land*.

"After a century of research," I'd hear her say on the phone, as I was waking from a Librium-drugged sleep, "psychiatrists still haven't agreed on the causes of schizophrenia or of the manic-depressive state, they can't even draw a clear *line* between the two. . . ."

Her intimate tone let me know that she was talking to the concerned, puzzled Vincent.

"Have you heard of the nature versus nurture controversy going on about schizophrenia, Vincent? Quite fascinating, really. Nature school views psychosis as a strictly biochemical imbalance independent of environment, only responsive to chemical treatment . . . whereas nurture school goes back to the Platonic concept that mind and body are separate entities, thus blaming mental illness on an unhealthy childhood environment. . . ."

"Well now, Vincent, we can't go along with Plato on *this* one, can we? I love her, I gave her all I knew to give . . ."

(Much tremor in the voice. Suppress, suppress, she couldn't do it this time.)

Long pause, Uncle Vincent must have been up until three A.M. studying the last issue of *Psychology*. As he understood it such lapses were usually triggered by a specific event . . . Sala's death . . . the pressure of Paula preparing for a theatrical career while striving to excel in her college work . . . he'd also read that people who became schizophrenic have often had isolated childhoods with no more than one close friend. . . .

"Don't be ridiculous, Vincent, look at the lovely summers we gave her with Nicolas! . . . What else could we have done, sent her to one of those swimming camps where she would have become another *average* child?"

Another morning, waking me painfully from my newly prescribed euphoria of ten-milligram Librium: "The most recent evidence, Vincent dear, points to the prevalence of *genetic* and *chemical* factors . . . schizophrenic symptoms can arise no matter *how* perfect the patient's environment. . . ."

Often I couldn't follow the thread of her words, trapped in a dumb, drugged, peaceful void in which I imagined that I was still cradled in Sala's thick black arms, hearing her say, "Child, there's nothing in sight but births and weddings and deaths, births and weddings . . ."

Another day, dawn: As Mother's expertise increased she woke her confidant at six, seven A.M. The heredity theory is also growing by leaps and bounds as a factor in Paula's kind of illness, she'd say to Vincent. No elaborations needed on her own mother's curious behavior, a talent for sudden, erratic departures had marked generations of her family—her maternal grandfather abandoning a flourishing

career in diplomacy to devote himself solely to the raising
of hybrid bees in a Welsh hamlet. Great-grandfather Hars-
grave, leaving his family at the age of fifty-one and becoming a hermit in some granite hovel on the Isle of Skye. . . .

Alone with me she was as tender and serene as ever,
putting on a superb show, prattling about the details of the
profession. "Chanel's line will win out after all, Pumpkin,
I've been predicting it for decades. . . . Oh, do get back
to your drama studies and pull yourself together in time for
my Saint-Laurent party, darling, let's get into a cab to see
Dr. Kubie. . . ."

Dr. Kubie was a jovial, excruciatingly social shrink in
his middle fifties, with Gucci shoes and a perpetual Caribbean suntan, whom I went to see three times a week.
Here's a pillow, he'd say. Talk to the pillow, Paulie, pretend it's Mother. Get mad at Mother. Punch the pillow! I
guess he expected me to hit it very hard, but as I stared at
the dumb, pink thing I felt a dumb, drugged anger that had
nothing to do with Mother. I just held it, staring. Well,
pretend it's not Mother, who else could it be, Paula? So
I'd hit the pillow several times pretending it was Sala or
Nicolas, yelling why did you leave me, leave me? At that
point the phone would ring and Dr. Kubie would be busy
for some minutes answering phone calls from the mayor of
Boston or the Albert Lasker Foundation. That gave me
time to improve my act. I'd steal a look at his notes or
dive into my mind like a trained seal, trying to come up
with some nice tidbit to please the doctor. I prattled on
about the origin of palmistry millennia ago among the Joshi
caste of northwest India, world's most ancient wisdom, its
recognition long past due—the only science that can detect
the faults in mankind and redeem them—lines of the hand
unlock the cabinet of character, improve our lives by lib-
erating our most hidden energies and talents—(anything to
keep away from my forbidden games with Nicolas or Sala's

death)—I can save thousands of lives by reading the future in the palms of hands, doctor, only way to self-knowledge, self-mastery, the improvement of mankind—

. . . Regressive rebellion against the appearance-conscious society in which patient was nurtured . . . Paula's desire to be invisible alternates with bouts of extreme exhibitionism . . .

The greatest pleasure I received from studying Dr. Kubie's notes was that he described me as a "rapid cyclist." When I first went to see him my "cycles" of mood occurred at speedier rates than in any patient Dr. Kubie had treated in the last few years. However, after three months of continually increased Librium treatment, I was being turned into an increasingly slow cyclist. By then I'd ceased preaching any mission about how to get a better deal in this life or the next. I'd lost all control of my voice and was ashamed of using it; my voice came out piping high like a five-year-old's or raucously low like Orson Welles playing Iago. Remembering the simplest facts—Aunt Babs' or Uncle Vincent's names—was like attempting to read Sanskrit, each time I tried to concentrate on something my mind glided off like a car swerving off the road into a deep safe field of snow. I lay in bed all day, numb and wise and dozing, or else I locked myself in the closets of Mother's apartment. That fall, after Nicolas and I had played out our fates, I'd stayed closeted for a few hours at a time. But in my second bout my retreats lasted for a day or two. It was so nourishingly dark, so warm and private in that velvet darkness, I was the small furry animal waiting for spring's return, I sang Sala's old hymns or addressed Nicolas in our old language of *The Tempest*. "Four legs and two voices, a most delicate monster. . . . Dost thou forget from what a torment I did free thee . . . took pains to make thee speak. . . ."

At first Mother had tried to get me out of the closets all by herself, standing outside the door, her smell of jasmine warm and welcoming, calling me all the names of our shared childhood. Come, rabbit, what do you think you're doing there, it's time you stopped playing, puppy love, when will you stop being funny, mousy darling? (Mother never meant funny haha. She was British there, funny meant batty.)

But in the last days of my freedom she turned to her friends for help. There came a closeted stay when I'd slept well enough between what I supposed had been two daylights—a good twenty-four hours. The air was getting a little stuffy. I'd grown a bit more lucid without the numbing drugs and I was enjoying thinking of how Grandmother Fitzsimmons had hidden from the world in the desert. She too was said to have had visionary powers, a few times she'd walked into Mother's room in the country crying out, "Nada, Nada! Don't ride today!" And each of those mornings one of Barkham Hall's legendary horses had thrown its rider, causing grave injuries. . . . I was enjoying myself a lot with Grandmother in between my lovely sleeps until Mother finally decided to get help from the Little Family.

Babs could have taken off her stiletto heels and tiptoed toward the closet with the softfootedness of a Plisetskaya, I still would have known her approach by the cling clang of her huge bracelets, the hot violent smell of Diorissima, "so delectably beyond nature," as she'd described it in *Best*. Sometimes I heard a soft whisper from behind my door and knew that she had one of her beaus at her side. I enjoyed inventing him, he might be called Vero Prosciutto and have long green hair, a dagger at his side with which he painted large pictures of Saint George. Babs had devised a hilarious language for her task of uncloseting Paula, some

weird mixture of British lingo and field hockey school-
marm which she'd decided was appropriate for balmies.
"Hop hop and hallow, how's the old sport doing, having
a swell time in there?" At times she sounded like a British
colonel of the Indian Raj coaching a team of teenage native
polo players. "Bit of an act you're giving us, hey? Well,
cheerio, old girl, jolly good proposition I have to make
you. We'll lunch at Grenouille and go to Broadway to catch
Brando in *Streetcar,* rather more fun than calling in the
carpenters, right?"

Culture wasn't working, so Babs resorted to Emotion.

"Paula," she wept, "come back to the family!"

I always waited for the family bit, that was a howler.
You've never heard a bunch talk so much about family as
the loners who made up Babs' and Mother's world, they
all had the weirdest notion of what it was. Dior said that
his family consisted of Bobby, his dog. To Givenchy it
was his cook and his gardeners, so sweet. To Balenciaga
it was the two Madrileño fops who cut his broadcloth and
his lace. Loners like us didn't hook up with normal people
who had friends, they chose a few other loners and made
up some oddball group they called the family.

"Paula, darling, come back to the family!"

So I just continued to crouch there, enjoying the increasingly warm darkness, waiting for the baron to fish me out.

For since Sala's death only Uncle Vincent could do it,
the failed poet who still dared to weep and bare himself
before others, to whom I embodied the romance and shat-
tered dreams of his own youth. "I miss my little *Mädchen*
with the long brown hair," he whispered. "I pine for her,
I wither like a leaf on a storm-stricken branch, I am the
bridegroom knocking at an empty door. . . ." His incan-
tations were couched in a florid German which I later realized were botched, ill-remembered lines from the favorite
poets of his youth—Heine, Hölderlin. And toward the end

of his entreaties he would sing to me in a sweet, high falsetto verses of those poets set to music in Schumann's lieder. My favorite one began, "You are my rainbow in the woods . . ."

He once tried Schubert but I didn't like it as much. I'd begun to get choosy there in the closet. "Schumann," I cried, "I only want Schumann!"

And after hearing the cracked strains of his song I reemerged. Mother wheedled me into drinking a little orange juice. "What ho," Babs would exclaim. "Come back to pasture like a jolly old horse!" As soon as I saw people around me I turned catatonic again, swung my hair into a thick curtain over my face, refused to speak. I was swaddled into shawls, taken back to Dr. Kubie. He stuck a needle into my arm. "Doubling the lithium dose. Our new wonder cure for the blues. She'll be nifty in no time, good as new!"

Lithium doses tripled, quadrupled, quintupled. The rapid cyclist riding faster and faster into her lowest downs, I'd finally crossed into that new body I'd wished for since childhood, I'd dived through the surface of the time lake and tasted the darkness that lay on the other side, but it had none of the stillness and peace I'd expected, it was daze and rage and unredeemed solitude; sometimes I wondered how much of a choice I'd had in all this, whether I hadn't left the stage to play a new role that would isolate me even more from the footlights of *Best*. . . .

Chanel was staying with Mother the day I was committed to a hospital for the first time. I'd just turned nineteen and Chanel had just come back from Texas, where she'd received a huge gilt statue from Neiman-Marcus for her contribution to the World of Fashion. I'd taken the statue into the closet with me and she was furious. A fourth voice, Chanel's yellow-fanged hiss, joined the familiar three voices whispering behind the closet door. But she was talking to them, not to me. "A success you're making of your career, *ma belle* Nada. Are you going to allow that muddy little gypsy to ruin your life? Bunch of cowards, what will you *look* like if you don't put her away?"

Of course, WHAT WOULD THEY LOOK LIKE!!!

Babs pretended to plead for my safety as she joined Coco's demands: "Save her from herself, from herself!"

One last look at Mother: helpless, distraught, dreading all confrontations, dreading the present and the future. She clutched my hand. She did something amazing. She kissed my hand. "You must go," she whispered.

Even the baron retreated. "As a philatelist, I feel incompetent to give an opinion in this matter."

Even he had abandoned me.

I WAS DELIGHTED WITH THE FIRST DAYS OF MY HOSPITAL stay. So much to hear and see. Many imaginative people wandering around playing my old reincarnation games saying they were Jesus Christ, Herbert Hoover, Shirley Temple. I could sit at the breakfast table and do polite introductions saying, Sal Mineo I'd like you to meet Albert Einstein; stop people in the hall explaining that I could teach them how to be anyone they wanted to be in the next life, Woodrow Wilson, a crab, Babe Ruth; listen to patients talk about their travels to every planet in the solar system. I was delighted by all the new words I learned in the nuthouse—the nurse in constant watch over me was called a One on One, I was on C.O. for constant observations and forbidden to do anything A.M.A., Against Medical Advice. I was a likable loony when I got to the hospital, not a paranoid nasty one. I'd recently added astrology to my expertise in the occult; as soon as I left the family for the hospital I wanted to read as many palms and horoscopes as possible, make more and more converts each day to my science of the future, I insisted on going into every pa-

tient's room to help them save their lives through my wisdom and when that wasn't allowed I paced the floor of the
ward, singing the opera arias Mother had learned as a child.
My favorite was the one she'd listened to on Grandmother
Fitzsimmons' crimson-petaled gramophone, *"Ah se una
volta sola . . . "* My elation approached a state of ecstasy
when I got several people together to listen to me. I told
the doctors I had no time to go to bed or sleep because
there was too much work to do.

And then the growing outrage.

Being wheeled into a tall white room, now this isn't
really going to hurt Paula, just a little burning sensation in
your head . . .

It's just like going to sleep, some people *like* it Paula,
bite down on the wire . . .

Throwing the gasoline on Paula when she couldn't
wouldn't sell/ lighting it . . . white flesh mangled insect
screams shot up to the sky in a rubbish heap of flesh
smeared over the rotting phosphorescent bones . . . men-
dicant words falling like dead birds into the darkness/no
more/ no more/ darkness wiping me out like chalk on a
blackboard . . . then bring in the cool the freezing morgue
waking from the dead with the taste of rotting metal in my
mouth. . . .

Until one day I played the greatest role in life, Escape.
I strung myself from the hospital window with a sheet in
the middle of the night and started running again. With the
forty dollars I'd hidden in the seam of my mattress I bought
a bus ticket to Chicago. I'd always wanted to see "La
Grande Jatte." I believe not only in reincarnation but in
Providence.

Sleeping on that bus for hours I opened my eyes and saw
a face that I remembered from another life, from a particular day when I was still a good girl playing all the roles
dearest Mummy wanted me to play, when I used to curtsy

and smile in posh restaurants saying *"Je voudrais la sole
meunière s'il vous plaît . . ."*

I'D TURNED SIXTEEN THAT DAY; IT WAS A YEAR AFTER
Nicolas' flight to the navy. Mother and I were having lunch
at "21," and on a red-brocaded banquette in front of us
sat a man wearing a navy blazer whose sleeve was tucked
into a pocket. His eyes were dark brown and guarded, three
fine scars crossed his left cheek. The beautiful woman sitting at his side was cutting his meat. As his companion
went at his meat with her fork and knife, the stranger studied the room with a pleased, distant gaze. Mother nudged
my elbow and whispered, "What an extraordinary-looking
man!" I'd been playing Ophelia again at the Academy that
year, I enjoyed regaling mother with new lines: "He is the
glass of fashion and the mold of form." I would never
forget his pale haughty face, and for months after that first
glimpse of Julian Symonds I'd even remembered the delicate way in which he ate his food after it had been cut up
for him; slowly and delicately, with the fussiness of a cat;
not looking much at his companion yet answering her with
a quick smile, brief words that made her laugh. It was
when he threw his head back, exhaling the smoke, that his
eyes first rested on us. He placed the cigarette on an ash-
tray, stared at us for a few seconds, whispered to the
woman at his side. She nodded with an air both interested
and annoyed. Mother was prodding me to rise and leave,
let's not waste time, darling, I've twelve more pages to lay
out before the weekend. As we walked toward the door
Mother waved goodbye to Elsa Maxwell, blew a kiss to
the editor of *Daily Wear,* said hello, Maude, we're dining
on Tuesday to an Englishwoman dressed in a Balmain suit
that Mother had rated earlier as unfit for Liverpool. We'd
hailed a cab to take her back to her office. I'd wondered

which one of us the one-armed man with the soldierly gaze had admired.

It's from the sunnier side of my time lake that the stranger reappeared, on a bus bound for Chicago. A face above mine, furrowed cheeks, delicate bones. He gently placed his hand on my head. The weight of his chill and total comprehension. The certitude that he could bring all healing. The only one who would want me dusty and discarded, who would love me tattered and thick-tongued in my beggar's rags.

JULIAN MIKOLSKI SYMONDS WAS BORN A DECADE BEFORE me, under the sign of Saturn, the son of poor, alcoholic parents who left him orphaned at the age of eleven. Between his twentieth and thirtieth years he had been a war hero, a divinity student, an Episcopal priest, and a biographer of saints. At the age of twenty-nine he had written a best-seller on the life of Saint Francis. I'd managed to be rescued by a complicated, driven man.

OCTOBER 1960: MARQUEES, SWEETMEATS, GUESTS, dolled-up bride, still-at-attention groom in his scrupulous wedding suit, Uncle Vincent weeping. A mysterious telegram from Nicolas, who was putting himself through college in the far reaches of the Northwest after having left the navy: "But yet thou shalt have freedom—so so so."

Jean Dessés and Jacques Fath flew from Paris for the wedding and Balenciaga sent a Goya etching as a wedding present. Saint-Laurent, who sent a Moroccan rug, had raised hems by still another two inches at the fall collections. Babs wore one of his knee-high camisoles, totally made of birds of paradise. Mother had chosen my wedding dress, which was about to be on the cover of *Best*. "Love at first sight and forever when he glimpses you in this dream of white lace," Babs had written about it. "Isn't Paula smashing in her Balenciaga,'' Mother prattled to the guests. ''Isn't she a beauty. Her treasure of a husband was the star student at Union Theological Seminary, a place in Harlem they also call the God Box.''

''Lost an arm in the Korean War,'' Babs added, ''first Purple Heart in our family. The image of Leslie Howard . . .''

JULIAN

WE SPENT OUR HONEYMOON IN ROME. IT WAS Mother's suggestion as an ideal wedding trip, and Julian had agreed that it was the best possible idea.

Early in our marriage Julian wrapped me in such privacy and peace that my memory remains blurred, like trying to recall nursery years, when one changes very fast within a closed and tiny space.

I mostly remember the starved way in which I absorbed the details of Julian's past. Illness had left me blank and docile as a newborn, at times I was so happy with my new life that I felt no more self and wanted none. I resided in another one called Julian, the way I used to feel part of a wiser, beautiful self called Mother.

We stood before paintings of the conversion of Saint Paul, and my husband described how faith had once seized him on the battlefield, in a whorl of pain and blinding light. We stood before the dome of Saint Peter's, and he talked about the anxiety he'd known when he had left the priesthood.

Walking in the streets of Rome I often stopped to look at babies; they seemed made of cream and attar of roses, they were as fat and luscious and perfect-skinned as the bambini in Christmas crèches, they opened their fists and moved their mouths at firefly speed to tell you of their perfect happiness. I stared down at many carriages, cooing at babies alongside their mothers. ''I want a lot of children,'' I told Julian. ''I want to live in the country, I want to give them a childhood exactly opposite to mine.''

''You'll have a baby soon,'' he said, and gently ran his hand through my hair. That was his most direct gesture of affection during our walks, running his hand through my hair while he looked at an altar or a painting or some other sight of Rome.

I learned early on that he was restrained and brief of words. The battered, impoverished orphan renamed Julian had chosen to hide most of life's joys and pains under a stoic mask of cool and calm. I had to have great trust in his love for me.

I'd understood it all when he began to talk about his childhood. About the way he kept scrutinizing his face in mirrors, as a small boy, to efface some expression of anger or fear that might trigger his parents' drunken rage. About a woman standing in a slovenly little Ohio house, his first mother, swigging her rye into a storm of shouting and abuse; the father, a sullen car mechanic, cringing glumly at his wife's curses. First memory little Joe Mikolski had of his father: he'd run the boy's hand down the scar that crossed his forehead, saying feel it, that's what she left me the one time I tried to stop her drinking. . . .

Julian still had a special way of looking at himself when he passed a mirror, lifting his head sideways a bit to the left with a cold, critical glance. What did he see? A shock of brown hair came down in a peak to the center of his forehead, which was high and very pale. Pensive eyes, dark and thickly lashed. The wary, bemused gaze of one who has not yet decided how much of himself to reveal. Three fine scars ran down his temple, acquired in the same battle in which he'd lost an arm.

He was often studying something, a difficult book, a new language—German, Greek, he seemed never to feel complete. He walked down streets very quickly, head bent forward, hand in pocket. Sometimes I'd scare him by hanging back and seeing how far he could walk without noticing he'd left me behind; when he saw I wasn't at his side he'd run back to me, laughing, put his arm around me as if I were a child.

He had a shy, ironic smile, a way of saying "terrific," barely moving his lips, which I loved to mimic because he'd acquired it at Harvard.

Rome was full of saints, Julian's favorite subject; we visited many churches, he loved to tell me about the martyrs after whom they were named, Cosmas and Damian, Santa Sabina, Santa Agnese. He favored the saints with the most tempestuous lives, the ones who'd undergone the most dramatic forms of suffering and conversion. Cyprian, Bishop of Carthage, hung and quartered under the reign of Valerian. Santa Cecilia, beheaded under the reign of Diocletian. Desperations and tormented visions, desert fathers burning fast under African suns, maidens thrown to lions or agonies of flames, Julian was drawn to all such heroism and excess.

All those serious phrases from his seminary days—or from a sane vast world very new to me! The scandal of the Incarnation; cosmic longings; the folly of the Cross.

Solitude wrapped him like a cloak. I sensed that he made friends with the greatest difficulty, that it might demand too much of what he called "the dreadful vogue of baring our souls." And I enjoyed the thought that I would have him to myself.

He said he'd loved me, searched for me since that very first time he saw me, seated at a fancy restaurant at Mother's side.

Julian always preferring to make love in the dark, his stump of missing arm warm and familiar as one of my own limbs.

I kept returning to the story of his early childhood; since he very seldom wished to talk about it I recited it to myself, with wonder and tenderness, it was like reading a Dickens novel. The time he'd joined a church by himself, aged six, to be away from his brawling home for a few more hours of the week, walking miles through blizzards to attend service; neighbors marveling, that little Mikolski kid walking by his lonesome through the snow to get religion.

Or the times he was confined to his room during his mother's drinking bouts and he read through sets of ancient magazines it was his father's solace to collect, visions of fashionable folk and distant resorts—the collection included, of course! a famous one called *Best*—ladies in delicate silks and bobbed hair leaning on ships' railings, drinking tea beside potted palms; portrait of a delicate, long-limbed woman riding horseback in the British countryside, pale hair, faintly arrogant violet eyes, he believed he'd even seen a picture of Nada Fitzsimmons in a 1937 issue of *Best*. . . .

Julian loved to talk about his second father, an Episcopal priest who had adopted him when he was eleven after his first parents died in a fire from which he was miraculously spared. He described Reverend Symonds' long mirthful face, his quotes from Virgil, the tidy, genteel parish parlor in which Julian and Mrs. Symonds filled out applications for prestigious schools and scholarships. Both his adoptive parents had died by the time Julian was twenty-six.

It was from the Symonds' history books that he chose the name Julian. "Princes of Rome, sumptuously dressed prelates," he said with a smile. He sometimes poked fun at his taste for luxury, tradition. I was realizing that he might much enjoy the style and finery *Best* would offer him.

"We live in constant rapture," he wrote Mother on a postcard. "My treasure is in excellent health and spirits. . . ." He admired Mother beyond any woman he had ever known; those days it didn't really bother me.

He'd once asked me, gently, to tell him more about my illness. But I couldn't yet speak of Nicolas, I could barely speak of Sala's death. Doctor Kubie had flunked out and sent me into flames; lurking under my newfound peace I only felt dumb anger, some botched, ill-digested memories. Not now, I said to Julian, maybe later, not now. So there were things about our past we each had to hide from the other, and that suited my husband's temperament very well.

We WERE SITTING BEFORE THE PANTHEON. LIGHTS SHIMmered on the marble tritons of the fountains, lovers embraced, serious English ladies studied guidebooks. Julian was telling me about more of his early despairs and miraculous rescues. He'd expected a priesthood to go on like that, tempestuous, painterly. And then he'd been assigned to a drab working-class parish, he'd learned that life's not made of hailstorms and conversions but of some dreary commonplace dust, the dust of everydayness . . . he'd hated it.

"You weren't a fit priest because you couldn't bring yourself to love the poor," I said; "that would have meant loving yourself."

He gave me one of those glances I would try to avoid for many years of our marriage—fear, annoyance in those eyes.

"Anyhow you'll soon get tired of me," I pacified. "I've

always craved the commonplace. Blackberries, babies, beagles.''

"Tired of you?'' he smiled. "There's so much to renew in you, such palaces and gardens. . . .'' He ran his hand through my hair, looking at the columns of the Pantheon.

I could sense his need to be seized and transported, his appetite for what he called the rapture of excess. So at times I feared that I was growing too mute and docile with happiness, that I would wear off the way his conversion had.

"Imagine, Paula,'' Julian used to tell me about Saint Francis (he spoke marvelously, like a great teacher, I loved to imagine him on the podium or the pulpit, preaching with large dramatic gestures of his arm). "Imagine this. A young rascal robs his father's store to pay for repairing a crumbling church. He leads a band of ragged friends who beg throughout the countryside, only accepting the blackest, hardest bread offered them. He's called a thief, yet before you know it he's gotten ten thousand men to follow him, that's what faith is about . . .''

It might be very hard, he said, to write another book. Saint Francis had been his *mea culpa*, his atonement for leaving the Church. He'd thought of writing on Saint Ignatius, Saint Thérèse of Lisieux but no new theme had really seized him yet, he seemed to be always waiting to be seized, he might wait a long time. That longing in his eyes when he said that—it gave him what Mother called "a marvelously tragic air.''

I KNEW THAT GRANDMOTHER FITZSIMMONS WAS BURIED in Rome, in the British cemetery. For when she fell very ill she'd informed her daughter of her whereabouts, she'd asked to be taken to Rome for her last months, she died peacefully in her daughter's arms in a room overlooking the Piazza di Spagna.

But I'd forgotten to ask Mother precisely where that grave was. After twenty minutes of searching for the tombstone I began to cry, I wasn't sure why. Rome had to do with Georgia Fitzsimmons' last days, perhaps Mother had sent us here on the occasion of our wedding to honor her memory. . . . I began to cry and Julian immediately wanted to take me away, I wanted to continue searching but he insisted on taking me away and I obeyed. I believed in being a docile exemplary wife, the opposite of most women I'd ever known.

WE CAME HOME. WE LIVED FORTY-FIVE MINUTES OUT OF town, in what Babs and Vincent called the dreadful suburbs, a plain little white house, perhaps the parsonage I'd dreamed of. Healing blessedness of early marriage, motherhood, recovered sanity—hunger to create a being absolved of all our imperfections—that first lovemaking after our daughter's birth, lust feeding on weeks of abstinence, on the shared sight of the cribbed treasure—passion and pounding of breasts aching with new milk—I sorted Julian's socks, hung his Harvard summa cum degree over his desk, made jam from berries stolen from a neighbor's yard, spent three hours on pates feuilletés for the editors who published his articles, I was a blast, I was a housewife—I waited on him at lunch every day when he came in from his study, looking forward to his silent embrace, to his musky smell of English tobacco and lemon soap—Julian the exemplary family man, always up early to do the first diaper shifts, calling Mother every two days to tell her how we were, urging me to study a little drama again to rest up from the housework—we took our vacations in small boarding houses on the Cape, for hours on end we could cuddle on a bed watching our baby, Georgia, crawl and take her first steps, how we relished our isolation and purring peace—Julian would brush his hand quietly through my hair and what serenity flowed through me, those were sweet days, sweet days. . . .

IN A FEW YEARS, FAILING TO FIND ANOTHER SAINT TO chronicle, Julian made a fine living as a journalist, documenting those who were finding God in Ways as New and Original as Possible. His column was the Best on God. I followed Julian to Texas, where he wrote for *World Report* about astronauts who had found Christ in the deep cold blue of space; to Cambridge, where Julian ingested psilocybin in the company of fifty Harvard divinity students, and found that he was the only volunteer who did not experience any component of the mystical state; to Chicago, where he received standing ovations for his lectures on "The Concepts of Sainthood in William James"; to the Anglican churches of his profession, where he knelt every Sunday straight-spined as a knight, waiting for Something to return.

I would want another child but it was denied me by Julian, by doctors, by the family. We carried Georgia everywhere like a papoose, inseparable, I nursed her for long over a year, enjoying the delicate look of horror in Babs' eyes when I opened my blouse in the middle of lunch or teatime visits. Uncle Vincent had been very moved, whispering German verses about the fount of life. . . .

But the gaze in Mother's eyes toward the end of such visits, that was something new and strange, the same pained remote look she'd worn the day of our wedding. She stood at a door, waving goodbye with a gaze of feigned bemusement, the dome of silver hair frozen upward like a creature in flight. What would happen to her life now that I was "beautifully settled," as everyone put it? Standing at the door at such moments, blowing Georgia a kiss, she seemed to stare at something new and terrifying within herself, perhaps at our freedom from each other.

But at the time I didn't give it much thought. Only one thing mattered when I married the elegant, God-starved Julian. I believed that I was finally safe. That I was free of Nicolas, and of the world that had tried to bring us up.

PART II

So the actor has a double task—that
of living in his role and at the same
time judging his own effects in relation
to the audience, so as to present an
apparently spontaneous, living being,
in a pattern carefully devised beforehand, but . . . bound to vary slightly at
every performance.

—John Gielgud, *Stage Directions*

ANNIVERSARY

THERE ARE CERTAIN WORDS IN THE ENGLISH LAN-
guage that had always cast a spell on Julian Symonds, that affected him as powerfully as "sex"
affects a fourteen-year-old, as "mother," "childhood,"
"self" might have affected his wife, Paula. Julian's words
of power were "family," "style," "tradition," "faith."
Save for the last, which had tended to grow elusive, he had
acquired all these talismans through his marriage. In Nada
Fitzsimmons he had found the kind of lineage he'd always
yearned for, fulfilled those childhood longings in which he
fancied himself born to gentility, with centuries of ceremony to recite. He had eased into her world the way a war-
battered soldier might settle into a theater seat to watch a
play about the antics of royalty. What a spectacle, he often
thought to himself, what a comic, splendid mummery!

(Seated with Nada and Vincent on a Sunday afternoon,
playing backgammon over tea. Three doubles in a row,
why Nada, someone is being unfaithful to you. Her delicate laugh. The Agnellis are coming in from Torino Mon-

day . . . Babs makes the mistake of the Viennese, she puts too much emphasis on sex . . . I haven't told you about that inn I found in the mountains an hour from Salzburg. . . .)

As for his missing faith, Julian would be extremely slow to diagnose its waning. He would be reluctant to admit that he had been drawn to the priesthood, in part, by his taste for all sumptuous and ancient rituals. He continued to long for the elation of his first calling, which had briefly fulfilled his great yearning for rootedness, community.

(Many nights he still woke into the violence of the Korean battlefield, when a shot had felled him and he'd rolled on the muddy ground, overcome with light and lightness, falling downward, knowing only that the blow had come very close to his heart—fainting and half-waking and fainting again, reaching for his left arm and touching only a pool of blood—and in his last fainting a novel burst of faith, liquefaction of all will—heavens rent like a curtain of milk, celestial horde hovering above him draped in hues of lavender and almond—he still woke at night, the odor of metal in his mouth, missing the certainty accorded him in that moment, unable to account for its loss.)

Julian's dread of confessions and confrontations had made him innocent of some transformations undergone by Paula and Nada after his first five years of marriage. Nada, while praising the health to which Julian had restored her daughter, had grown ever more quizzical and aloof, as if harboring great changes in herself which it was not in her nature to disclose. As for Paula, she had lost that helpless serenity and dependence he'd once cherished, had grown increasingly restless and defiant. Julian attributed her disquiet to her frustrated need for a career. It was his way to dismiss other possible sources of unrest, to joke and prod her to more frequent drama lessons, to steep himself all the more arduously in a refresher course in Greek or Hebrew.

So consider the impact of these events on a man who'd rather lecture six hours on the concept of martyrdom in medieval times than hear a moment of confession, confront another's disarray: on a summer day in 1970, Nada Fitzsimmons disappeared. She had suffered a heart attack the previous spring. Shortly after she was enough recovered to return to her office, she left her apartment one morning, leaving Paula a long, affectionate letter without telling her where she had gone.

Do these Fitzsimmons women settle on a disappearance, Julian began to wonder, the way others might choose madness or suicide? A few weeks after Nada's departure, Paula had returned to one of those disturbing mental states whose details she had seldom discussed and Julian had never probed. Paula, as Julian delicately put it to the world, had had to leave for a little rest.

So the problems that confront Julian on an October morning in 1970 are made all the more perplexing by his great dread of others' minds. On this October morning Paula has returned from the clinic, and is sitting on the rim of his bathtub, watching him shave. Upon coming home she has changed into jeans that are unkempt and frayed; she sits by him with her knees spread wide apart, leaning forward, elbows on knees—a boyish, assertive, unfamiliar posture that makes him uncomfortable.

As Julian slides the blade slowly, carefully about his cheek he frequently looks at his wife's reflection in the mirror. Tenth wedding anniversary today, she didn't seem to remember it, he hadn't really expected her to.

He stares at her relentless violet eyes, at the hair that has grown matted and ragged again during her weeks at the clinic and that he's decided to trim that very day. He is meticulous about hair—his own, others'. My grace, my poem by heart, you hold much of the wisdom and sweetness I'll ever know; no emotional forays, he thinks at the same time, no tusslings or confrontations; domesticity, paternal care, his most trusted expedients. He looks in the mirror at the love of his life, thinking, as soon as I have made her lunch I'll give her a marvelous haircut, blunt and short, the way it was when I found her again, the lost girl of my dreams.

PAULA SAT ON THE RIM OF THE BATHTUB, WATCHING JULian make up his face. Julian's bathroom was the most elegant room in their apartment. Lacquered walls of chocolate brown, an extensive array of men's colognes, posters from many exhibitions of sacred art. Over the sink, the reproduction of a painting of Saint Sebastian. Delicately leafed trees surrounded him, arrows entered some twelve places of Sebastian's body, on his face was a certain expression of chagrin. It was a Saturday, and within a few hours Paula was to accompany Julian and Nicolas to an antiwar demonstration. Julian was taking more time shaving than usual, he had tilted the mirror to observe her better and was shaving very slowly, averaging four seconds for his own face and one second for Paula, four Julian, one me. During her last brief hospital stay Paula had started counting everything in sight, buttons on the nurses' uniforms, starlings settled on the tree outside her window, and now she counted the intervals at which Julian looked at his face and at hers. He concentrated increasingly on himself as he swept the razor over his upper left cheek, near the fine scars that swept down from his temple.

Paula sat on the rim of the bathtub toying with a small case of jewelry she had taken from her dresser that morning—all that was left of two generations' gems—her grandmother's, her mother's. There are certain women, she'd kept telling herself in the past weeks, who with the threat of advancing years must strike out for a new life; split, run, leave all they know and love behind. Forty years after

Grandmother Fitzsimmons' disappearance Nada had flown from New York, leaving Paula a delicate silk case containing remains of the family jewelry, a note in her large, eccentric hand: "I want you to have these, darling, I'll let you know where I am as soon as I'm better . . ."

Compared with the last two battles Paula had fought for her head, this last one was a cinch to figure out, she'd become an expert in the lingo. "Alternate desire to reject Mother and cling to her . . ." "A relapse often occurs in the patient's late twenties or early thirties, after a serious loss or rebuff . . ." Paula looked up briefly at Julian, stared down again at her legs. The thinness of her ankles made her feel more like a child than ever, she'd always been someone's little girl, Sala's, Nada's, Julian's, passed on from one pair of arms to the next. How wretched for me, she often thought, that Julian was born looking so distinguished. What with his finicky Dunhill suits, his Medici profile (Babs' metaphor), he would have been equally irresistible to the family if he'd been a dentist or a mortician. "My son-in-law Dr. Symonds, a most gifted author . . ." Paula had wanted to be swept away on a long one-way voyage, and instead Julian had offered her a round trip. Julian and the Little Family had found each other so entrancing that after a few years of domestic happiness she'd been vacuumed right back into the world of *Best* as into a black hole—whoosh, less Paula than ever. When Julian was made senior editor of *World Report* and they moved back to New York, Julian grew to enjoy Nada's parties, he passed the canapés just the way Paula used to as a good little girl, he was particularly enchanted to meet Balenciaga, he often sat with Uncle Cristo on Nada's black settee discussing Spanish saints—Ignatius, Teresa. Uncle Cristo told Nada he'd never met any man with such *innate* elegance and such an accurately *tragic* view of life. . . . Paula raised her eyes to the bathroom mirror, one two three 45678

Julian was still shaving, staring at his left cheek. What can you do with someone born in Capricorn with Mars in ascendance, they're the fellows who'll never leave well enough alone, perfectionists, sufferers, virtuosos of self-improvement.

JULIAN PUT HIS RAZOR DOWN ON THE EDGE OF THE SINK and carefully rinsed out its blade. He would wait for Paula to break the silence. Her face was uncommonly calm and still, immobile as the eye of a storm. There was a heightened defiance in her gaze that he couldn't fathom, and that made him cringe. In such difficult moments it returned to him with clarity and longing, the broad simplicity of their early love. That small Italian restaurant they had sat in a decade earlier, soon after their chance meeting on a Greyhound bus, Paula reading his palm, pretending not to notice the slight trembling of his hand. "Why it quite contradicts what I first saw in your face," she'd exclaimed. "I'd considered falling in love with a lunar being, someone who heads for the night side of things, as I do, but you're very terrestrial!"

She'd clucked her tongue disapprovingly, shaking her head.

"Aha, there it is, right in the middle of the plain of Mars! You *think* you're drawn to religion but that's really much too modest for you unless you could hold the attention of many thousands, like Billy Graham!" Large circular gesture of her hand, a scolding smile. (He had told her nothing about himself save that he was a teacher of sorts, "presently unemployed.")

"Impatience, and that stubborn, dominating thumb! Always looking for someone new to reform in order to wield still more power. . . . A great early success which you'll try hard to recapture, but you're utterly out of touch with what my old nurse used to call the patience of the Holy Spirit. . . ."

She brought his palm close to her eyes now and compressed it as if kneading dough, massing its flesh inward to create lines and mounds he'd never seen before . . . come love with me he hummed to himself, studying again the delicacy of her face, the pale throat that rose like a crystal stem from its base of frail shoulders.

"Oho, I get it!" she exclaimed. "Line of Apollo moving straight up toward the ring finger, a veritable craze for aesthetic perfection. But how much more security and smart furnishings do you want . . . have patience, when you marry you'll rise even higher in prestige, whatever *that* means."

She'd made a grimace of distaste while he thought, You idiot, I'm doing everything in my power to curb myself from asking. . . .

"Yet you only pretend to be cold," she said softly, shaking his thumb in reprimand. "Actually you idealize love to a perfectly ridiculous degree, and all you'd expect of a wife! Total everything, scary!

"And yet, alongside your mundanity . . ." she was musing long after he'd ceased to listen, admiring those ruthless eyes.

Alongside all his mundanity, part of him still yearned for the most immaterial complications, God, surrender. . . . At the end of the reading (she was tired, rehearsing an old skill she'd ceased to practice), she laid his hand down on the table and patted it once gently with her own palm. "There's something I'll mention once and never again," she said softly. "At some stage in the first third of your life, I don't know whether it's behind or ahead of you, you come very close to meeting what Henry James called . . ."

"That distinguished thing," he finished for her.

"Right."

"It's behind me," he said. She'd lifted her head with a calm gaze.

"It's all behind me," he had repeated, shaken by the girl's precision.

THE RADIO BLARED BRIEFLY ABOUT TWO HUNDRED THOU-sand Americans being expected in Sheep Meadow that afternoon to protest the Vietnam War. Sheep Meadow, it would be the first time this fall Paula would see Nicolas again. She thought with alarm of Nicolas' shrewd winsome smile, wondered what his first words to her would be. Paula watched Julian's pectoral cross swinging gently on his chest as he splashed water on his face. She had given him the cross for their second wedding anniversary, just after their daughter was born. He winked at her in the mirror this time and smiled, a mannerism he'd adopted in the last years of their marriage when he saw her looking angry and bored at one of the parties Nada took them to. Besides the art posters of saints on the bathroom wall, there hung pho-tographs of Paula and Julian Symonds dancing at the April in Paris Ball, the Just One Break Ball, the Walter Winchell Cancer Fund Benefit Ball. Throughout their marriage Nada had bidden The Children to accompany her to such events, and in the past years Julian had accepted with an enthusi-asm that Paula had found puzzling. Until she'd realized that this was what he'd longed for much of his childhood—to stare at people like Princess Radziwill, the Earl of Litch-field.

In these past few years the family had been grateful to Julian for making Paula dress well again. Babs would get her size eights from Seventh Avenue for nothing. And Jul-ian would carefully study her before they left for parties, saying, "Just pearls!" Or, "No jewelry tonight, beautiful, perfect, nothing!" And then would observe the effect his

stunning wife made. In the last two years Paula had secretly begun to resume drama classes, pretending to the
family that she was at the library researching a biography
of Madame Blavatsky. So the events recorded on Julian's
wall showed Paula looking bored and furious, wishing she
were home with Georgia, rehearsing Strindberg, while Julian sat by Nada, thoughtfully gazing at the whirligigs Paula
had dreamed of escaping since he'd been twelve—Mrs.
Something Vanderbilt, Doris Duke. Paula had tried to for-
give him those outings because of the horrors of his early
childhood—its filth, shouting, beatings. And he did not
mingle with those crowds, his gaze was simply one of
meditation, of slow imbibing. At those New York parties
he might have been the perennial student again, studying
Beautiful Manners this time, fearing that he hadn't steeped
long enough in gentility. What else could Julian hope to
get from the *Best* crowd's junky savvy, from the conversations that often centered on what country you flew to to
have some part of your face or body lifted. Brazil is the
place for breasts and thighs, England unsurpassed for eyes
and noses, Emilio You-Know-Who had his chin done in
Paris at the same time as his mother and grandmother, a
three-generation facelift, what a lovely feature story you'd
have there, Nada darling! Pauline Trigère, Captain Molyneux, I want you to meet my son-in-law Julian Symonds,
religion editor of *World Report* . . .

Julian had finished shaving and was splashing some lo-
tion on his face. He lit a cigarette, same gesture she'd
observed the first time she'd ever seen him, seated on a
banquette at the "21" Club with a redhead at his side.
Toward the end of that lunch he'd laid his fork neatly on
his plate and taken out a cigarette from a slim gold case,
tapped it quickly on the table. Bending a match in half he'd
quickly struck it with two fingers while holding down the
tar with the pommel of his hand. A deft gesture; Paula had

wondered how long it had taken him to perfect it. He'd inhaled the first few puffs very deeply, with a way of throwing his head back that was not unlike her mother's. "Now there's a superb man!" Nada had whispered.

THE NAME OF THE YOUNG WOMAN WHO HAD TAKEN JULian to "21" that day might have been Marietta, Daphne, Claire. She was a divorcee with long, splendid thighs and worked in the firm that had published Julian's book on Saint Francis, written toward the end of his brief career as an Episcopal priest. Five months on the *New York Times* best-seller list, the attention of several women, at last a home of his own. He had furnished his first flat in an Empire style that he'd always admired (consoles of lacquered maple with gilded griffin feet, dominant color scheme of royal blue and malachite green), had invested in a Rouault drawing and some first editions of G. K. Chesterton. But these bounties had confused him, for they were tainted by many recent losses.

During his first year at the seminary, shortly after he had returned from Korea, Julian's foster mother had died in a car crash in their home town of Liberty, Pennsylvania. Doris Symonds had lost control on a patch of icy road and been hit by a truck, the trunk of her Plymouth laden with posters announcing a bake sale at the church of which her husband was the pastor, grocery items favored in her household—Julian's fettucini, Reverend Symonds' Social tea biscuits. Mrs. Symonds was found dead with her shopping list still in hand, all its items crossed out save for the emblematic word Joy.

To these second parents of spruce, radiant presence celebrating the joy of life was a virtue as central as charity or faith. Mrs. Symonds: gentle, freckled face, bun of ashen hair, rose hues of cashmeres and modest tweeds, hovering with admiration and cheer over Julian's adolescence. The

little china church on the dresser of her bedroom in which
she kept her hatpins, knitting needles, Julian's glowing report cards—a sign, like the last word she'd left before death,
of the serene seamless space that contained her life's faith
and its most menial details.

And Reverend Symonds, the windows of his car kept
open wide throughout the seasons so that he could roar out
his greeting to every passing acquaintance. The jovial,
cherished big man's laugh with which he responded to pa-
rishioners' problems. How amply these guardians had tried
to flood Julian with their own serenity, expressed their gratitude for the way he'd blessed their previously childless
lives!

Two years after Mrs. Symonds' passing, after that brush
with death in the trenches of Asia that had brought him the
promise of eternal life, Julian had been ordained to the
Anglican priesthood in the presence of his foster father.
Kneeling on the sanctuary steps, the trembling weight of
other ministers' hands on his scalp, he had glimpsed Father
Symonds in the front row, clutching a large handkerchief
to his face.

He'd often thought back to the gesture. Was Symonds
suffering renewed grief for the loss of his wife, shielding
the emotion of having offered God still another apostle? Or
was he hiding a smile, knowing that the young man he'd
saved and raised already looked a bit silly kneeling there
in his black robes, that Julian Symonds was quite unfit for
this vocation? Which had turned out to be the case.

His brief ministry had been a disaster (only for him,
since he was both honorable and theatrical enough to appear impeccable to others). It had been a secret disaster
because he had experienced much drudgery, little euphoria
or belonging in return. In the glum working-class parish of
upstate New York that had been his first assignment, he
had stood single-armed and bright-eyed every Sunday,

leaning with fervor toward the farmers, mechanics, sales-
men who reminded him bitterly of his origins. He had tried
to infect them with the elation that had first inspired his
own ministry. He had inherited his foster father's gift for
sermons and other dramatics, had packed the church and
stood at its door amid his flock's grateful smiles. With a
heavy heart he'd watched them walk back toward their cars,
pot roast dinners, Sunday sports pages.

"Suffering can turn us into romantics rather than cyn-
ics," he had written Father Symonds that first year.
"Imagine living one's first two decades in the high winds
of Damascus, accustomed to brushes with death, miraculous rescues, and then suddenly becalmed, like a sloop in
a windless pond. . . ."

"I'm fighting the most serious of all sins," he wrote
Symonds again, more at ease with high language than raw
truth. *"Acedia,* melancholy, what the Church Fathers called
the devil's ambrosia . . ."

And so he had tried to comfort himself by spending
sleepless nights writing about the faith of some Great Others. It was in this new avocation, as biographer of the saint
of poverty, that he had sat in a gilded New York restaurant,
aged twenty-nine, amid those very rewards the Gospel has
warned were most deceitful—success, wealth, pleasures of
the flesh.

There was a moment toward the end of lunch when he'd
glimpsed the two women sitting across the room from him:
a lost-eyed adolescent and a silver-haired beauty he'd recognized from fashionable magazines. While the mother was
making her regal goodbyes, he'd studied the girl as she
rushed back to her seat to pick up a forgotten notebook.
She pirouetted once or twice in midroom, as if she'd lost
her bearings, seemingly confused about which door to follow her mother to. And in this furl of classroom cotton and

soft chestnut hair she expressed some state of inner despair that he had an immediate, inexplicable desire to heal.

The girl had obsessed him for some weeks. At first he'd thought of scanning telephone books for the address of the famous Nada Fitzsimmons, taking his coffee near the street corners where his vision might get on or off the bus. Over the months the memory of the lost adolescent waned in sharpness but often recurred, often enough to fill him with joy when he found her again.

Traveling west after a service in memory of his adoptive father, he had wandered to the back of the bus where it was calm and he could hold to his grief in quiet. And then he saw her, or a shred of what she'd been. She lay on a back seat, dressed in a torn gypsy's skirt, pale cheeks smeared with an ashen dust, the face of one fleeing from a fire, a sudden flood.

But even in her misery that delicacy unparalleled: she was a dandelion wafted by wind between blue sky and greensward, the rare flower burning blue on icy mountains that men climb dozens of miles to find. . . .

PAULA STILL SAT ON THE RIM OF THE BATHTUB, RUSTLING the jewelry that lay on her lap. In the 1920s Nada had spent many months looking for her own mother—after hearing from her she had finally joined her in a small village on the edge of the Sahara where she was helping to run a small French hospital for the Berbers, one of those settlements in which the desert sand drifts up a foot a month—We must all search for them, hell is let loose by the mothers who leave us—you've abandoned me, thinking that I was at last safe. . . .

Start over, Paula, who hasn't tried to teach you stoicism? Suppress, she'd play their game, she'd decided that morning to impress Julian with their freezing family game.

She replaced the rings and bracelets in the delicate silk case. The packages were very sad, very pretty.

More photographs hung on the walls of Julian's bathroom: their daughter, seven-year-old Georgia, holding a kitten in her arms, staring out with Grandmother Fitzsimmons' questing eyes. A picture of Uncle Vincent in Paris, seated at the Crillon, struggling over his copy. "Ah, do not dismiss snobs, dear girl, snobbism is a form of despair."

Uncle Vincent had died of a stroke eighteen months ago, Nada and Paula had each held one of his hands in the last hours. There had been no funeral service, Vincent had no friends beyond the Little Family. Nicolas had come back from Africa, where he'd been stationed with the Peace Corps. Nicolas had returned to weep at Vincent's grave. His plane had been late, he had met them at the entrance to the cemetery. He offered a brief, cool hug to the three women and shook Julian's hand. It was a raw March day. Babs was the first to cry. "I can't bear the void. We loved him so." As the coffin was lowered Paula looked up at Nicolas. Blond hair grown quite long, and disheveled from the day's haste. Lashes deep brown and sleek over his castdown eyes. Cheeks flushed from the cold, pink as they'd been when they'd skated outdoors, aged eleven. She'd hoped that he would be grown and transformed beyond recognition. He was disturbingly manly, disturbingly the same. Her alarm quite overcame her grief, and she felt guilty.

As the earth was thrown upon the coffin they all tossed in a branch of lilac, Vincent's favorite flower. Now there were tears on Nada's, Julian's, Nicolas' cheek. And when Nicolas' eyes finally rose to meet Paula's—blue, fetching, clear—it struck her that the serenity of recent years was like a lit candle in her hand. She'd carried it down a still,

windless corridor, and suddenly she stood somewhere outside, drafts rising, threatening.

Oh, Nicolas would become wily, the way he'd endear
himself to Julian and begin to move back into the family.
She'd fiercely avoid his visits, but Nicolas had been as
shrewd as ever, dropping in to visit Julian and Georgia
while she was out of the house taking drama classes. . . .

Over the bathroom sink there hung a picture of Julian
and Nicolas walking together in a park, Julian making one
of those sweeping pulpit gestures as he preached to his new
friend about mercy or self-discipline.

Julian was drying his face with a thick brown towel. "Be
subject to no sight but thine and mine," she recited toward
him. " . . . invisible to every eyeball else," he finished
the line.

They did not continue with *The Tempest*. Julian swirled
a drop of makeup base on his temple and tapped it lightly
on the barely perceptible scars of his left cheek. Then with
a pair of sharp curved scissors he trimmed delicately at his
sideburns. Narcissism, Babs had written, the last refuge of
civilized men. The gravity of the frivolous, Nada said, the
spirituality of dress. Paula was waiting for Julian to put on
his tie, a feat of dexterity she'd once enjoyed watching, his
thumb and forefinger working like pincers on a piece of
fine silk. But it was a weekend and they were off to Sheep
Meadow; he reached for a turtleneck lying on the shelf
above him and pulled it swiftly over his head. Finally he
turned away from the mirror and stood tall above her, staring into her eyes.

He wanted to say: Paula darling, what can we do to get
Nada back home?

But he didn't say it. He feared that she might resort to
her frequent bouts of nihilism, reply what can we do if
she's in Beirut, Bucharest, Kathmandu? So he waited.

"Well, happy anniversary, Julian darling," she said instead.

He smiled and held out his arm to her. But she remained sitting, eyes as impassive as her mother's.

"I came home to see our daughter and go to some demonstration with you. How long has Georgia been with Nicolas?"

"Since last night."

"Let me guess. You had an article on God due in this morning. The one baby-sitter you trust is down with mono. And Nicolas has been asking to have Georgia all month?"

Julian smiled, sprayed something on his hair and said, "You're psychic." For an instant his eyes lay upon hers, brooding, gentle, irisless in their darkness. And then he left the room.

JULIAN DISLIKED DOING KITCHEN CHORES ALONE, HE wished Nicolas were there to help chop vegetables for Paula's lunch. While trimming the lettuce he looked up at the calendar of saints tacked up above his stove. October 17, 1970, Saint Ignatius, Bishop and Martyr: "When sent in chains to Rome and thrown to the beasts he had exclaimed, 'May I be agreeable bread to the Lord.' " October blood, the blood of martyrs. There were still some instants of splendid liturgy or recollection when he was filled with clean and beautiful newness, his thirst for belonging fully quenched. But how infrequent these moments, how short-lived! So he still marked to himself, almost every morning, the feast of saints. Heralds, troublemakers, leavens of a better order, beaked and taloned graspers of our souls, how their tempestuous lives could relieve the dryness of a day! His eyes swept over the month of October. Father Symonds' favorite apostle to be honored tomorrow, Saint Luke. The month had begun joyfully with the feast of Francis of Assisi, October 4. "In his youth renounced pleasure, fine clothes, all wealth and toward the end was rewarded with the stigmata . . .'' Obverse of Julian Mikolski Symonds, born to rags and aspiring to the finest finery. He'd dedicated his only book to his adopted father, two years after his death. "The Holy Spirit is the Biggie," Reverend Symonds always said. Julian had celebrated his last mass on Pentecost in memory of his beloved guardian. Kneeling at the altar of his little church before the service, relief sweeping over waves of guilt, he'd rehearsed the spectacle beforehand, rehearsed it theatrically, the way he'd wished all life to be. (Fire beginning slowly among my flock, whispering flames for hair and fingertips, upturned faces bursting into flames as all cry out, "Men of Judaea, it is the Lord who speaks . . .")

"Listen, Paula," Julian called out. Paula, Nada, Babs, Nicolas, listen, one of the few ways of praying left to him, conversing with the Spirit that lies dormant in the most imperfect others. Be lenient to all for He is in them. What he feared and envied most about Paula was her gift for discerning malice from purity, soul's light from dark. Whereas he still persevered in only detecting the comfortable, the curable, the good. The remainder of his calling, discerning Spirit in the most inscrutable, jagged others, Babs with her brazen gall, Nicolas with that anger and mother-hatred he had set out to cure. He was drawn to such extremes, he had listened to Nicolas' rages with loyal interest and Paula had behaved appallingly. Had sullenly fled from the house whenever Nicolas came to visit, pretending she had to visit a friend, go to the library to study Ibsen. In the past weeks of her illness—her last and only one, he'd pledged to himself—he'd realized the depth of his dependence. He had come to love the world she enjoyed hating, had drawn her back into it, with dubious results.

It is possible that I've always wanted to be too sure of everything, he thought, sure of never being battered, abused, deceived, alone again, sure of being needed and necessary to all.

"Listen, Paula," Julian called out again.

She came toward him now with that defiant set of chin she had in moments when she was determined and absolutely well. My love, I must rescue you from childhood, from illness, from myself; one must be very careful today, he was thinking at the same time. Thoughts of death came back to him at the oddest moments; there was a Hasidic notion that in paradise you could return to that moment of life in which you had known the greatest happiness; so after death he could revel again in the Eden of early marriage and first fatherhood, in those years when Paula had laughed and teased and chatted, when they'd sat in stark Cape Cod inns gamboling with little Georgia; he'd revel in that small span of time whose serenity he wished had never ceased. . . .

"You still don't know where Nada is?" Paula asked. "You're not keeping anything from me?"

"I've told you all I know, Pumpkin." He heard her breathing, felt it as part of his own breath.

"Perhaps Babs has found out," she said. "Perhaps I can weasel it out of her."

Paula left the kitchen and went to the living room. She sat down on the floor, facing the window that gave out onto their small dusty garden. That tolerance of Julian's, that clemency going out to all and sundry—she'd first thought of it as a form of pacifism, a compassionate force that others could melt before and capitulate to, like that of Dostoievski's Idiot—but later it had become a nuisance, an obstacle to her freedom. She took off her sweater, glided her hands over her upper back, feeling bones she'd never felt before. Sharp sting of wings on either side of spine, vertebrae pointed as fish's fins. Julian was in the kitchen and soon he'd be trying to make her eat. There, too, Paula detected Nicolas' devious intrusion into their household. Smells of fennel, coriander, arcane touches Julian wouldn't have thought of by himself. It was almost noon, Julian was combing his hair while his curry simmered. A Saturday, another demonstration, Julian carefully parting his hair.

Paula stood by Julian's desk, feeling hungry for the first time in weeks. On the shelf above it lay little plaques, certificates, awards for best reporting on this or that. Alongside his Olympia de luxe typewriter, reprints of articles on those contemporaries Julian called his secular saints—Cesar Chavez, Dorothy Day, a group of Franciscans working among Navajo Indians. A few new books by the typewriter: *The Spirit of Poverty. Does God Exist?*

"Le déjeuner est servi," Julian called out.

She started eating her lunch. Or rather, Julian fed it to her. Her moments of "instability," as the Little Family put it, had included the symptom of refusing to eat. But this time Paula opened her mouth obediently for the delicious food Nicolas had taught Julian to make. Over the years Julian had even acquired the Fitzsimmons' distinctive way of laughing. When something had amused Georgia or Nada Fitzsimmons they'd screwed up their faces and let their shoulders shake slightly, without making a sound. As Paula told Julian about her weeks at the hospital, he occasionally bent his head and silently shook his shoulders in the way of a laugh. While his eyes rested on her with relief, tenderness, fear.

"This doctor wasn't any Park Avenue jerk like Kubie, Julian, he was the real thing, a sharpie shrink from L.A. who got to the center of my troubles . . . refuge in singular, dramatic language, memories of Nicolas when we were fifteen, that's what he managed to pierce through. 'Any lines from Shakespeare you remember from your childhood, Paula,' he'd ask. 'You are long withering my revenue of patience,' I'd answer. 'Fine, fine,' he'd go, 'we want more anger.' He kept fingering a string of Indian beads, turquoise blue. 'What do you remember best from the time you were fifteen, Paula?'

" 'Nicolas. His large pale hands.'

" 'Anything else about him, Paula?'

" 'The big lonely house we spent the summers in together. Mother loved its isolation. There was a portrait at the head of the stairs that reminded us of my grandmother, it hung right off the door of Nicolas' room . . .''

" 'And what do you see there . . .'

" 'I refuse. Someday, doctor, not now. Sala loved me, Sala sneaking a new book on palmistry into my room on my thirteenth birthday when I was practicing my lines, opening a split of champagne, saying *Toi est grande fille,* I'm giving you a present; we sat there getting high, hiding from Nicolas, who was calling for me all over the garden, big black Sala always protecting me from Nicolas . . .'

" 'There you are,' the shrink says.

" 'Are where? Sala looming at my door at night, candle in hand, the whites of her eyes rolling, lighting the darkness that made me cry out at night when the three of us were alone . . .'

" 'We're doing beautifully today. Can we return to Nicolas?'

" 'In July and part of August, when our mothers were in Paris, Nicolas and Sala and I saw no one but each other, Nicolas tried to steal everything under the sun from me, my soliloquies, my sacred animals, we clutched each other on the grass, arguing, ''I am passing fell and wrath at this your theft my lord . . .'' '

" 'I see,' the shrink would say. 'So this went on . . .'

" '. . . you are a very beauty and a prodigal, my fair Miranda . . .'

" 'This is our third week, Paula. We're going to move very slowly if we keep on talking that language . . .'

" 'After great pain a formal feeling comes.'

" 'Bottling it up again?'

" 'Forget it, doctor.'

" 'Your mothers worked together, neither of you had a father?'

" 'I was nobody and just another thing.'

"But then I remembered a lot, I may have remembered all, Julian, and I wept a great deal.

"The first time in years I've cried," she added coolly. "I'd learned the craft of stoicism from you and Mother, Julian, not liked it but crammed on it. 'What kind of Oedipal fixation is that,' I once asked the doctor. 'I married a man who resembles my mother to a T . . .' "

Not to a T, Julian smiled to himself, shaking his head. Nada had been too busy writing about Dior's courageous bronze greens to feel the need of much rescue work. Perhaps only the rescued, having eaten the humble pie of gratitude, crave to feed it to others. There, have a bite, see how odious it tastes.

I've gotten it together in the past month, Paula thought. I'm ready to up the ante. "Listen, Julian, you've failed me on several counts. First you tried to sweep me right back into the crowd of creeps I had to go loony to escape from, and that didn't wash."

That was like a slab of meat thrown on a table, violent. Had he loosened his hold on her as he'd spread into her kin? Sudden terror that she might in turn let go of him.

"Then you let Nicolas settle right back into our lives, and he's the one who sent me up the river in the first place. . . . Nicolas has always tried to take a lot from me, but he can't have my child any more than he can have you or me. . . ."

"When did you rehearse this little outburst?" he asked. He wore an apron. His eyes were a furious dark brown.

"The world Nicolas and I came from is a beast, Julian. Might never let you go. Best luck to all of us."

"There's the doorbell," Julian said. "There are Nicolas and Georgia, all ready to go to the park."

NICOLAS II

NICOLAS WALKED DOWN 77TH STREET TOWARD PAU-
la and Julian's apartment, relishing the warmth of
Georgia's hand in his. "The sun's clouding over,"
he said to the child, "it smells like rain." He looked forward to rain, to the possibility of being spared still another
demonstration. He was fed up with Trotskyite lingo and
Dr. Spock's ancient jokes, he wished they would all stay
home so he could cook for the family again, a delicate fish
and fennel dish, a startling recipe for zabaglione. As he
untangled the string of a red balloon he had just bought for
Georgia, he curbed the bitterness he sometimes felt before
her parents' love, decided that all today might go well after
all. Paula, lost angel of his youth, she'd gone about life in
the most daffy ways. Her candor was her undoing, she'd
constantly needed to seduce her mother and the regiment
of fops who'd poisoned their childhood, with Paula all had
been pacification and pretty smiles, *Bonjour oncle Christian, cette collection est vraiment la plus exquise du
siècle. . . .* The story of their lives is that she'd gone crazy

for both of them and spared him the misery. What's sanity, Paula darling—sanity is to say No and fuck you to pater and mater, that's if you know who pater is—and take the lonely road of confrontation and deceit. . . .

At the age of thirty Nicolas was a tall and handsome man who was still terrified of being forgotten in the corner of a room. In order to creep out of childhood he was needing to think of himself as iron-armed, Leviathan, uniquely and excessively lustful. It was his only way of conquering the great fear of women that had marked his first years. His early memories of an adult world—hordes of women riding roughshod over his body, laughing loudly and holding high the whips of their voices, all about them was spiked and blazing, a prehensile tribe trampling the world with startling opinions, gleaming gimmicks and flagrant frippery. How is it selling, they demanded, their colors glaring, their voices yelling, their power swelling. . . .

Of course Nicolas exaggerated much, exaggerated superbly, even to himself. Most persons bred in the world of *Best* tended to drama, and like Paula, his appetite for attention was particularly fine. "It is scandalous," Babs used to say, "to enter a room without effect."

Paula and Nicolas had been set apart by their mothers, for in that generation women in Nada's and Babs' positions were unique. Other mothers they'd known during their childhood had played bridge, bought trinkets or treasures, counted their linen, filed their nails, scolded their servants, dabbled in charities while waiting for their husbands and children to come home. Babs Hollins and Nada Fitzsimmons had never waited for anyone, anything. They had straddled the ocean telling those very women how to comb their hair, keep their men, button their coats, feed their guests. Had told them what boats to take to which resorts, what paintings to hang on their walls, what poets to namedrop at lunch, what books, plays, beaches to discuss at dinner. Babs and Nada had had children amazonically; whatever men were in their lives seemed as superfluous and interchangeable as the belts and gloves they eulogized in the pages of their magazine. They earned a small fraction of the income of the women whose tastes they ruled, and lived superbly, publishing empires furnishing them with all the clothes, staterooms, four-star hotels anyone would ever want. Yet the grandeur of their lives was an illusion, which was the very stuff of their vocations. They were perennial outsiders, doomed to ephemeral friendships and a certain solitude; for in that pragmatic, hard-dealing world they were mostly sought out for their influence and favors. Women like Babs and Nada preached the gospel of achievement and instant gratification ("Needed immediately!" . . . "In and new this very fall!"). Their offspring remained childlike all the longer by taking such seductive imperatives to heart. And however stridently they raged against *Best*'s frippery (sometimes feigning, loving it) they would crave to partake of their mothers' power.

Nicolas, from the beginning, had lived and breathed rebellion. It was taking him as long as Paula to settle into adulthood. For much of his energy was channeled into provoking that brazen, inventive specialist in histrionics, his mother; much thought was given to inventing tactics, assuming roles, that would embarrass her more deeply than the last. He had continually striven to live in worlds as radically opposite to Babs' as possible. After a few idyllic years under Nada's care, he had roamed about the Pacific as a guest of the U.S. Navy, gathering many romantic memories, most of them highly magnified, of his alleged dissoluteness. Staying high on grass, nutmeg, Spanish fly, dark rum (so went one of his more extravagant boasts), anything I could get my hands on between my frenzied bouts of flesh. Aged twenty-one he had washed dishes, corraled horses, cooked in diners while putting himself through college. Even an honorable schooling had to be as distant from his mother as possible and as startling. He'd opted for Oregon State, and majored in home economics. Then on to the Peace Corps, to teaching in storefront schools in Harlem. Like many who have known early solitude he was sensitive to kindness, and easily moved to gratitude. So these worthy occupations were in part intended to recapture the esteem of Vincent, Paula, Nada . . . he thought of Nada, quite accurately, as the provider of the only youthful happiness he'd known. And he so savored charming that part of the family with a new performance, irritating Babs with a new incarnation, that it was always a joy to rehearse still another role.

Children born into the Best are reluctant to admit their craving for the luxuries of their parents' world. Nicolas had invented many strategies to hide his. He'd started feigning as a tot, taking care to mask his great enjoyment of the sumptuous clothes, food, women constantly paraded before him. Little Nicolas had sat by *Maman* at Patou's, Givenchy's, most particularly Dior's salons, delighting in the soft dove-grey velvet under his naked knees, the flare-skirted cocktail dresses of magenta *peau de soie*, the bouquets of tea roses spread out in gilt and marble vases, the hot dry odor of Diorissima which Babs Hollins had described as "so hothouse, so indoors, so delectably beyond nature." How he looked forward to those February days when a new spring line was about to be shown at 30 avenue Montaigne—jammed babbling oven of the salon, crowded elbowless space, airless perfumed air, fashion devotees packed like scavenger birds all the way up the stairs, *vendeuses* in white smocks spraying walls, chairs, each other with still more Diorissima . . . eight, nine, ten-year-old Nicolas had feigned boredom and disdain, yawning and popping bubble gum, inventing many ways to attract attention and purge himself of the ancient childhood fear that his mother would forget him at a street corner while fawning on still another man.

Little Nicolas (he would have been the last to admit it) had grown to be as kind as he was obstreperous and sly. He felt happiest when he was able to wield his principal source of power over others—his great talent for nurturing and giving pleasure. He was of charitable and nomadic nature. And independently from his need to annoy Babs and regain the Little Family's love he had been very moved by the arduous tasks he'd pursued since returning from the Peace Corps. In Harlem he had dealt with children who came off the streets, their wizened faces all eyes and dark shadows, whom he'd fed a cupful of soup every few hours because they were too weak to hold down any solid substance—these were the beings who had offered Nicolas the greatest sense of worth he'd ever known.

So he would temporarily give his all to these vocations, in both spirit and style. Blond hair and beard worn long when he'd worked for the Peace Corps in Africa, this month he was clean-shaven, his hair short-shorn as a football coach's, to teach black children in Harlem. Today he wore a black beret covered with antiwar buttons which he kept handing to Georgia so she could read their slogans. He had grown to be tall, wide-shouldered, barrel-chested, his eyes were a periwinkle blue, he knew how to walk down the street on any occasion with a friendly, welcoming smile.

As he walked toward Julian and Paula's apartment that October Saturday he hadn't seen his mother for long over a year, since shortly after Vincent's funeral. No pleas of Nada's or Julian's had moved Nicolas to reconciliation. Avoiding contact with powerful mothers: an instinct many need to follow in order to come of age. The principal goal Nicolas had set himself that year was to recapture the affection of Paula, only member of the tribe who had not shown him any renewed trust, had failed to acknowledge his honorable recent vocations. Paula will come around in time, he thought, as he came within sight of the Symonds apartment that morning; Paula might even be won over today; up to now she had not given him a scrap of a chance, not a minute alone, they'd barely exchanged a word. He'd waited for two years to have a quiet day with Paula and Julian and Georgia. . . . He looked up at the sky again, hoping that the afternoon would bring rain so they could all stay home together. "We're going to see Mummy again!" he exclaimed to Georgia as they approached the front door. And he rang the doorbell, looking forward to the cheer and comfort he seemed to be able to bring to just about anyone in the world.

SOLITUDES

THEY ENTERED THE PARK AT 65TH STREET, NEAR THE zoo. A frail young woman with large violet eyes, holding a child by the hand; a man in early middle age wearing a pectoral cross on his black turtleneck; a man some ten years younger with merry eyes and torn jeans who kept exchanging a red balloon with the child.

This is the first time we're trying it out together, Paula thought; this is the Little Family, new version, Nicolas sneaked back. She felt very calm and empty, like the eye of a tornado standing still in the middle of its hullaballoo.

Georgia seemed to have grown even in the past month. Paula stared hard at her whenever the child didn't notice, when something in the crowd or the men's talk drew her eyes away from her mother's.

Paula thinking: One thing I'll insist on for my daughter, Georgia won't grow up wanting to please and pacify, women's curse through the ages, whores, poodles pleading and primping for love and shelter, Paula for thirty years begging for approval, that was over once and for all. . . .

At the edge of the Central Park Zoo Julian hoisted Paula onto his shoulders, you're too weak, Pumpkin, to walk to Sheep Meadow, and then Nicolas said upsy-daisy and raised Georgia onto his shoulders, too. Earlier today when Nicolas brought Georgia home the child had lunged toward her and stayed in her arms for many seconds without moving. Nicolas standing over them, Paula kiss Uncle Nick, I want a kiss too. Two young wolves trying to stake out their territories, he'd leaned his cheek toward Paula and she'd refused, so he'd brushed her forehead with his hand and said you are the sum total of my earthly desires. One thing was clear, in the past years of rebelling against his mother Nicolas had stopped stuttering, that ruse replaced by urgent rapid speech. We bought the balloon at 86th Street and Lexington, you remember Paula, the corner where we used to meet on Saturdays to take the crosstown to the Planetarium, before that we had a fine breakfast at Longchamps didn't we, Georgie, three blueberry muffins . . .

I WANT TO WATCH THE SEALS, THAT'S MY REAL VOICE, Paula's, imperious. Julian's body below me, stopping by the pool like a horse pulled by a bridle. I look down at him, I touch the fine scars that cross his temple. I stroke his forehead, gestures foreign and familiar as rediscovering my own bones. He brings my hand to his mouth and kisses it and lingers over my palm, head lowered. . . . The sun is out but it smells like rain. The fall leaves burn like molten gold. The seals swoop in and out of the water, sleek and tubular, ribbons of blackness gliding in and out. One of the last times I'd seen Mother before she left she was in a hospital room, tubes in her nose and arms and winding down about the bed, here straight as rails, here woven in coils about the furniture of the hospital room. Scissors lay on the table across us. One could end it quickly. What a calm, calm way. Needles in veins and arteries, vital signs monitored by a box full of beeping, blinking lights, like the control panel of a space ship. Mother raising her head, sipping some tea through a straw. You must realize I can't stand being seen in such a condition, darling, I'm ringing for the nurse, could you please leave me alone a minute. . . . The barren gaze that follows me out of the room, not yet goodbye in those eyes but I don't want, I refuse to be seen in this state, her pride, her honor, her horror. . . . The next day she picks up her spectacles to see me better, hand delicately bypassing the tubes that enter her arms. You look ravishing today, darling, I adore your hair that way. Why can't you always keep that curl in, it's so very becoming. Closing her eyes for an instant, exhausted, fed up with her life, afraid? No one could know.

A day later she feels well enough to send for her floral sheets. She feels well enough to tell me what a big fuss was made over sheets by women of fashion in the thirties. A group of them would pack onto the *Train Bleu* at four P.M. to go to the Côte d'Azur, Elsie Mendl, Daisy Fellowes, Dawn Porter would get into their peignoirs at five and decide to go to bed and dine in their compartments . . . their maids made up their berths while they'd plan to have cocktails at Elsie's, the main course at Daisy's, dessert with Dawn to visit each other's linens. . . . Daisy had white and blue printed batiste and quilted cover to match, Elsie's scheme was brown silk moiré and beige crepe de Chine, Mrs. Cole Porter had linen in several shades of pink silk topped by a sable throw . . . Mother smiles wryly and she stares peacefully at her own sheets, a field-of-violets Porthault designed for her in London in the thirties. Did she have them brought because she wants to live or die in them? Each of her needled arms supported by flowered pillows and her face reposing on several more, even as I stand by her bed she seems to lie very high above me, transfigured like the mother of heaven on the altar of a baroque church, she stares at me with her large indifferent eyes through violet-tinted glasses, what peace in those eyes which say I shall soon leave all this . . .

ON THIS SUNNY AFTERNOON NICOLAS EAGERLY WATCHED the pretty lasses passing by him in the park, there goes one with her wild red hair flying, green-stockinged legs delicate as a colt's, still on the borderline of childhood like Paula when we first took each other, strawberries of breasts sweetly jumping under idiot slogans of T-shirt, Peace Now, Free Grass, Free Angela, Out Now . . . In Now I say, catch up with the darling and pin her down, seize her right here on the tar of the pavement, black tar and naked whiteness, no, too beautiful, not permitted (these were the kinds of rakish images Nicolas loved to conjure). What a fine sight this afternoon, girls out by the thousands, pears of titties praying to the sky, peaches of softest down sunning themselves in lovely October, queenly mammalia paraded with dignity, and many girls with the shimmering flanks of perfect animals, one over there with a collar of peace amulets round her neck, splendor of curls swishing toward barely nascent breasts . . . damn it, a guy, one never knows anymore. His name might be Myron, Ezekiel, Leopold the Fourth . . .

You're always finding a new way of protest, Julian often says, Nicolas shrugged his shoulders at that. Protest so built into his bones that he was barely toilet-trained when he rebelled against the name Babs had first bestowed upon him, Beau Hollins. Beau is what Babs had called her offspring, striving for something "Historic, unique." But her wonder boy soon sensed the problem of tramping through life with a name like Beau; by the time he was five he was demanding a new *nom de guerre*, shouting "I am Nicolas, Nicolas!" That was the name of the man whom Babs was courting that season, Uncle Nicolas remained a highlight in family annals, he even lasted long enough to take Babs' darling to the Central Park Zoo. So Babs capitulated to a new baptism and from then on it was Nicolas do be amusing, Nicolas come give Uncle Hubert, Luigi, Edmundo, Giorgio a good-night kiss, do be original Nicolas . . .

That's where I may have gotten it, my beautiful primal lust, sulking about Mother's boudoir hearing her moan out next door to Giorgio Cristobal Wolfgang Benvenuto Heinrich Gianfranco—to dive into other flesh, melt and be born again, the only self-knowledge—O splendor and glory of that Vietnamese beauty who sat behind me in her tub of steaming water scrubbing my back and singing, and then the deep bed hung with thick green netting, *ah doucement mon Nico, lentement, lentement*—wishing at times that sex organs could sprout all over me, a multitude of throbbing cocks to enter twelve, fifteen, twenty paradises at a time (Nicolas was truly happy with that metaphor), my body gang-banged in one go, then off to capture a whole new tribe of wenches, seducing, leaving and seducing, anything to escape that respectability dear Nada always egged me on to—you must crystallize your great talents, Nicolas darling, Nada standing in her New York living room, saying hilarious things like when are you going to put an end to this curious dissipation, Nicolas dear, there used to be ways for preserving purity, a simple diet and a fear of sin— Mocking eyes, shrewd smile letting me know that my excesses were not exactly hers. . . .

"No soap, auntie darling, you'll think me a failure if I'm not president of Revlon or Bonwit's by thirty-seven and what would that offer, duodenal ulcers, o.d.'ing on tequila at the Acapulco Hilton among a convention of toupeed jerks? . . ."

You call Nicolas to order, dear family, but he demands search and wildness, he wishes to perform to excess, without his gorgeous wantonness he'd be like a forgotten pack-

age in the Milan, Paris, London airport. Having been
frequently abandoned, Nicolas wishes to be embraced,
swallowed, submerged in female flesh. . . .

"LET'S PLAY WHY NOT, UNCLE NICOLAS."

"Okay, sweetheart. Why not cover all of your walls in
precious, nearly extinct snow leopard."

"Why not wrap yourself in a gorilla and keep it on 'til
next spring," Georgia shouted.

"Why not send the gold fillings in your teeth to Kenneth
Lane's for smashing new cufflinks," Paula said.

"Why not send all your bedsheets to Afghanistan to have
them rehemmed by hand," Julian said.

PAULA PERCHED ON JULIAN'S SHOULDER, HER BODY AS
warm as a summer sun. Life's wonder and treasure, even
that first glimpse of her in schoolgirl frock could have led
him to forget all of Heidegger, Saint Paul. Detached, in-
corporeal, yet she was all bluntness, candor, the candor of
those eyes that seemed to slice through air and refuse all
illusion . . . to possess her he'd have sacrificed his hard-
won little fame, the scruffy honor with which he'd clawed
out of childhood misery . . . yet how ill-prepared he was
to show the depth of any love. J.S., he often scolded, Slavic
prole renamed Wasp dandy, did you have to adopt the ill-
nesses of your new world when you crossed from the Symondses' scrubbed parlor to the gilded zero of *Best*?

Youth churning and milling about that day, Free Angela,
Free the Presidio Seven, Veterans For Peace. Memory returning often, his own fall in a muddy field of Asia, instant
of near death when he'd fainted and waked and fainted
again, knowing that the blow had come very close to his
heart. Struggling to his knees, crawling toward a field filling with large yelling birds, wading toward his friends'
bodies, waiting for a moan, a sound, all was silence. Then

seeing his corporal, best buddy, the only being he'd trusted
with details of Julian Mikolski Symonds' brief life—groin
a mass of crimson bubbles, but features untouched, eyes
skewed and open. At such times strange things come to
mind. As freshmen at Harvard we'd recited Housman,
"Shoulder high we bring you home and set you at your
threshold down." If I lived I'd have to write his father,
dear sir I had the honor of sharing several philosophy
classes and a tender friendship with your son, *Dulce et
decorum est pro patria mori*. Falling in anger beside his
body, crawling from him into the safe spotless verdure.
Elation of succeeding hours, striving to recapture it for
years to come, one-armed divinity student studded with
shrapnel and decorations. . . .

CAREFUL WHERE YOU PUT YOUR FEET, GEORGIA, DON'T
step on the people sitting on the grass, listen to the
speeches.

Sing me another song you had in church, Daddy.

"In the glory of the lilies He was born across the
sea . . ."

HER HAND IN HIS, HIS CHILD, PERHAPS HIS ONLY ETER-
nity—eyes filled with such hope and fervor, children's confidence preserved throughout millennia of our crimes—
repeated treason of their dreams, nascent flowers fucked
over, generations of children's hopes sold out everywhere
and always, at least he was spared that early trust and its
demise. Three people needing you, Georgia, trying to recapture the childhood they never had. . . .

Well, damn it, that morning had been difficult, that
morning had been a mess. Throughout his youth, even in
the Symondses' tidy parlor, he'd wished for a family similar to Paula's, he'd fantasized vivid eccentric relatives like
Babs and Vincent, amusing difficult cousins to counsel like

Nicolas, a mother-in-law of superb grace like Nada. And what was Paula doing but refusing him the shelter and drama of a tribe.

He wanted to curb his annoyance, tried a simple Zen exercise he'd learned years ago when he was experimenting with the Eastern way to peace. You keep your mind totally empty for many sets of ten consecutive breaths. If a thought intrudes you push it firmly away, punish yourself by starting all over again at breath one. The exercise went well for a few minutes. He managed several sets of breaths unsullied by thought, felt considerably calmer, recalled a phrase of his wife's: "You're so lenient with others, so severe with yourself."

JUST THINK OF ALL THE OTHER SOBRIQUETS THE DIVINE Babs Hollins could have dumped on me before I renamed myself Nicolas—Styx. Caliban. Hitler. Horsie. Pasadoble. Amoretto. Sweet Potato. Cupid. Cupid Hollins, that tag would have been in character for either one of us. Men going in and out of *Maman's* life like luggage on an airport carousel, little Nicolas sitting at cafés in Florence, Madrid, Marrakesh watching the frenzied glint of her gaze settle on every male who passed by—isn't that a divine policeman over there with the thick blond mustache and blue eyes just like the Duke of Windsor's, you never saw such intelligent witty bright eyes like David's. . . .

Don't hate your mother, Julian always says, hatred is a waste of something, hatred is a lack of imagination.

Just think how much we still have in common, Paulie, we were seven years old when the New Look was born, Uncle Christian pinching in miladies' waists and making their boobs pop up again like Syrian pomegranates—the New Look is when little Nicolas began his incarnation as a fashion addict, seated with Mother amid dozens of press harpies about to preach the waist cinch and make titties

bloom over the Western world like tulips in springtime—
10:15 A.M., shrieks of the *directrice* as she reorganized the
seating, shooing the pipsqueaks from Holland and Japan
from seats reserved for *Flair*, *Le Figaro*, bewitching Babs
Hollins of *Best*—and at 10:25, the hush that fell as if mass
were about to begin, Mother's upper-crust gang seated on
gilded chairs in the front row, all legs crossed at the same
dainty angle like chorus girls at the Roxy. Nicolas sat by
Maman longing to hear what kinds of names would be
given the collection this year, Uncle Christian was original
with titles, would we get a parade of exotic places, Mad-
agascar, Buenos Aires, Zanzibar. Or famous artists, Tou-
louse-Lautrec, Dali, Michelangelo. Or more musicians,
Verdi, Pergolesi, Albinoni.

Looking forward to the human tide that would surge toward Uncle Christian at the end of the show, crying, "Sublime, a ravishment, the best you've ever done! We are
speechless, so moved!"—and then butlers rushing about
the room passing champagne over the heads of the crowd
and Uncle Christian coming out of the *cabine* looking like
a country curate made of marzipan, hands folded over his
plump stomach, bald little head cocked modestly to one
side saying *merci, merci.* . . .

There was sweetness at the collections, having Mother
to myself for a few hours; there was fun in Paris pretending
I hated the whole glorious spectacle of the salons, planning
new tactics.

Confining my protest the first year to such exclamations
as "Hideous!" "Badly cut, he knows nothing about
sleeves!" But that had simply caused a typical anti-Ameri-
can stir, another Yankee brat doing his thing, far from the
complex commotion I wished to create. . . .

So Eureka! one year little Nicolas decided to change
tactics, why not go for broke and break wind in the middle
of the show—Uncle Christian had opted for poets that year,

ministerial voice announcing *"Numéro Quinze*, Baudelaire,"* witches' coven whining "heavenly, adorable," and I let go with my exquisite concert—finally sensing the attention of the folk from *Yes!* and *Daily Wear* settle on me with distress, vexation, pity for a child given the trots by the lousy postwar Paris diet—all faces turning then toward *Maman*, wondering how dear divine Babs is going to handle it, as the attention swerves to her I give it my best, give it my all . . .

"La Rochefoucauld" and I send out my finest toot—begun in a low demonic hiss and growing to a faint buzzing like that of a distant telephone ring, swelling in delectable crescendo to an apocalyptic roar . . .

"Emile Zola!" Another valiant trumpeting for Alla, the Slavic beauty who's said to have received an egg-sized emerald from the wealthiest tin king in Argentina—"Gustave Flaubert!" The *vendeuses* crane their heads toward the windows as if the din is being caused by some delivery truck lumbering up the rue François Premier; Uncle Christian's bald pate emerges from behind the curtain of the *cabine* (unprecedented sight) to detect the origin of the commotion. . . .

Throughout all this, Mother sitting impassively as ever on her dainty gilded chair, taking frantic notes and abstaining from applause or any gesture of emotion so that no one will know which little numbers she will choose for the hallowed pages of *Best,* paying no attention to my efforts. Perhaps hoping that the fracas will be traced to the acolyte from *Flair* seated in the next row—*Maman's* cheeks immobile fields of chalk-white powder, gash of pink mouth—after some minutes of my aerial spectacle she turns her face to me without even a raised eyebrow; she has no eyebrows left to raise, she's kept them plucked for the Oriental look as long as I can remember; neither can any other of her features express startlement or indignation—she had such an impeccable facelift when she was thirty, only by staring into her eyes can I recognize the original Mummy who'd occasionally bent over my crib—the expression some enterprising surgeon fixed on her face is one of delighted surprise, as if she's about to exclaim *Ciao! Comment vas-tu? Tout est formidable!* So as she looks down at me in the midst of my concert, what do I get but the same ecstatic face with which she greets her pals in Paris salons. How delicious to see you! Sheer heaven! Expressions of encouraging reward, so in a fracas of adoration—Balzac!—twenty-one-gun salute for Lia, freckled-faced Hispanic darling who sashays the short cocktail numbers with an immense white smile, as if about to burst into a fandango complete with castanets. My exquisites, my enchantresses, how much more I could offer you now. . . .

And then it came, memorable year, Mother promoted to draw Paris blood for the crucial October issue of *Best*, and we sat across the runway from a gloriously beautiful, sullen child my age, who actually fainted when the wedding dress swept in. Unimaginative, Paula, A for performance but C-minus for content. You were so absorbed in your act that you didn't even notice me; acted a year later as if you'd never laid your eyes on me before; yet I wanted to give you a pep talk about method then and there, angel face, melodramatic, too earnest, a real soap—if you go for attention give it some outrage—to just plain faint, that was Pumpkin all over, always greedy for approval, pretending you freaked out of sheer emotion. And here you are fresh from the nuthouse, sweetheart, here you are in the arms of the man who's trying to rescue both of us—I alone can teach you that sanity is to be a brutish two-fisted bravado fighter, sanity is disguise, imposture and double-dealing cock a doodle-doo. . . .

FREE OUR POLITICAL PRISONERS, FREE ANGELA, HOSpital Workers for Peace, too many hospital workers, too much white—there was that first day in the hospital, Paula remembered, when it had taken three doctors to strap me in—attack beginning like those of ten years ago, manic agitation, a very urgent message that must be shared with all. This time it had to do with being separated from Mother, I'd shouted much about no one having any fathers, the uselessness of fathers, women's duty to keep the tribe together until the end of time— As they'd strapped me down I'd felt sewn into the fleece of an animal, the walls of the room a palpable, hairy skin pulsating about me like a heart. And then two small figures had come swaying toward me whom I recognized as those of my mother and my child—in perfect proportion to each other yet fetal in their smallness, the height of small chairs, blunt oval snout of newts where a face should have been. They wore Edwardian dresses with small hoops in back, like those in photographs of Grandmother Fitzsimmons when she was young. I should have been there between them, a right of blood, a right of lineage— The figures disappeared and I was thrown back into pulsating layers of animal fleece, I broke one of the straps that bound me and started biting the doctor, drawing blood. He was a blond Swedish intern with pale hairless arms. Paula, are we going to make it or aren't we, he'd looked like Nicolas and I'd yelled don't touch me never touch me again, yet looking at Nicolas today carrying Georgia so gently on his shoulders I began to wonder which would have been better, growing up with him or without—Nicolas had understood me, we'd shared a childhood, we'd shared much folly—could I ever escape that sharing?

LISTEN TO THE SONG I USED TO SING WHEN I WAS LITTLE, Georgia, ''Oh when the saints . . . go marching in . . .''
    More, Daddy.
    ''Oh Lord I want to be in that number . . .''

Fearing violence today and always, dreaming last night of my first mother's last revenge—running home from church on a snowing night and seeing from blocks away the sky brightened by a blaze of light, sirens screaming, running against a searing wind and learning that my parents had burned all in their wake, brought end to the terror of our lives—little Joe Mikolski running nearer still, watching the fire beast lick its tongues into every crevice of his childhood, timbers and plaster shooting downward in sheets of flame, they'd finally done it. Then in a swift collapse the walls crashing in on all like a waffle iron, end of the violent farm girl and the bland tortured man she'd shared her curse with—handfuls of dust now in the exploded house, all memories and lies charred beyond recognition, child standing before the conflagration, shoulders held by solicitous policemen and cowering neighbors. . . .

Then breaking loose from the strangers' hands, that moment of clarity in which I prostrated myself before their pyre, acknowledged my total solitude—there must have been a moment of helpless drunken awakening before the final trapping of the flaming walls and those seconds would haunt me for life—my love, my dream, that night years later when I found her on the bus. She sat up in fright like a sleeper violently shaken, her eyes weighted me toward some new center where I'd never been. She softly touched the empty sleeve of my jacket, you are a soul in torment. Yes, I said, common prayers committed to memory, weekly mass still, taking my spirit for forced walks in the park of gestures, like Schopenhauer with his poodle, an hour a day, rain or shine. . . .

A wren was settled on the pine tree before him, Julian saw it nestled into a hollow of the trunk, seeming to seek its sleep. It occasionally struck its beak against a branch as for reassurance, clack.

A rosening sky on the last warm afternoon; a bird gone to sleep in a pine branch. Peace.

Someday faith—God—whatever it was—might return to you like a thief when you least expected. Or like sleep or a forgotten tune. All radically different from the brutal seizure on the battlefield that he'd dreamed of recapturing for a quarter of a century.

It was even possible that the glowing moment in the trenches had been a delusion, that it had never offered him true faith. Ah, what a fine event to look forward to—accepting the fact that he'd never had any faith to lose, that he'd never lost a thing!

JULIAN WASHING AND CUTTING MY HAIR AFTER I'D COME home from the clinic this morning, finishing it off with a funny flourish of his arm, there you are, a new girl, even Nada would approve. Next he made me change my shoes and stockings before Nicolas and Georgia arrived, I feel tightened, more orderly, legs dangling below me like those of a puppet with the strings gone loose. The costumes had much interested Mother at these demonstrations, she'd studied the students in make-believe workmen's overalls, Mao jackets, motorcycle gear, and said this crowd is so amusing and diverse, Vincent is quite right, we're seeing the death of fashion; no more rules she sighed, she'd pinned an Impeach Johnson button on her black Balenciaga. . . .

Georgia grabbing my hand above the men's shoulders, Georgia's so delicate, with my mother's pale hair and eyes and that crazy way of wanting to pick every flower and leaf in sight and taste it, maybe Grandmother Fitzsimmons was driven to that in the desert, grabbing lemons and blossoms off the trees in every oasis she reached— We're still watching the seals, the women on the men's shoulders, when Nicolas says Uncle Nick has to go spend a penny. Georgia repeats that, laughing. That's the way he'd said it when he knocked at the door of the bathroom we shared during Long Island summers, he needed to barge in whenever I used it during the night as if he were constantly watching me, waiting for me— It could have been three A.M. and he knew I was up, he'd be pounding at the bathroom door, Nicolas aged twelve in his pajama bottoms, rubbing his swollen, distrustful eyes. . . .

Nicolas' father dead, right after he was born. Or so Babs says. I'll go see Babs after the demo, talk about old times, talk about Mother. Every chance that she'll be at her office on a Saturday afternoon, taking Mother's place as the world's *numero uno* arbiter of fashion— Sits in Nada's black and white office scribbling late into the night with a bottle of vodka at hand. Kind silly Babs, never knowing how to show her love, provider of magnificent presents, I'll go in there and she'll be writing her manifesto for the January issue, "Consider the evenings when it's imperative to be not merely beautiful, but cataclysmic—" Then the oracle will stare Paula down, "Shorten your bangs and celebrate your eyes, *chérie,* there's little left in the world to celebrate save for beautiful eyes . . ."

Nicolas almost as beautiful as his father, Babs used to say. At least no lies about my father, a man in my life Mother called him, so I've been free to invent him, an Arab father in white robes. T. E. Lawrence, where I got my clairvoyance. Nicolas trying to make me read his palm on rainy days, Sala's fritters fragrant through the damp summer house, Sala, fortress, how often I ran to seek refuge in those thick black arms— Mother after tea quietly writing her fashion notes for a November issue. Take the cue from Chanel, on black cashmere try six or nine strands of beads in onyx or pale rose— A toothache in the summer, train trip to New York with Nicolas and Sala, going to see Mother and Babs at one of their famous fashion sittings, cover girl frozen before camera, Dior Corolla line, heart-

shaped décolleté, electric fan blowing to give the skirt more
flare. Mother striding across the room with Amazon steps,
saying don't be ridiculous you *can* give me more wind,
more width to the skirt! Six more fans appearing, Babs
always trying to keep up with Mother, crying out we want
more wind in her *hair* do you hear, we want her hair all
the way out to Outer Mongolia! Nicolas' delighted smile,
never saw him so happy all summer, he loved *Best*, hiding
it well but happy as a cat in cream in that world of theirs,
that's why the bastard's sane. . . .

Nicolas puts Georgia down to go to the bathroom. Julian's face impassive, eyes filled with love. He puts me
down too, raising my leg above his head like a doll's,
sliding me gently down his right arm. Nicolas walking away
from the seal tanks toward the polar bear cages. Under-
neath it Nicolas is kind, Julian often says. Julian takes
Georgia's hand and I her other hand and for a moment she
is ours and I'm happy again.

MANY BLACKS IN DASHIKIS, MANY WIDE-EYED YOUNG-
sters reminding Nicolas of the places to which the Peace
Corps shipped him. Peace Corps, now that was one high
colonic of joy I gave the Little Family gratis one Thanks-
giving Day—"Our boy" (Nada, slyly approving), "off to
save the world for democracy!" "Peace Corps!" (Babs)
"Are you going to turn Buddhist next?" Well there was
no way Mother could have kept up much with the Peace
Corps, she'd been placing all her bets for the redemption
of the world on Yves Saint-Laurent, little horn-rimmed kid
who looked like an anemic bank teller and went bananas
after two months of French army life, that year he was
cutting make-believe motorcycle jackets out of crocodile
skin, "The genius of it! What aura, what mystique! Yves
is to the sixties what Picasso was to the thirties!" Mother

could barely mention that twerp without shedding tears of genuine emotion, little Yves had kept Mama very busy.

So down there in Dar-es-Salaam I'd often sit by the ocean alone wondering what sort of work I was truly fit for, seeing the kind of Little Family I came from. . . .

It would have been hard for Mother to ever pay attention to any one of my karmas, she'd always been too busy writing her *chef d'oeuvre,* "Why Not." She could even have called me Whynot—every few months when she concocted a new batch of Why Not's she'd go into the blue think tank in our apartment where you had to take off your shoes as if entering a Hindu temple, walls upholstered in Kashmir shawls, floor freshly relacquered dark blue every year, "a strong, Czarist blue," she demanded—that was one time the most lusting lover wouldn't have been allowed to disturb her, she'd have foresworn flesh for a month for one line of good copy. I used to peek through the keyhole and see her sitting there, eyes closed, pencil poised in air between each of her delirious *trouvailles.* "Why not pour brandy on your hair and set fire to it for a spectacular new entrance . . ." "Why not steal twelve charming communion cups from your local church and serve mint juleps in them for your next party . . ."

But the storefront school uptown, that was my providence, that crowd of needy children to nurture and be loved by in return—within a few months the children climbing and tugging at me as if I were some tree of life, and how I blossomed under their touch, gentle, teaching them manners, Bobby, you've got to learn how to share, Justin, how many times have I told you . . .

Even now a little one at my side . . .

"Smell this rose, Uncle Nicolas."

"It's not a rose, Georgia, it's a nasturtium."

"Well I call it a rose."

"You've got it off the ground and you're putting it in

your mouth, that's disgusting; throw it away right now, you hear?''

Loveliest few hours of the past month, taking care of Georgia during Paula's illness when Julian's held up at the office or flying off somewhere in search of some hot new satori— Taking charge of Georgia, that would be my answer to Paula—only member of the tribe who's refused to acknowledge the new Nicolas, not shown an ounce of trust since that hour we first owned each other, two children on a hot white beach— I'd resisted her first, but not fiercely— In the shade of the large rock where we'd spun out our dreams of future lives, in the next days and weeks her playful cunning way of evading me, heightening my desire, hiding from me in the woods, teasing with her wily voice so I could seize her with all the more fury when I found her, the fierce, heated repetition of it— So you, Paula, who stole any room with your mere entrance, toward whom all eyes turned, ''Ah what a star she'll be!'' You were finally in my power— Too much for you to bear so we fled from each other and from all we knew, I out of sight and you out of mind. . . .

Last month after Nada left, leaving us adrift—a visit to the hospital, seeing you sitting by the cold, white bed, fear flickering in and out of your eyes, and when you smiled your eyes seemed to splinter into tiny particles of light which flew to the high corners of the room— That was the time I could step in. Let Julian know that I could be the lifeline to your presence, seep you back to him on the thread of our shared past— Fetching shopping cooking, making myself useful while Julian traveled about rubbing himself against every holy man he could find to catch the virus of their faith, junky of sanctity flying about the country seeking no one but himself. You haven't been enough of a prodigal to earn true grace, dear Julian, you preach

learned tracts on Saint Augustine and you've never stolen
so much as one damn pear.

THE SUN WAS SHINING HOT AGAIN, CLOUDS DISPERSED, IT
hadn't rained. It is startling, Julian thought, how little attention we've paid to this demonstration. It is quite true
that many go to such events to cure ailing marriages, wield
a better profile in society, gain self-esteem. And what luck
that this has kept us from staying home and having a simple
little argument. Julian had tried to push out of mind the
tensions Paula had started that morning; there might be
another conflict later between Nicolas and Paula and he
didn't want it to occur, it was his turn to enjoy decorum,
repose.

He passed a food vendor's stand, hung with leaflets and
antiwar buttons, briefly glanced at himself in the mirror.
Earnest, sunken face made pallid by libraries, insomnia,
tobacco, odious deadlines, the face of one who couldn't
ever have given himself to life in the streets . . .

"From all the cells the sick came swarming out" (Saint
Francis, Julian Symonds' own words) "and on every one
of the hands that reached out he imprinted a kiss." Memories of Nicolas at his mercy work uptown, playing out his
perpetual game of being needed—Julian had realized how
unfit he'd been for his first vocation, Nicolas' fling with
Lady Poverty had helped him to know that he'd moved on
to another world in which he felt more honest, more at
ease: the bright world of visible rewards and pleasant spectacles, the seduction of a comfortable, unanguished middle
age.

RETURNING

THEY ONLY STAYED AT THE DEMONSTRATION FOR AN hour or so. After the crowd had finished singing "Amazing Grace," Julian said come you're tired, time to go. He leaned down to help Paula up, Nicolas said giddyap as he swung Georgia onto his shoulders again. They started walking toward the West Side, where Paula and Julian lived.

The crowd was just beginning to disperse. The afternoon was damp and hot. Julian was sweating under his black turtleneck. Nicolas had taken off his T-shirt. Paula stared at his torso, finely muscled, ruddy-haired.

"Let's play Why Not!" Georgia cried out.

"Why not be hypnotized and acupunctured while standing on your head," Nicolas said.

"Why not wear a Tibetan wedding robe to your best friend's funeral," Julian said.

"Why not go all out for yellow," Georgia said. "Yellow daffodils, yellow nails."

"Why not wind your hair into a swastika-shaped chignon . . . I'll see you all in a couple of hours," Paula added.

She had let go of Julian's hand and started running alone. She heard the voices behind her calling, Paula! Mummy! If they still think I'm batty that's their business, I'm fine at last. She wished she could reassure them that she was perfectly safe, just going to Babs' office for a visit; but she didn't want them to catch up. She ran past the hot dog vendors, the hawkers of peace buttons, the Trotskyites with granny glasses waving issues of *The Young Socialist*. Within a few minutes she was lost in the crowd that was flowing out of the park, and she headed east toward Madison Avenue to enjoy the shops.

She hadn't been alone in a street for a month. She reveled in the festive Saturday crowds, walked through red lights, smiled at the cab drivers who yelled out, Watch out lady, you want to kill yourself. She loitered with pleasure past window displays, admiring hand-embroidered sheets and Georgian silver, paused to study some expensive pipes. Very soon she must buy Julian a luxurious meerschaum, it would ease him out of his cigarette habit. "The Chairman's pipe offers the Best for your smoking pleasure. . . ." She passed a boutique that sold secondhand Victorian dresses, saw one to do Ophelia in, oh no she wouldn't play Ophelia anymore, she'd play Nora, Nora slamming the door and striking out for a new deal in life. She wished to curse and rage and rule on stage, to play the powerful she must understand power, one must know Versailles to know the king, imagine Elsinore to play a Hamlet. . . .

It was three o'clock, Saturday afternoon on Madison Avenue. Many women were walking poodles. The October issue of *Best* was displayed in the window of a news store, and Paula went in to leaf through it.

There were only twelve pages or so of Paris collection

reports. Paris had much declined in importance since the late 1960s. Nada had found this "interesting" and "refreshing." Babs had always been the Paris fanatic, she'd said that when Paris died only the *outrageous* could make news. In this October *Best* many women's hair was bound up in Dynel loops dyed to shades of green and orange, looking like some late Roman fertility goddesses gone psychedelic; others looked like transvestite gauchos on a Las Vegas stage, done up in cowboy hats, high laced boots, foot-wide suede belts with fringes to the ankles—the magazine had seen some bad times since Nada had left it, the cold cereal king who owned it had given Babs a year to get it back on its feet or else she'd get the boot. So October *Best* featured women with green lozenges smeared on their foreheads, half moons of purple on cheeks, "Why not paint yourself all over as creatively as the Buddhist idols of Kathmandu," Babs' lead editorial read. Boy did I ever look prophetic and normal at that party of Mother's twelve years ago, Paula thought, they're the ones who've been balmy all along—here were Mau Mau tribeswomen in gaudy ten-inch-high beaded collars choking them from chin to shoulder, Cherokee maidens with great rings of white around their eyes, purple feathers glued to their lashes—green and yellow eyelashes, ringlets of hair dyed poppy red, Chagall blue, Parma violet. . . .

Oh, no, Babs, this freaky stuff will never do. Paula wanted to look once more at the serene, sensible women who had modeled Nada's fashions. She needed to see her mother seated next to the baron on their Long Island terrace, murmuring over her quiet, pellucid notes: "The tranquillity of pink. . . . With a black cashmere sweater nothing in the world will do but pearls. . . ." But those serene sensible women were gone too. Every aspect of *Best*, past and present, might be crumbling. These days it was becoming gauche to show off finery of any sort, in a few years the only In style might be the Bag Lady look, the Japanese Beggar look, soon the chicest magazine in town might be called *Worst*. Leave the sinking ship the baron used to say. Nada Fitzsimmons had escaped from the world of escape, timing her exit superbly.

Paula had reached 48th Street and the building from which Nada had dictated much of American fashion since World War II. She walked through the towering glass doors and into the empty, tomblike elevator. She looked at herself in the mirror. Her best blue jeans, a T-shirt saying Out Now, a leather belt into which she'd punched several new holes that morning. Here I go, back to the dying tribe from which I came. You can't imagine how rigorously everything was defined in the days I was growing up, Mother used to say, ladies slapped their cheeks and bit their lips to heighten their color before entering a ballroom. . . . The ultimate liberation of Chanel's elegance, Mother used to write, Chanel's revolutionary vertigo of black. . . .

Nicolas had always said that when Babs got too old for men she'd take seriously to drink and start to look like Peter Lorre, but that was one of Nicolas' typical embellishments. Under the stress of age and threatened failure, the mythically ethereal Babs Hollins had simply grown a little plump. She sat at Nada Fitzsimmons' desk, frowning and shuffling through pages of copy. Round, Kabuki-white face, brilliant pink cheeks and lips painted with great care. Under the desk Paula glimpsed delicate snakeskin shoes that emulated Nada's.

"Hi, Aunt Babs," Paula said. Sanity is to choose your roles. She'd chosen a light, firm voice, a voice she liked.

Babs raised her head with a swift, sullen motion, like a guard caught napping on duty. On that familiar face Paula detected some desperation, some pleasure at her entrance.

"Our own Pumpkin! Back so soon!"

That was so casual, Paula could have spent the last month at La Grenouille instead of a clinic; one never knew to what degree they rehearsed their lines. Babs was scrutinizing her with an acid, critical glance that started at the feet and zig-zagged slowly toward the head.

"I like the anorexic look, it's sensual, draggy. But do pull your top down *over* your hips, darling, you need a low waist this fall."

Paula pulled out her shirt, adjusted her belt over it.

"Voilà le look," Babs clapped her hands. "What a difference two inches of hip can make . . . it could change the world, right?"

"Wear the right belt and you'll get everything in life," Paula smiled.

Familiar phrases, curiously soothing in the familiar room. The black and whiteness Paula had loved and hated as a child was gone from Nada's office. It was repainted canary yellow. And several desks stood about the room, as if Babs had brought assistants into her office for some kind of team work.

"I see you've been to that demonstration, one of those sit-in's?" Babs had gone to the cupboard to open a bottle of vodka. "Who did you sit with? Oh, your two gallants of course. . . . How *is* my son, that charming hybrid of Don Giovanni and Saint Vitus?"

"Nicolas is working . . ."

"Not interested, not interested," Babs interrupted. "He'll come back in good time, he'll make amends. Let me look at you, angel . . . why don't you wear a peasanty cotton skirt instead of those clichéed jeans? You need a casual, throwaway look, very in this fall."

She rolled up the piece of paper she'd been writing on and hurled it into the wastepaper basket, scowling. "Yes, everything is for throwaway, times are very difficult. . . .

Listen, Pumpkin, I'm dashing off some thoughts for my New Year Memo, you're just the one to share them with."

"Carry on, Aunt Babsie," Paula said cheerfully, "I'm listening."

Babs lit a Black Sobranie, profiled herself against the coromandel screen in the authoritative pose Nada used to strike for her press conferences.

"Do you know what our times are signaling to me?" Babs began. "Signaling nothing less than the end of ravishment, the end of all *Style.*"

She took a sip of vodka, inhaling on a long, white cigarette holder.

"Ever since the beginning of civilization style has depended on dictatorship, has needed an aristocracy that *imposes* a certain mode of dress. And what do you see these days in the Hamptons, that Deauville of the bubble-gum set ruined by discarded singles from Maxwell's Plum . . . women decked out for the evening in workmen's overalls or Victorian nightdresses, women in thrift shop trash wearing the discarded clothes of dead strangers. . . . I call that a loss of faith in humanity!"

She had the same smoky voice and swift gestures Paula remembered from her childhood; her pale-skinned gaudiness now gave her the air of a handsome, aging, tropical bird.

"And when you come home to Seventh Avenue you're told that the seventies generation is into separates and body suits. . . . Who can *dictate* separates? How can Mr. Bran Flakes, sitting in his group-sex modern digs in Chicago expect me to run a magazine dedicated to the Best in body suits? When there's no one left to *decree* style, *impose* the fall and rise of hems, is it worth going on living?"

"Poor Aunt Babs," Paula said. "I know just what you mean."

A swerve of suspicion, surprise.

"What do you mean you know what I mean, Paula Mary? You've never before in your *life* known what I mean."

Paula thinking: Babs had never been nasty; just suspicious, crazed with ambition, insecure; all those women who needed *Best*'s frippery must have tiny egos. They feared they were nobodies, they were terrified that if they weren't constantly seen Everywhere making spectacles of themselves they might simply cease existing. That was the greatest illusion *Best* had to offer, the escape from being no one.

Babs had lain down on Nada's Empire couch, which she'd reupholstered in a bright shade of crimson. "Oh, you're looking at a tortured woman," she sighed, and closed her eyes. Paula paced through the room and saw that each of the desks in the office was dedicated to different departments of *Best:* "IN with indirect lighting to make you look delectably younger," the Homes galleys read, "OUT with every lampshade in the house . . ." "IN are strong astonishing rooms devoid of a picture, OUT are the Rothkos and de Koonings we're all fed up with . . ."

Beauty desk: "The luscious, rich-red mouth will become, without question, the fashion symbol of the seventies . . ."

No assistants worked at the other desks, Babs had simply taken the whole of the magazine into her hands in an attempt to rescue it. And she could well succeed, there might be no way of sinking *Best*. Acid rain swamping the country, cities' ghettoes filling with machine-gunning hoodlums, underground gangs learning to make atom bombs in their cellars, National Guard called in to rule the cities, *Best* might still survive, its models looking increasingly burned out and drugged, sequinned lids and slack mouths dribbling onto their tons of body paint; *Best* was as much part of the human condition as all our dreams and doubts and nightmares. . . .

Reclining on the red velvet couch, her head thrown back in Nada's smoking gesture, Babs had begun to muse about her past summer.

". . . except for France I fear Europe is finished, Pumpkin, Italy and Spain have become trailer parks filled with hairy-legged Swedes. . . . So now the Third World might be the only getaway left. Off to India next year, lovey, most *luxe* hotels left on the planet . . . the Grand in Calcutta particularly recommended if you can beat your way to the front door. . . . Yes, Calcutta Grand, marble bathrooms the size of Rockefeller's terrace, three-course meals brought to your room at two A.M. a few minutes after you ring for it, the world's most heavenly massage and pedicure round the clock, you want it you have it. . . ."

She took off her shoes and rubbed her pretty little feet.

"Feet are of the utmost importance," she declared. "It's trifles that make for perfection, trifles . . . guess who said that?"

"Baudelaire," Paula ventured.

"Nonsense, angel, Voltaire. Dear Vincent was right after all, travel to the Third World for unsurpassed luxury. Moroccans are so efficient that Yves' villa was finished in a matter of weeks, he even built three kitchens side by side in order to keep his chef happy. What taste my sweet Saint-Laurent has, Persian carpets all over the outside terraces, where they belong, a private chapel totally hung with silver damask. Now there's a place where you can still enjoy sublime food, impeccable domestics. Ah, what genius for life dear Yves has . . ."

It's not the time to hear all about Yves again, Paula thought. "What about Paris?" she asked.

"You *have* regained your wits, darling, I was keeping that for dessert!" Babs raised her glass of vodka to a picture of Dior that still hung over Nada's former desk. "Our dear Paris isn't quite as defunct yet as your poor mother thought, that '68 nonsense was a lot of left-wing poppy-cock. . . . But *Best* might well be a sinking ship, your old Babs and the entire West will go down with it, so when in France why not go out for all the classiest, most decadent things. . . . Last summer I flew down to Cannes in Charlie Chandon's private jet, waiters pouring out his '56 extra brut—a living dream, that Chandon, looks like Valentino, shoots grouse in Scotland, plays polo in Brazil, would have been my ideal fling a few years ago but I'm aging, Pumpkin, a free drink is all I can hope for these days. . . . Then on to the Laffittes in Burgundy and guess what's new there—Marie-France has installed twenty-five closed circuit televisions in her bedroom so that she can study the flower arrangements in each part of the chateau from her bedside! And she does have the greatest nose in France, a different mix of potpourri custom-blended for each room, scent specialists spending *days* creating new fragrances for her . . . not to speak of the Laffittes' cuisine, you've never tasted such filet en croute, ah there's the secret of the good life, a first-rate butcher!''

She put out her cigarette, looked wryly at Paula. ''It's not so bad getting too old for sex, darling, you simply switch your attention to other little pleasures and they begin to count for *everything*. You go down to Monte Carlo and sail in the Revsons' yacht, *Ultima II*. Thirty movies for the cruise, a new one shown every night after dinner. Fifty or sixty people for cocktails, when you dock in a fun place, you put on snappy clothes and head for some good jazz club . . . the in game on the Côte d'Azur is Who Would You Like to Be Frozen With? Merle Oberon said she wants to be frozen with her hairdresser and her jeweler, ever heard of anything more trite?''

Paula sat very still, hands folded in lap. Babs had always loved her audiences.

"But forget the face-cream crowd, none of it compares to Eugénie's costume ball in Paris!"

Paula thought hard to remember who that could be. Ah yes, the thick-lipped hustler who'd captured the wealthiest man in France some fifteen years back.

"The fantasy, the pure waste of it, that's what's so glorious about her Paris parties! We've gotten so stingy with our lives, we're forgetting that Western civilization is based on endless, beautiful waste . . . well, that event was *sublimely* wasteful. Go take a look at my December spread, that's what I call great copy. . . ."

Babs had pointed to the Society desk, on which there lay a six-page spread of the Baronne de Lefkowitz's last costume party, called the Head Ball.

The Vicomtesse de Ribes had real snails and ivy stuck to her face and throat, winding their way down onto her chest.

Madame Guerlain, heiress to the perfume fortune, wore a record player on her head.

Countess Barberini was hatted with cabbages and had powdered her face in shades of cerulean to match.

Hubert de Givenchy wore an aviary covered with fine mesh netting, inside which flitted a dozen real butterflies.

Fifty extra policemen had been hired to guide the guests through a make-believe Black Forest—five hundred feet of corridor hung with a dense thicket of black velvet ribbons.

Barbara Hutton arrived in a wheelchair in the company of a twenty-five-year-old toreador to whom she had just offered forty million French francs and a Mercedes-Benz.

The director of the Crillon Hotel had enclosed his head in a birdcage. He'd refused to greet Barbara Hutton, who had asked to have three extra ice boxes brought into her Crillon suite to hold the forty Coca-Colas she imbibed every day.

Paulette Goddard had spent the morning at Alexandre's

having daggers sunk into her head, and the afternoon at a makeup artist's, where drops of blood were painted down her cheeks and chest . . .

The menu included truffles en croute, wild boar and black currant sherbet. It's just a little dinner the Baronne had said, not a ball, since that last bombing at rue Copernic we can't afford to . . .

. . . PARTIES ABROAD ARE BECOMING INCREASINGLY RAU-cous, Grandmother Fitzsimmons had written Nada from Rome in the 1920s, before leaving for Africa. The Mar-chesa de Casati appears in society holding a leopard on a leash and is flanked by a Negro servant painted head to toe in gilt, the Duke de Verdura gave a party to celebrate the canonization of Joan of Arc, the snakes writhing on the floor of his palazzo were quite unnecessary.

Grandmother had also attended a costume ball in Rome at which Countess Volpi planned to appear as an electri-cally wired Saint Sebastian; she wore an armor pierced with hundreds of arrows, each arrow was studded with glit-tering bulbs that were to light up upon her entrance . . .

But the costume short-circuited upon first rehearsal, the countess suffered an electric shock that sent her into a high backward somersault and she did not recover in time to attend the party.

"I DON'T HAVE THAT MUCH TIME LEFT TO ME, DEAR heart," Babs was saying. "People are still inviting me be-cause they want their name in *Best*, but next year there may not be any more *Best*, and then . . . pfoooooot . . ."

She made a long downward gesture with her hands.

". . . then I'll have to spend my retirement going out to dinner once a week with my favorite walker and watching Betty Bacall showing off at La Grenouille again, who wants *that*. . . . You know something, Pumpkin, New York's

Beautiful People are becoming the OTB's, and I don't mean Off Track Betting, I mean Old Tired Bores. I know my crowd, they're a bunch of vain, stupid snobs. I'm also a vain, stupid snob but I have one thing they don't have, I've worked all my life creating a *style,* you remember my motto, I *risk,* therefore I am . . ."

Babs slammed a fist into her desk. "Oh I wish it had all been totally, totally different. I wish I could have been frozen at the age of thirty-nine, at the height of all pleasures. I wish the 1940s would return and we could still dance the rumba, the strict, difficult, demanding rumba, instead of just standing in front of each other and shaking like spastic idiots. Or I wish I'd lived in the eighteenth century so I could have made friends with Dr. Johnson, I'd have talked much of the day to Dr. Johnson and I could have met Beau Brummell, imagine Beau shipping off his laundry to be done in Paris every week, now that is class . . .

"Oh I'm out of my time, out of my time," she sighed. "I've never had so much as one unattractive thought and all is disillusionment, pure, unadulterated disillusionment . . ."

"You've had love," Paula said gently.

"Oh, *that!*" Babs cackled, looking at Paula as if she'd suggested that the bottom of evening trousers be worn rolled up. "Peanuts, crackerjack for the masses. Wealth, power, beauty, more important than love, and there I was always a little outside, looking in . . . well at least I didn't marry Bill Paley, everyone tried to marry Bill Paley."

Her hoarse belly laugh returned, the plump little woman's laugh that finally had begun to suit her body.

"The three of you are still so romantic, you and Julian and Nicolas, with your perpetual ideas of marrying each other . . . who ever thinks of getting married anymore save for a few priests and homosexuals?

"Guess what the French government gives as a wedding present to each couple after their civil ceremony?" she continued. "A copy of *Madame Bovary*. Now that's style. . . ."

Then she rose from the couch and yawned, with the little gesture of hand to mouth that indicated she'd had enough of a conversation. The interview was over. Babs had turned back to the copy she was writing for her New Year's issue.

Back for Keeps: The Neck! Enchanting, alluring, demanding . . .

This is The Year of The Boot . . .

Fashion is the Triumph of the Ephemeral . . .

"Do something for me, darling," Babs whispered to Paula, looking up from her desk. "Startle me terribly. Nothing is unthinkable to me but sameness. The allure of life depends solely on surprise, and I simply haven't had one surprise all year. . . ."

Paula looked at herself in Babs' mirror, and was interested to find how much she looked like her mother. She saw that driven expression Nada had when she was working on a very difficult project, a nothing-will-get-in-my-way look. Here we go, Paula, this is it.

"Where's my mother?" Paula asked. "Only people in this office might know, Babs. Where is she?"

"Your mother?" Babs' face didn't move, remained a lake of white powder punctuated by two dark brilliant eyes. Those eyes darted toward her visitor, mischievous and blinking. "We just heard a few days ago . . . don't worry about her, dearest; a well-groomed invalid lives on for years."

Paula knew her Babs; she was playing it right.

"Only you can tell me where she is."

Babs rose and patted Paula affectionately on the cheek, as she had years ago when she approved of the way she'd dressed for one of Nada's parties.

"If you really want to know, she's in Rome," she said languidly. "I simply can't think of a more stupid place to go to nowadays. Imagine going to live in a country where you're even mugged for wearing a Balmain and false pearls into the street, where Princess Corsini has to hire two armed chauffeurs for protection even though she masquerades in jeans.

"And I'll tell you something else about Nada," Babs whispered. "She's working in a hospital. . . ."

AFTER GRANDMOTHER'S DISAPPEARANCE GRANDFATHER Fitzsimmons had talked to his friends about those "untidy mystical torments" that had plagued his wife for many years. Paula had always loved that word, *untidy!* Friends on the Continent understood her better—Cocteau commented on "the glory of this premeditated, voluptuous withdrawal!"—*"Mais ça a un chic fou d'aller dans le désert!"* Coco Chanel had exclaimed to Nada—"It's her Slavic soul," explained Patou, who had lost one of his best customers.

Well I certainly didn't miss much while I was away looking for Mother, Nada used to tell Paula about her two years' absence from London and Paris. Nothing more hideous than the early thirties' taste! All those mortuary white calla lilies and everyone plundering churches for their decor—Piguet's shoulders were hideous, Schiaparelli's turbans were the living end, and even Coco was going through that ghastly Byzantine phase while she was living with her Russian prince.

Nada's eyes would screw up slyly and she would silently bend her head down and let her shoulders shake, her mother's way of laughing—when her eyes rose again Paula saw them filled with sorrow, longing, the discipline and pain of suppressed sentiment, God knows what else. . . .

* * *

"DON'T YOU THINK IT UNBELIEVABLE TO LIVE IN A CITY where you can't even make it to a luncheon because some stupid demonstration is always blocking traffic to the Torre Argentina," Babs was saying. And then she brusquely added, "Well, Paula Mary, *now* will you read my hand?"

It was another of the hands Paula had refused to read since childhood. But here it was all of a sudden, stretched out and supplicating. Paula sensed Babs' solitude. She turned Babs' palm outward and gently palpated it, kneading it under its mass of tight gold rings.

"External appearances matter little to you," she said, "you go straight to the moral principles that lie behind illusion . . .

"Heart line long and fretted, intense sensitivity to the world's suffering, to the feelings and needs of others . . .

"Mount of Venus—goodness, how flat and fragile! Don't be too much of a Puritan, Aunt Babsie."

Paula held that hand with interest and tenderness, sensing for the first time in years the familiar heat, the suspension of time that occurred in her best readings.

"This could be the hand of a nun, a revolutionary leader living a life of extreme asceticism . . .

"Watch your liver and your heart, Babs dear, those are your weak points. I'd say that from now on you must be very, *very* careful."

I'D ENJOYED WATCHING THE DISTRUSTFUL, AMAZED LOOK in Babs' eyes. I sensed that she only had a few years left to live; I also knew that either my science had been a lot of bunk or Babs had brilliantly played many roles to survive—the shared fate of every member of our so-called family.

There remained the matter of the gun. I'd found the gun in a drawer of the Fashion desk, where I had a hunch Babs would be keeping it, rather than in Beauty or Homes. I'd considered snatching it while she went to her closet to pour us a vodka. It was a small Beretta of Uncle Vincent's, with an amusing history. Some fifteen years back, while working late into the night on her crucial October issue, Babs had been held up by three amateur hoodlums who had assumed that the clunky costume jewelry she wore to the office was the real thing. Uncle Vincent had come into her office, his own little Beretta in hand, attired in one of my mother's hats, singing a Schubert lied in his high falsetto voice, and the robbers had been so startled that they'd fled out of the window before anyone could even call the police. It was this pearl-handled toy of Uncle Vincent's that I considered putting into my purse as I prepared to leave Babs' office for our apartment, I knew Nicolas would be there getting my family settled for the evening . . . but I decided against it. I had other tactics in mind.

THE KITCHEN AND THE BATHROOM WERE SIDE BY SIDE IN the ground floor apartment that Julian and I had shared for three years. The windows gave out on a small back garden which was accessible through an abandoned lot in the center of the block. So if I crouched low under either of the two windows, I could easily slink back and forth unseen, watching my family in both of the two rooms . . . for I'd decided that in order to get the key to the next stage I should lie still and hidden for a while, imbibing the surf of enemies and friends inside. Sit and watch carefully for a while and the future might just come to you like a trained squirrel in the park.

Our garden was dotted with a tiny patch of green which shone brilliantly on this October afternoon. Nicolas had been hard at work trying to grow a few vegetables for Julian, salsify, arugola. Staring at his summer's work I realized that Nicolas' true vocation seemed to lie somewhere in the domain of victuals. The way Nicolas had first charmed me with his dinners or distributed ice cream cones to neighborhood children whenever Babs gave him money to get rid of him for a few hours, rewarded by their smiles, their recognition. And what had the Peace Corps and that Harlem school been but another way of seeking much-needed love and attention; we offspring of *Best* each find our dramatic way of seduction. Look at Nicolas just now, playing house over the kitchen table, doing something complicated to a piece of fish.

"Did you know that Scotland is still the only place that knows how to smoke salmon properly," he was saying to Julian and Georgia. "Norwegian and Irish-smoked brands only substituted through deviousness or ignorance. Scotch smokers treat their fish with salt and molasses to give it a subtle ying-yang of sour-sweetness . . ."

"Where does salmon live?" Georgia asked. She was sitting on the floor, doodling restlessly in a picture book.

"Lives in salt water . . ." Julian began.

". . . and spawns in fresh or brackish water," Nicolas finished for him. "Also did you know that some American firms ship Nova Scotia salmon to be smoked in Scotland and then have it reshipped to New York? So in fact it's Scotch *smoked* salmon rather than smoked *Scotch* salmon."

"Amazing," Julian said. Impassive, hunched over a notebook. He might be planning a trip to visit Jesuits in Goa, writing an article on Rome's newest edict on masturbation.

"Whenever you're served salmon with a deep reddish color instantly send it back, the best Scotch salmon ranges from the tender pink of a dawn sky to the pale orange of sunset . . ."

"You do wax poetic," Julian noted. "Where in hell do you think Paula went? I mean, when should we start calling?"

"Call who?" Georgia asked.

"Just friends, sweetheart."

"We only left that demo an hour and a half ago, Julian, let's hold off a tiny bit before we start broadcasting our problems."

My husband sat at the kitchen table, smoking. "Let's be careful about Julian," that was a phrase often heard in the family. It was related to his solitude—he was still the orphan pressing his nose to a window, admiring worlds that were not his. It had to do with that great charity which often made us feel crass and guilty—he was always trying to bring us together, reconciling me to Mother, the family to Nicolas. "Let's be careful about Julian"—there was something magic, untouchable about Julian that had to do with his having saved me.

"If the heart of the universe hummed one great song and we could suddenly hear it," Julian asked Nicolas, "do you think we could dance to it?" He beat out a quick rhythm on the kitchen table.

"It sounds like a samba," Nicolas said. "I suppose we could, I'm not sure what you're talking about."

"I bet Grandma could dance," Georgia said.

"She's right, Nicolas, Nada would hear it before anyone else, she'd see right through to the dance."

"Don't let's talk about goodness," Nicolas said, "that could bring out the worst in all of us. Nada's got something more interesting than goodness but I'll be damned if I know what it is . . ."

"I'll bet anything Paula returns in time for this delectable dinner," Nicolas continued as he squeezed a lemon. " *'La donna è mobile.'* Can't trust women as far as George Washington Bridge, can you, Julian? And I've known my share of femmes fatales. You know something, I'm perfectly satisfied to be a happy, fulfilled dilettante. I just never want to be alone anymore."

"Obviously," Julian said. "None of us wants it. That's

why we're here, in this kitchen, watching you torturing a fish.''

"What's for dinner, Uncle Nick?" Georgia asked. She was scribbling in her coloring book, not looking up. "I don't want dinner until Mummy comes back."

"Why not serve pork to all your Moslem guests," Nicolas said, "they never get it at home. Actually, we're having poached filets of salmon tonight, with a caviar sauce. Excess, extravagance, *that* is *class!* as my hallowed mother would put it.''

Nicolas lit a cigarette and stood profiled against the window for a second, blowing long plumes of smoke. His hand was shaking slightly. I knew he was as worried about me as Julian, putting on a fine show, keeping the family as calm as he could.

"Now let me teach you something about caviar, Georgia," Nicolas resumed. "Beluga sturgeon provides the largest eggs and is only found in the Caspian Sea, that's the southern part of Russia, sweetheart. Now to the serving! We've seen it dishonored by garnishes of chopped egg or minced onion, all additions are very gauche beyond a squeeze of lemon . . .''

Julian said "Damn, damn," and tore a piece of paper out of his notebook. He threw it to the floor and paced up and down the kitchen, hands in pockets. "Honestly, Nicolas, where do you think she is?"

"We'll know in an hour or so," Nicolas said quietly. "Maybe she's shopping on Madison Avenue."

He brandished his kitchen knife in the air with a flourish. Georgia lost her anxious look and giggled.

"I'm determined to remain honorably occupied with externals," Nicolas continued. "I'll tell you, Julian, one of the differences between you and me is that you're interested in the mystical, whereas I'm only interested in mystique. . . .''

"I'm not a mystic, chum," Julian said with his wry smile. "I'm just a cop. Protecting certain traditions which for some curious reason I wish to see preserved."

"Beluga caviar has mystique," Nicolas said, "pressed caviar doesn't. Lenny Bernstein has mystique and Nureyev lost his. Norman Mailer's kept mystique, Capote had it and blew it . . ."

I CROUCHED THERE, LISTENING TO HOW PREDESTINED WE all are: tiny eggs come into being with all future instructions embedded in their nuclei. Nicolas might be as incapable of purging himself of our mothers' world as I was. Both of us stamped and doomed, *Best* sucking us up like a galactic vacuum cleaner, however far we'd strayed from it. Was this a tale about the fragility of the individual and the might of the environment, could I ever break the code, reshuffle our instructions?

Julian had left the kitchen and seemed to have gone to his room, Georgia had followed him. Several dinner courses were ready for the oven, covered with aluminum and Saran wrap. Nicolas was cleaning up, soaping every dish and knife, rinsing, drying, I could see his long lanky arms, the bright pale blue of his eyes. He called out to Georgia saying bath time, bath time. I rolled over like a cat toward the next window to watch them, crouching very low. I'd always found it thrilling to prepare the timing of delicate entrances, like that night I'd squatted at the entrance of my mother's flat, chimpanzeed gypsy staging her first disappearance. . . . Twelve years later I was dressed in sensible jeans, ready to return to the stage and change my life again.

There was a quick shuffle of feet in the bathroom, a rumble of faucets, water spurting out of the handsome brass fittings of Julian's tub. Nicolas' voice reminding Georgia to fold her clothes neatly on a chair, Mummy will be home soon to get you a fresh bathrobe. Georgia testing the bath

and finding it too cold, too hot, Nicolas helping to adjust
the faucets, lap of water against porcelain, Georgia's birdlike voice as she lowers her body into the tub. I've raised
my eyes to the level of the window. Georgia's hair is tied
up with a rubber band, without its heap of brown curls her
slender face shouts out the Fitzsimmons clan louder than
ever, Grandmother's wide-spaced questing eyes, Nada's
wry, upturned mouth. My daughter stands in the tub, dous-
ing herself with water from her plastic toys, dribbling water
over her head. Okay porky pie, cut out the monkey business; Nicolas is going in and out dressed in denim shorts,
his legs are lean and powerful, no more the heavy, shy
boy's legs of his adolescence. Georgia giggles as Nicolas
tells her to wipe her ears and neck, soap her shoulders. He
dips water in her toy ducks to help her rinse, she splashes
back. . . . Julian would have been less gifted at such tasks,
not through physical impairment or lack of love but out of
disinterest in life's more prosaic chores, his distaste for
anything that reminds him of his own early childhood.

But Nicolas is helping bathe my child with efficiency and
tenderness, Nicolas might be chaste as Saint Francis while
boasting of a thousand conquests, virginally shy of women
while talking like a stevedore, that's how I'm figuring it
out tonight, but he's so crafty I could be all wrong.

A last burst of splashing and giggling, cut it out you
funny beastie, time to get into your p.j.'s. . . . If I'd
brought that Beretta of Uncle Vincent's I could be cocking
it at Nicolas just now. I don't want Nicolas and Julian to
bring up Georgia, I don't want them to carry on without
me and turn her into a wonderfully safe, fashionable girl.
Julian would send Georgia to Chapin rather than Brearley
because it's more Old Families, and she'd mingle with the
brats of Republican National Committee golf buffs. Later
she'd be like the goons who'd waited for marriage by hanging around Mother's and Babs' office, downing sedatives

while struggling to write dazzling captions about the newest bikini. On Saturday nights she'd deck out in borrowed Galanos chiffons and court clean-shaven young Wall Street brokers who didn't know Ibsen from *Idomeneo*. Or else Julian and Nicolas would glut Georgia with all the safety and normalcy the three of us didn't have as children and turn her into a tennis-jock Locust Valley matron who says dearie to everyone she meets. I don't want her to be like myself or any of those women, I want her to retain the eccentricities of the earlier Fitzsimmons women, remain an adventurer, a seeker, whatever the risks.

Nicolas has draped Georgia with a large bath towel. The child sings a song, tries to make him dance with her the way I'd danced with Uncle Vincent, my little feet docile and happy on his big black shoes. Enough, sleepy lady, go dress for dinner. She puts on her serious scowling face, runs out. Nicolas is seated on the rim of Julian's tub now, scouring it with a large stiff brush, I see only his strong adolescent chest, the picture of Saint Sebastian looking chagrined over his blond head.

THAT AFTERNOON OF OUR FIFTEENTH YEAR I'D ADVANCED toward him on the hot white beach and at first he'd been terrified. Stood with his back to the oak tree, hair disheveled, eyes pale with anxiety. We'd been arguing about how to speak Caliban's lines, "The isle is full of noises, sounds and sweet airs. . . ." I'd pressed my body against his, pressed him hard against the tree and pinned his arms behind him. He'd bent his mouth to mine, pink and passive, not yet knowing what to do with it. And I'd thrust my thighs against his, moving slowly until his breath was short.

AT LEAST THAT'S THE WAY IT MIGHT HAVE BEEN. I DIDN'T remember all that clearly. That's the way it came back to me that October evening as I stood at the window. The success of my next tactic depended on impeccable timing. I had to leave on an important errand for a few weeks; but first I'd let them know that I planned to return very soon, remain quite in control. If I'd brought that gun I could have pretended to shoot Nicolas as he bent over the tub, sprinkling his brush with green scouring powder . . . instead I opened the bathroom window, rose to my full height and shouted out at Nicolas.

"Paula!" he cried. "Stop this nonsense!"

I'd intended to startle Nicolas out of his wits. I'd looked forward to seeing him cower before me, like the stuttering child who'd crouched in a corner of my mother's living room, yearning for love and sandwiches.

But it didn't turn out that way at all. Nicolas was standing tall before me, looking threatening and angry.

"You owe me an explanation," he said. "You owe me a few well-chosen words. You owe me an hour of your time, right now."

"Why not?" I didn't know what to say.

Nicolas pulled himself up to the windowsill, jumped down into the garden beside me. "You and I are going back to the park for a walk. You and I are going to be alone together for a little while, at last."

By the time we'd sat down on a grassy, secluded patch of the park we were very quiet. We'd done a lot of groundwork. We'd heard several things that we'd never spoken before.

"There's something about a first love that stamps you for life," Nicolas had said, "neither of us might be able to fight it."

"But we've changed a great deal."

"That's just the point," he said, "we've barely changed at all. We've changed amazingly little. We're still trying to upstage and amaze each other, like all the goons in our mothers' drawing rooms. And you're still trying to manipulate me, and I'm still putting on many masks to try and gain your love."

"I'd always thought that you'd attacked me," I whispered, "and then abandoned me."

"It was all very mutual," he said gently. "Everyone around us was in the business of seduction, only family trade we were taught. And we had so little in the world outside each other."

IT WAS AFTER SIX O'CLOCK, A VERY WARM OCTOBER DUSK in the city of our childhood. We sat by an oak tree under the ledge of a large rock. The leaves above us glowed like a canopy of gold. I picked a leaf that had fallen on Nicolas' hair. He took my hand.

"Always keep this in mind," he said. "You might try to love others, you might succeed, but you'll never really belong to anybody else."

"One must remain honorable," I whispered.

"Quite so. But there's only one life, unlike the way we figured it as kids."

"Right. No next time round."

"I'm not asking anything of you now. I'm just warning you that someday you might return to me."

WHEN WE TOOK EACH OTHER AGAIN, SHORTLY AFTER those words, fifteen years melted on touch. As our bodies renewed each other's on the dark grass, I knew that Nicolas was offering me the grandest fantasy any reunion can bring: the illusion that our flesh can remain unchanged throughout decades, that we are arresting time. In the warm grass of the October dusk our flesh was as starved and familiar as it had been on a lawn of our summer house, in those fervid days of our fifteenth year. As the darkness cloaked us, as we ceased and lay still, I was at peace and wiser.

Nicolas had spoken little while we made love, no I love yous or other banalities most men would feel entitled to. And in his silence I sensed again his great shrewdness, that catlike being who knew precisely when to pounce from a sill, pry open a door, charm anyone into sharing a dish.

The most dangerous or clearest thoughts occur afterward, when we lie quietly in the other's arms. It is then that we risk to pledge away our freedom, or else receive a burst of wisdom, as I received that evening; during those peaceful after-minutes I learned that Nicolas would always retain the awesome power to abolish time and bring me back to childhood; that I must avoid at all cost living again under such a spell; that I would never choose between Julian and Nicolas, would only choose some path equally independent of both men.

I felt more than ever the need to go abroad and attend to my mother.

WE WALKED HOME HOLDING HANDS, SHARING MEMORIES of Sala and *The Tempest* and Uncle Vincent. Only an hour had passed, and it felt just like that—an hour. Nicolas had looked for me and found me in the park.

After sharing Nicolas' exquisite dinner with my family I went to the phone and booked myself on a flight to Rome.

ABROAD

MOTHER'S QUARTERS IN ROME: A SMALL ROOM WITH only a bed, a chair, a desk, a standing clock.

No longer a matter of Elegance is Refusal. An austerity not willfully chosen but lapsed into. Musty green walls, clean plain coverlet on the bed, faint smell of mint and disinfectant. On the single table, when I first entered the room, lay a few books on the history of Rome and a bottle of medicine. As I stared at her refuge I thought of the solitary hours she must have spent in her single chair, I thought of the mystery this woman had presented me for thirty years.

As far back as I could remember I had not wanted my mother's life. I'd come to realize that she had not loved it either; and that I'd taken many risks to cop out of it before she did.

Standing at the door of that room in Rome, her mystery deepened. I knew that I could not have suffered her new life any better than the previous one.

WE HAD BEEN REUNITED IN A HOSPITAL ON THE JANICU-
lum where she volunteered to help a few afternoons a week.
My first vision of her had been in the dispensary, where
she was washing luncheon dishes. She stood bent over a
chipped sink amid grey-robed nuns, dressed in a wool
smock, her hands making calm, repetitive gestures over the
running water. We were thirty feet from each other. The
indifference with which she raised her eyes toward mine
put me into a state of panic. My mother had gone mad,
had lost all memory, was rejecting me even more totally
than I'd feared. But after a few seconds her curiosity was
aroused, she wiped her hands on her apron; hesitated, took
a step forward; and with eyes first unbelieving, then joyful,
she began swiftly walking toward me . . . I realized that
her eyesight might have begun to fail.

She threw herself into my arms. I placed my hand over
her head, swept it over her furrowed, wasted face. I cried.
She did not. "Why did you leave me," I asked. "I am a
misfit," she answered, "I have known sixty years of fear."

SHE HAD LIVED THE ILLUSION OF AFFLUENCE MUCH OF
her life, and now she was leading the life of a studious,
frugal expatriate. At the hospital, taking temperatures, carrying bedpans, serving meals. Bringing flowers to my
grandmother's grave in the Protestant cemetery. Visiting a
few times a week with acquaintances from the 1920s, aging
contessas of her mother's generation who huddled in shawls
in the corners of chill palaces. I slept on a folding cot in
her room. We ate many of our meals in trattorias near
Trastevere filled with large families, bawling children,
disheveled waiters doling out tepid pasta.

After dinner I obediently followed her new evening
schedule. I accompanied her to institutions that offer free
lectures to the dilettantes, indigent scholars and lost souls
who make up many of Rome's foreign residents. Seated on

spindly chairs at the British Academy, the Villa Medici, the American Academy, we listened to numismatists, life-long annotators of one medieval manuscript deliver passionate papers on their life's obsession. During such evenings I indulged in fantasies in which my mother would have been an educator, a teacher of arduous and arcane subjects. I fancied her having stayed on at Oxford, an early feminist in shabby tweeds and sensible shoes. She might have conceived me with the aid of a Spenser scholar devoting his life to deciphering one book of the *Faerie Queene*. . . . I dozed off at Mother's side during lectures on "Mithraic Cults of Ancient Rome," swathed in a limpid boredom and the greatest peace I'd known in years. "You may not need this," she would say during her diligent note-taking, glancing at me over her powerful spectacles, "but I am here to improve myself, to rid my mind of all that junk."

In the daytime we walked many miles each day. She walked a little stooped now, with jaunty swings of an ebony cane she had found for a song in Rome's flea market. She had discarded her Balenciaga chemises, her black and whiteness, her drama. She wore loose, plain vestments acquired in the city's department stores. We walked and we admired. Museums, monuments, statuary. She had a way of moving too close to the work she was studying, laughing because she'd almost bumped into it, backing away a few feet, changing to another pair of spectacles. She'd lean on my arm, settled into her arduous gazing, often asking me to read a passage from our guidebook.

Mother's mind had often reminded me of some beautiful unfinished town in which gazebos stand gaping in the middle of empty squares, houses thrust flowered, half-built terraces onto the street. In her latest bout of dabbling she'd set out to become an expert on all things Roman. She instructed me on the subject with the finely tuned sentences that had been a trademark of her writing. "The Farnese Palace, presently the French Embassy, where I'll soon take you to tea, for I've met its occupant, was built by Pope Paul III out of two thousand five hundred and twenty cartloads of travertine from the Colosseum. . . ." "Agostino Chigi, the Norton Simon of his day, used to serve his guests dinner on services of gold plate, which were then thrown into the Tiber . . ."

I suppose we were walking to all the places she'd visited with her own mother in those last weeks before Georgia Fitzsimmons' death.

I suppose that was in great part why she had come here, to die amid memories of her own mother.

I imagined these two inebriates of style riding slowly in a closed car, the dying woman filling her eyes with those Roman sites the British had loved best: the fir-lined avenues of the Borghese Gardens; the Fontana Paola on the Janiculum, the green piazzas of the Aventine Hill, suffused with the soft chanting of psalms emerging from its convents.

Grandmother Fitzsimmons had developed a particular interest, in her last months, for the work of Bernini. She'd been especially fond of a certain sculpture in a small church at the bottom of Trastevere. It depicts a woman lying on her death bed, cloaked in a flow of marble drapery as in furrows of gushing water, face raised high as if reaching toward a source of light. Several times a month Mother would stand close to the statue, squinting, while a sacristan held a large candle to shed more light. "Read to me, please." "Blessed Ludovica Albertini," I complied, "died of a long illness after a life of good works and Franciscan piety. Note the clusters of floating cherubs pointing like arrows at the convulsed figure, the artist's symphonic treatment of physical suffering and pain . . ."

"Perhaps she's also in a state of sexual ecstasy," Moth-

er ventured one day, "that's what your grandmother believed." Oh God, I thought, what did either of them know
about that . . . "No, no," I said, "it is about her expectations of eternity." "I understand," she said.

In these first days of our greatest friendship we often
answered each other with such phrases: "I see." "You're
right." "I understand." We coded our emotions through
statuary, the fate of friends. Our speech remained as oblique
as our guilt—our sense that we had not overtly done wrong
toward each other but had done wrong nonetheless.

"Be like this, be like that, be like me!" her voice had
shouted inside me, full of her own self-doubt.

"Watch me play Portia, watch me make you happy,
watch me rebel!" I'd shouted back.

And many other tactics: Perennial choreography of seduction, mothers and daughters strangling on guilt and love.

We lunched almost daily on the sunny side of the Piazza
Navona, staring at gypsies hawking their children and
flowers, sultry girls in leather jackets huddled over their
coffee and their men. Lovers perennially kissing at the feet
of the river gods. Beautiful schoolgirls walked by us in
droves like legions of vestals, eyes cold and metal-irised,
hair frozen into a multitude of wiry ringlets. Mother put
on her strongest spectacles to stare at them, rekindling her
interest in the splendor of human surfaces. . . . Youths
raced their motors with a sexual frenzy, women's voices
shouted out from the rivulets of nearby streets, filling the
air with the din of their tears, laughter, reprimands. Volks-
wagens passed us steered by white-coiffed nuns, priests
whizzed by on motorcycles, black robes flying in the autumn breeze.

We walked to visit Michelangelo's "Conversion of
Paul" in the Cappella Paolina of the Vatican, which I'd
visited with Julian on our honeymoon. Thick golden shaft
striking downward from Christ's head onto Paul's shoul-

der; apostle's tragic face, toppled to the ground by his rev-
elation. "Michelangelo's last painting," Mother noted,
"After this he just went on sculpting Pietàs over and over,
never quite finishing them." "Ah, that's Julian," I said. I
thought of Julian with a mixture of compassion, love, anger. He had reneged on a central pledge of all marriages,
which is to wrench us from our origins and make adults of
us. . . . "That great fear in Saint Paul's eyes," Mother
was continuing.

IN ROME'S ENGLISH CEMETERY THE GRAVE OF GEORGIA
Fitzsimmons lay lonely and tranquil, surrounded by roses
and lilies recently planted by her daughter. The space sur-
rounding it was serene, profuse with small wild daisies,
marked by the sense that many had come to this city with
the desire to be healed or to die a calmer death. British
drawn here for centuries in various conditions of illness,
persevering in illusions that put faith in the curative prop-
erties of Rome. . . . Libertarians, dabblers in sensibility,
amateurs in Caravaggio or the history of mosaics . . . reb-
els against the rural rites of a Grandfather Fitzsimmons
. . . persons like Georgia and Nada Fitzsimmons whose
brilliant facades often cloaked uncertainty and anguish, who
had little sense of their own worth. They had braved the
exile's solitude to bask in the mystic pull of Roman light,
to wallow in the beauty of a city where they were free of
all obligations and constraints, to enjoy the luxury of
choosing their end.

PACING THROUGH GARDENS OR PALAZZOS DURING THE
afternoons Mother was indulging in her little rites of ex-
piation, I sought for still other reasons why she had come
to Rome.
    The British come here to die, a tradition like scones and
tea. . . . Too abstract, try this one: family story repeating

itself; she'd waited until I was sane and settled and decided I didn't need her.

She'd repeated a test, I decided another day. I'd put her to the test of my madness; she'd put me to the test of her disappearance. And now we were even.

Or else Nada Fitzsimmons was looking for her mother, as I had come looking for mine.

As a child, when Nada had talked about the earlier disappearance, I kept asking what had happened to all those violins stored in Grandmother's closet? What had happened to those hundreds of pairs of shoes designed for her by a specialist in medieval costume? Mother had shrugged her shoulders with a stare of her own melancholy eyes.

What happened to all of Grandmother's furniture I'd asked her once, as we were moving into a new apartment in New York? The Adam chairs upholstered in magenta velvet, the gondola-shaped sofas, the crimson enamel gramophone? Even then, a wave of her delicate hand. "We all find other fetishes."

I undertook to return Mother to her former self. I filled her room with my perfume, small luxuries, advice. I bought basil and fresh cream for our cooking, flowers for her table. The doctor I took her to that fall certified that her heart ailment had been cured, but might have induced other injuries. "Irreversible tissue damage could gradually impair the patient's muscular and visual faculties." I woke in the middle of the night to invent a new dish, a new excursion. I was determined to reverse the process of decay, to strengthen her with nourishment and novelty. Another bowl of soup, darling. It's two o'clock, time for our walk, cover up well, don't forget your shawl. That skirt does *not* become you, Mother, those shoes are too severe. Wear your turban higher, it's covering your forehead . . .

We found a teacher of progressive yoga in the Via Giulia and sat on the carpeted floor of an old palazzo, third floor, as the teacher instructed us to become more aware of our bodies. Relax your shoulder, your eyes, your teeth. Breathe out your anxieties and exhaustion, breathe in pure energy. Imagine cool silver is running up your left side as you breathe in, hot gold is flowing out as you exhale. You're purging yourself of the hot male principle, filling up with the cool female principle. Mother sat on the floor in cross-legged position, smiling at the words but gazing inward, eyes closed. The ascetic posture became her, suddenly seemed fitting to each member of our family, to that celibate streak which marked most persons gathered about Mother, even Nicolas and Julian, that chasteness which might help us to live together in peace . . . I breathed by her side, feeling sheltered, safe.

Afterward, we rested in the sun of a café and watched more black-robed priests rushing by on motorcycles, more young Romans stretched out in parked cars on the verge of making love. "There's a sense of *kaputness*," she commented. I laughed at the word. *"Kaputness* about what?"
"About the world as we've known it. Did I tell you that Balenciaga is dying? In Valencia," she added, "surrounded by his orange trees . . . an era has passed."

I kept looking for a trace of regret, and perhaps it was also there. It would be the only mention she'd make of her former world.

NOVEMBER: A SMALL TRATTORIA OFF THE PANTHEON. GLASS of wine standing red as an ingot on the white tablecloth. And beside it Mother's long slender hands, now chapped. During our stay in Rome she'd heard a series of lectures on urban planning in sixteenth-century Rome, where nobles and beggars lived next door to each other, "in the mayhem of the human condition." (Mother trying to make me more studious with her eager snippets of history, I intent on restoring her lightheartedness.) Decaying cities and wealthy suburbs, she was saying, the American tragedy, why couldn't the poor and rich live alongside each other, as they did in Renaissance times. . . .

"When we go home I shall write a book," she added, raising her voice.

Oh, God, I thought, another one of those fashion magnates intent on purging the past, justifying the ephemeralness of a life. Redemption through recollection, there was barely a lingerie editor at *Flair* or *Yes!* who hadn't written her memoirs . . .

. . . So I switched the subject to clothes. I talked her into going shopping for the first time in months, buying herself a pair of shoes. "I'm a very difficult customer," she smiled. The next day we walked to the Corso and she chose a pair of delicate gilt evening sandals with girlishly high heels. She brought them home and instantly put them on. She danced in our little room that afternoon, her arms held up and out, as if she were holding an imaginary partner in a formal waltz. She had the arched feet and delicate insteps of a debutante, the ankles of a young woman who often danced late into the night. She danced with her past, floated about me, face frail and happy, humming Lehár and Strauss.

I'd wondered why she so often insisted on passing by the Farnese Palace, turning toward it with the ironic glance that usually accompanied some important memory. "Look at the way Michelangelo proportioned those upper-story windows. . . . I stopped there at length in the late 1930s, with a dear friend. . . . It must be seen at night, the new ambassador has totally redone the lighting on the frescoes in his office. . . . I must make that phone call," she said another time, "the ambassador will remember me well." And one day she made the call. Our host was an aging widower who chatted merrily about the figures twice his height that decorated his walls, saying this Salviati commemorates the triumphs of the Farneses, the frescoes in the dining room are Caracci's. "You stayed here often some decades ago with one of my predecessors," he said to Mother at the end of our visit.

"In summer '39," she said, "a few weeks before the war."

"Ah yes," he sighed, "some of my servants still remember the beautiful Englishwoman . . ."

WE WALKED HOME AMIABLY THROUGH THE DARKENING streets. What a funny way to be told about a father. "He was already married," she said as we reached the Tiber. *"La situation était grave,* war was breaking out, his wife had stayed home. We were to meet in Rome a year hence, but he died with the Free French."

We stopped for a red light, and she squinted at the banks of the Tiber, asking me to read the graffiti. *Maria cara ti adoro. Angelo ama Cristina. U.S.: Vietnam sarà il tuo Waterloo.* How tall was my father, what was his first name, the color of his eyes? Did you love him, did he ski, what poets did he read, what language did you speak together? There was a sense of pain and failure about such questions, of traumas past which had best remain half-healed, untouched. That evening at the restaurant I drank too much wine and chattered about Julian, Georgia, Nicolas, my plans to go back to the stage. Remember, Mother, how I used to love the parts in which I dressed like a man, funny child I was, liking roles of power, judges, kings . . .

She mostly talked about the book she would write, and about the Bernini of the dying woman, lying in billows of marble at the bottom of Trastevere. Do you think that's it, darling, the triumph of accepting death? Yes, I think that's it.

* * *

LETTERS FROM JULIAN AND GEORGIA ARRIVED EVERY week. I wrote them even more frequently.

In the third week of December the Piazza Navona becomes a gaudy marketplace of balloons and crèches, invaded by Santa Clauses riding festooned donkeys, vendors of sausages, Christmas toys and garish clothes. Children shriek, trumpet and drum, mothers shout orders, the young caress each other at the feet of the river god, motorcyclists rev their motors and slice through crowds like speedboats cleaving surf. We walked in the hot pink pandemonium of Roman Christmas and I said it might be time to go home. But Mother, standing under a flower vendor's awning, shook her head, saying not yet, not quite yet.

I didn't too much fear missing Christmas with Georgia for the first time; I tried not to fear it. I tried to trust that Julian and Nicolas could give her as happy a Christmas as ever. I began to look back with tenderness to the memory of Nicolas at Georgia's bath. Since that October evening I'd ceased to fear him, could love him again as the brother and only friend he once was.

For the first time in my life Mother was clinging to me, wishing to be alone with me a while longer, and that seemed to take precedence over all else.

For a few weeks she continued to sit in the sun like an ancient cat, blinking her eyes, perhaps enjoying her last glimpse of Roman light. I was often led to imagine Georgia and Nada Fitzsimmons in those last weeks together, wandering slowly through that vast compound of beauty and decay; led to recollect, also, the other sites of Grandmother's last years.

Throughout my childhood, long past my adolescence, I'd had a recurring dream of traveling to my grandmother's adopted home, it will be called Tafraout, a village of rose-red brick in the valley of the Sous, High Atlas—I approach it on a dirt path surmounted by pale silvery hills, spotted with cactus and palmettos; I've always loved the idea of an oasis; the land grows richer as we reach her home, gardens green and closely-packed, hills rich with olives, almond, fig and pear; asses and mules tread the wheat in large terraces cut upon the mountain's slope. (Corny, sentimental images. But that's the way the dream returns, female forebears conjure pastoral moods.)

At an angle of the settlement there is a small fortress of pink stone where the Moroccan chieftain lives with his pale British wife. "Our life is solemn, holy, wild," she would write.

When I awake I think of the sounds, the smells that must have filtered into Georgia Fitzsimmons' life: jasmine-scented moonlight; evenings seated on terraces under the stars, listening to men's voices wafting above the melancholy groaning of camels and the jackals' howls; lilt of the muezzin's song most solitary and splendid at four A.M., piercing the night's silence like a plum blossom in the snow.

At some point during her travels Georgia Fitzsimmons had journeyed among some mountain tribes of southern Morocco; and then her last adventure, for the first and last time she fell in love—a Berber chieftain with whom she begins the only domestic existence she'll ever know—she wears the traditional blue robe and *yashmul* of his tribe, she hovers about the campfire with the other village women, basting a roasting lamb with sheep's yogurt and wild honey. When visiting some distant tribe she seats herself at a respectful distance from the men gathered about the fire, holding the cloak of camel's wool her husband may need in case the evening cools . . .

Inch'Allah! the Lord willed it. She was in love.

And yet. Harder issues. She who had been admired and observed so intensely, did she become one of those women who walks to the well, holding an urn on her head, turning away from the traveler with a violent gesture, bringing the veil to her face whenever any man walks by?

Discipline, abnegation of vanity. Another priestess of beauty taking to a life of service, taking the veil.

"READ, PLEASE," MOTHER SAID AS WE STOOD AT THE Villa Borghese before another favorite sculpture of my grandmother's, Bernini's Daphne and Apollo. It had always reminded me of the Fitzsimmons women, that frenzy of flight, that long escape from the grasping male arms.

" 'Again Bernini chose the crucial moment. Just as Apollo thinks he has achieved his goal, Daphne's fleeing form begins to be encircled by bark, her fingers leaf out, her toes take root . . .' "

"I refuse to decide whether I like this sculpture or not," Mother interrupted. "I've had to support myself through a vocation whose principal purpose was to shape the opinions of others . . ."

" 'Since you can never be my bride,' " I read on, " 'my tree at least you will be! Let thy laurel adorn my hair, my lyre . . .' "

" . . . and to shape the opinions of others is to perpetually hide our true selves from sight," Mother ended fiercely.

IT WAS JANUARY. A SPRINKLING OF SNOW HAD POWDERED the palms and almond trees outside our window, a plume of rose sun lighted the city's roofs. We were packing to go home.

"Why did Grandmother leave so suddenly?" I asked.

"She suspected I didn't need her anymore . . . she was wrong."

I had come to trust her greatly, at last; I wished her to offer me the next words of her own will.

"I was wrong too," she added. She folded the last item

of her small wardrobe into her suitcase. "Do you believe in love?" she asked as she closed her bag.

"I think so."

"You have pieced me together," she said. "We could only have done it alone."

I knew that she was in my power, that she had become the child and I the mother, that she would be my captive for the rest of her days. I'm finally an adult, Paula thought.

TWO DAYS BEFORE OUR FLIGHT LEFT FOR NEW YORK WE heard on the radio that Gabrielle Chanel had died. We changed our tickets and went to Paris for a day to attend the funeral.

The service was held at the Church of the Madeleine. I recognized Dessés, Givenchy, Saint-Laurent, Balmain, Cardin, Fath, Madame Grès; with a few whispered words I pointed out each of them to Mother. But no greetings were exchanged. Mother was a frail woman in a grey turban and dark glasses, leaning on a cane in a corner of the immense icy church, and no one knew that she had once been Nada Fitzsimmons.

PART III

1978

Anyone not busy being born is busy dying.

—Bob Dylan

GEORGIA

S HE SPEEDS THROUGH WEST HARLEM ON HER ROLLER skates, dodging the traffic with rapid swerves at the corner of Broadway and 110th Street. A Walkman is clamped onto her head, Jimmy Cliff: "The harder they come the harder they fall/one and all. . . ." Georgia is sixteen and her reddish-brown hair is as jagged as a haystack. Her limbs are sturdy and awesomely muscled. She has her mother's forthright blue eyes but tends to stoutness, like no one in Fitzsimmons memory. She sometimes makes her evening rounds with friends called Tracy, Spencer, Kelly, equally dauntless athletes who wear very torn denims, spiked leather bands on their wrists and foreheads. Alone or with a friend Georgia skates swiftly in the thoroughfares of upper Broadway, enjoying the sounds of salsa and reggae coming from neighborhood bars or portable radios, speeding past stores advertising *Artículos Religiosos, Cerveza Fría, Especialidades Criollas.*

"There isn't a repressed emotion or opinion in that young

woman's bones!'' Nada often exults about her granddaughter.

Outgoing, intrepid Georgia is the star of her school's basketball and hockey teams, and frequently president of her class. She excels in social studies and in Spanish, the only foreign language she finds relevant. Her father calls her Woman Warrior. The young, he says, have become a nation unto themselves. Georgia is exasperatingly casual about her dress and diet, and tends to skip most meals cooked at home because gourmet cuisine is a drag. As her family sits down to a decorous dinner she is rambling up Amsterdam Avenue, stopping for a snack of *yucas* and burritos at the Deli El Barrio on Avenida Muñoz Marin. ''Just out enjoying the sights,'' she says when questioned about the jaunts. ''It feels so good up there.''

''She *must* learn to be more cautious about herself,'' Julian says over dinner. ''More careful about her safety, her diet.''

''One month of the cocaine habit she'll pick up on those streets and her figure will be just fine,'' says Nicolas.

''Nicolas, please!'' Nada says sharply. ''Let her explore the other side of the tracks.''

IN RECENT YEARS GEORGIA'S FAMILY LIFE HAS RADICALLY changed. After her trip to Rome, Paula had decided to make a career on the stage. Most parts offered her in New York were too small, so she began to travel a great deal. Julian and Nicolas decided that everyone should live together to take better care of Nada and Georgia. Resources were pooled to rent a brownstone in the West Eighties. Nicolas has graduated from the Culinary Institute of America, works as sous-chef at Le Pavillon's lunch shift, and rehearses his skills by serving delicate concoctions in Nada's family Meissen. Julian is doing much of his writing for *World Report* at home. Nada is devoting herself to Georgia and to her memoirs.

Like many who are bonded by solitude rather than kinship, the three adults' content, celibate lives are replete with domestic rituals. Decor, cuisine, color schemes, Georgia's education are favored topics of discussion, and Nada inevitably gets her way. Nicolas' preference for comfortable Victorian antiques has been vetoed by Nada in favor of cheerfully repainted secondhand modern. Julian's desire for white living room walls has been overruled for a warm dark taupe. Nicolas continues to be a perfectionist about his cooking and indulges in much self-criticism over dinner, the salmon just misses, it lacks the note of acid that would make it sing. They are each addicted to a television program—Julian watches "The Rockford Files" and "Kojak." Nada and Nicolas enjoy "Maude" and "Hawaii Five-O," calling them wonderfully vulgar. We're settled at last, their lives seem to say, leave us to our privacy and peace. Nada seldom goes out of the house save for a checkup. She sits by the window most of the day, her cane at her side, two pairs of powerful spectacles hanging on satin ribbons around her neck, working on a manuscript of her book. Her hand shakes too much to write clearly; she persuades various members of the family to take dictation, marking their typescript with a large felt pen. Over dinner she might describe a ball at King Edward's court, or the tribulations of the British suffragette movement. Nicolas will query the family about a menu for the following night. Julian tries to open windows on the world by discussing the perils of the missile buildup, or the ordination of women priests. And every evening one of them is bound to bring up the difficulty of supervising Georgia's French; her deplorable junk food diet; her mysterious dinnertime rambles. There the conversation will settle, for the stubborn, intrepid Georgia remains the family's most intractable problem.

Georgia is a problem because she is so excessively normal, leading her reclusive kin to ponder what, these days, normalcy might be. Nada had wished her to attend a progressive private school, like her mother, not realizing how vastly such institutions have changed since Paula's time. Instead of being forced to conjugate Latin verbs and recite Milton's *Lycidas*, young women in Brearley's junior class can take courses in Chinese and urban renewal, discuss "Gender Reversal in Contemporary Feminist Fiction" or the sexual implications of Kafka's *Metamorphosis*. Many of them snub their male peers, prefer jogging marathons to social dancing (Georgia is a leader of that faction) and worry that their generation is not political enough. Rather than spend their Saturdays enjoying the ballet, or stay home reading Jane Austen, Georgia and her friends have often followed some well-meaning teacher to a rally at City Hall protesting cutbacks in welfare funds, packed on a bus to demonstrate in Boston against the new draft law. Nada and Paula find these concerns remarkable. Nicolas fears that they show undue seriousness. Julian reminds them that following one's peer group is a normal instinct of any healthy adolescent.

More often than not, however, dinner talk centers on Georgia's most perplexing trait—an audacity that verges on recklessness. Is Georgia lacking a natural sense of fear? Or does she know fear well and find it thrilling? She has always had a taste for extreme sensations. (Perhaps hereditary? This too is much debated during Georgia's evening forays.) Remember when she was ten and begged to be taken to *The Exorcist*, sat through it three times in mesmerized delight? Remember the winter she was thirteen and bought herself ice hockey gear to play on some public rink in the park, lost two front teeth serving as goalie? Are her ventures into the city's Third World an extension of these childhood leanings?

"This generation is all out for kicks," Nicolas says, as he ladles iced parsley soup from one of Great-grandmother Fitzsimmons' Meissen tureens.

"Don't be ridiculous, they're just exploring their psychosexual boundaries," says Nada, who has been dipping into psychiatry.

"Let's talk again when she's been gang-raped," Nicolas snaps back, "or mugged by a teenager half her size."

Julian might say something like "Nicolas is right, we should be more careful." At other times he maintains silence. He misses Paula dreadfully and those ruthless eyes, that fierce independence of Georgia's so mirrors her mother's that he finds it hard to be severe. How different his life is from the middle age he'd dreamed of! He'd envisioned a peaceful, domestic time, a truce of shared years in which he and Paula would return to the haunts of their early marriage—Cape Cod, Rome—delight together in the beauty of a church or painting or evening sky. Instead, Julian usually shares his evenings and weekends at home with Nada and Nicolas, what with Georgia "taking in the scene," Paula away or on stage every night—Julian refrains from criticism.

And so young Georgia Fitzsimmons (her father wished her to keep her mother's surname) continues to skate her evenings away. She has half-promised the family not to venture beyond 96th Street, but what do twenty or thirty extra blocks matter; she loves the glare and violent colors of West Harlem, the fraternal mayhem of Caribbean voices shouting greetings. She prefers being surrounded by people totally different from her in language, getup, skin color; since discovering this part of town she's come to believe in reincarnation, she often thinks she once lived in some small Caribbean village amid the hot smells and hues that surround her in these streets.

Georgia sometimes stops in front of a small dingy store whose window sign says *Se Hacen Consultas Espirituales.* Inside are weird little objects of straw and wood, spooky dolls of ragged cloth and ribbon, numerous bowls of variously colored powders, the makings, she suspects, of voodoo and black magic. On a Sunday afternoon her mother once accompanied her on these rounds; she's often told Georgia about Sala and their expertise in palmistry but now she laughs and jokes as she refuses to read Georgia's hand, saying she's lost the art and anyhow it might have been a lot of bunk. So Georgia stares on with interest at the weird dolls and sinister masks, wondering. She often goes to have a snack at La Flor de Broadway Sandwich Shop on 138th Street, where she practices her school Spanish, *Qué pasa amigo? Dame un Seven-Up y una porción de patacones.* While she sips her drink she looks at her watch and knows that sixty blocks south the family has sat down for supper, perhaps roast pheasant on a bed of sorrel. Uncle Nicolas is asking the family to think of a name for the restaurant he hopes to open next year, they go on to plan a menu for the following night and Grandma says "You already loved to cook as a little boy!" and her father might interject that today is the feast of Saint Thérèse of Lisieux, a Carmelite nun who died at the age of twenty-four after spending nine years holed up in a convent and became patron saint of France alongside Joan of Arc. She loves her family but she can only take them one on one, as a group they drive her up the wall, all that talk about the household, never a new face at the table and those eyes observing, studying, dissecting her . . .

As she finishes her soda Georgia takes a look at her watch; she tries to get home at about the same time as her mother, who has returned to New York and is currently acting Off Broadway, playing *Hamlet*. A woman playing Hamlet, gender reversal all right! That's where it's at, that's something to be proud of. She's conscious of having grown three inches taller than her mother, who's suddenly become someone smaller and more fragile, like a sister she can advise, protect. Georgia slips off the seat of the soda fountain counter, says *Muchas gracias muchacho, hasta la vista.* Since there's an hour left before the theater gets out, she skates on across Harlem toward the Puerto Rican part of town, across Adam Clayton Powell, Jr., Boulevard and Frederick Douglass Circle and African Square, down Third Avenue to 112th Street where the ramps of the elevated train have been painted glorious brash colors of purple, turquoise, gold.

ONE PARTICULAR EVENING GEORGIA STOPPED A SHORT DIStance from African Square to study a block in which two abandoned houses stood like rotted teeth in the middle of a lot grown shoulder-high with weeds. She took a piece of paper from her pocket and jotted a note on the location— just researching that one vacant lot would make a terrific paper for her social studies project, with tens of thousands of homeless what was the city waiting for to build new housing here? She stuck her pencil behind her ear and skated back to the West Side, across 110th Street and Duke Ellington Drive. As she sped toward home it is hard to know whether she failed to notice the muttering men clutching bottles in the dark side streets, the citizens of all ages affected by one substance or another. Or whether she did notice them and skated on an extra half hour because such sights gave her a wondrous sense of being surrounded by the totally different, unexpected, strange. A cheerful young woman with plump, powerful limbs and a mop of unruly russet hair skated home through streets empty-dark or gaily lit; one may suppose that she was still compelled by a childlike curiosity, a restlessness made all the more savage by a family of doting, constantly observing adults—not just the usual two adults, as Nicolas archly put it, always needling away at this, rubbing it in; not just two adults, but three point one, seeing that Georgia's mother was so frequently away from home.

WRETCHED
QUEEN ADIEU

I AM PLAYING HAMLET. PAULA FITZSIMMONS IS PLAY-
ing the Prince himself. I pace the stage, brooding,
hands crossed behind me, waiting for Rosencrantz and
Guildenstern. "My honored lord!" "My most dear
lord!" The two blockheads join me, bowing and scrap-
ing, doffing their caps. I buffet them heartily in welcome, slapping them on the back with so much might
that they reel from the blows, fall back against the wall.
Good lads, how do you both? I whack at them again like
an Irish drunk greeting friends at the wee hours, pum-
meling them in the chest, the stomach. "The world's
grown honest," Rosencrantz mutters, cowering by the
wall. "Then is doomsday near!" I shout. " . . . Den-
mark's a prison!" The bunglers: "We think not so, my
lord." " . . . there is nothing either good or bad but
thinking makes it so," I insist, "to me it is a prison."

I leap to center stage, go at Rosencrantz with a swift
karate kick. He falls back to a corner, down on all fours.
"Dear friends, were you not sent for? Come, nay, speak."

I give Guildenstern a sideway armlock, send him reeling toward the footlights. We are still in rehearsal and I play the scene for all its worth of fury and revenge, for Rosencrantz and Guildenstern are our oppressors since time began, the traitors and slum landlords, the docile cops who put their chips on status and appearance, the Milquetoasts who sell out to all visible authority. They're the cowards who please their parents, get wait-listed for summer rentals in the Hamptons, invest their money in Dow Chemical, study sex manuals, impress their neighbors with wine labels, squeal on neighbors to the CIA. Those idiots I smack and kick about the stage are the spiritual dope traffickers of my mother's former salons, who hung out with Nazi collaborators, aped Coco Chanel's wallpapers, shortened their hems when Babs Hollins said knees were in, went on wild game safaris in South Africa, threw dinner parties for war criminals.

"Is it a free visitation? Come, come; deal justly with me." As I wallop Rosencrantz and Guildenstern about the stage I'm beating at all the hatchet men who'd sold me out for a quick buck, the fink shrinks who'd schemed to send me into flames while they picked up phone calls from Henry Ford, wrote out barbiturate prescriptions for Hollywood moguls, booked themselves for skin cancer sessions at the Rockefellers' Caribbean resorts.

"You were sent for . . . confession in your looks . . ." As I play that scene I keep remembering the suckers for display who'd conspired to lock me up as they hovered by the door of my closet, Coco Chanel out of meanness, Babs out of confusion, Vincent out of weakness, my mother out of innocence, all of them out of fear. I don't want to linger too long on that moment, so as I deal Rosencrantz and Guildenstern my next blow I'm beating at the remaining dregs of *Best*'s groupies, fops who got an erection at the sound of a British title and angled for invitations on the

Gulbenkians' yacht, ballet buff gasbags who gigoloed heiresses to Lincoln Center benefits and said Nuu-reee-yeev is the genius of our time—I whack away all the harder at those oafs because I could so easily have ended up with one of them and instead I'd fallen in love with Julian, who had seen through appearances and rescued me when I'd been discarded by *Best,* who had enjoyed its mummery for a while yet remained untainted, who had saved my sanity once and for all by giving me the courage to return to the stage.

HAMLET IS THE FIRST ROLE I'VE EVER PLAYED PROFESSION-ally in New York. I am thirty-eight years old. How readily we waste a life out of indecision, fear.

A woman as the melancholy Dane, what will they think of next! As I pass a karate chop to R. and G. I dedicate it to the outraged citizens protesting a woman's fitness to play Hamlet. A plain case of amnesia, Hamlet has been played by women since we were first allowed to go on stage, Georgia and I researched that in a matter of hours. Dr. Johnson preferred Kitty Clive's Hamlet to David Garrick's. Sarah Siddons took the part, as did Eva Le Gallienne, Judith Anderson, Siobhan McKenna, Sarah Bernhardt. "I cannot see Hamlet as a man," Bernhardt said. I suspect we've all wished to reclaim Hamlet from the macho style doled out by male superstars, portray him accurately as the tortured adolescent who refuses to face the risks of adult sexuality, who wants to remain a mad schoolboy and stay out of harm's way—I know a good deal about that state of mind.

In the more generous reviews I have been praised for rendering a "full range of ecstatic and depressed moods," for expressing "Hamlet's iridescent wavering between sanity and madness."

How blessed to know it again, the sense of having power

over an audience! Their fervor constantly renewing my strength, each second of power reinforced by the hundreds of eyes focused on me . . . that head-reeling feeling of being a shaman, a hypnotist!

The press has often asked me how I've retained my skills throughout the years I didn't act at all. I often speak about my idol, Ellen Terry, who took a ten-year leave of absence in the country to raise children, flowers, horses. She went on playing Juliet until the age of eighty.

MY HAMLET AT THE CHERRY LANE THEATER IS DONE IN early Victorian dress, 1840s vintage or so. I wear a tight-fitting little black cloth suit, "very Lord Fauntleroy," as Mother puts it. Julian and Georgia cut my hair beautifully once a week to give me that nineteen-year-old Heidelberg look.

Poor Ophelia! It is difficult to be brutal with her. I've played her too often myself, on and off the stage; she's so much part of me that I feel great tenderness for her. At each phrasing of "I loved you not" I become the traitors who've deceived and rejected both of us, I struggle for harshness in that moment and barely succeed.

"Get thee to a nunnery!" Rather than buffet Ophelia about in that wretched scene I lift her up and carry her about in my arms while berating her for her imagined wantonness. "Why wouldst thou be a breeder of sinners?" I hug her and set her down tenderly on a bench, pace before her, feeling the sorrow of treason. "Be thou as chaste as ice, as pure as snow . . ." I take her up in my arms again, shake her severely. "To a nunnery, go!"

When we rehearsed Ophelia's mad scene our director allowed me to stage it myself, teach her most of the gestures. "By Gis and by Saint Charity,/Alack, and fie, for shame!" I keep thinking back to my first illness, when I was fifteen and locked myself into closets. "He is dead and gone, lady, he is dead and gone . . ." I was rehearsing my own first Ophelia in that closet, knocking my head against walls to give my voice a more disjointed rhythm. "Good night, ladies; good night, sweet ladies . . ."

For those lines I had Ophelia sit on the floor, legs wide akimbo, her arms reaching up behind her and clutching a pillar of Elsinore Castle, the way I'd once seen a young woman sit in one of my hospital wards.

"Now could I drink hot blood . . ." that must be savagely savored, deep down in the violet velvet of the voice. I am preparing to meet with the Queen my mother in her bedchamber.

As I wait to confront the Queen I keep remembering the women in my past, the cool military clink of Mother's bracelet as she steered me into a taxi, come Paula dear, time to go to the hospital now. I remember a nearly manless world and the ball-breaking female horde in Diors and Balenciagas who'd bullied me into docility. I remember women, women, women.

Mother and I are finally alone on stage. The Queen: "Have you forgot me?" "Would it were not so!—you are my mother. . . . You go not till I set you up a glass where you may see the inmost part of you!" I shake her violently by the shoulders, wrestle her to the ground. Gertrude: "What wilt thou do? Thou wilt not murder me?" I drag her halfway across the stage by the folds of her purple velvet gown. After I've conquered Gertrude I lie on the ground beside her, weeping my sorrow and my rage. O sinister menace of the seductive demanding mother! Defeat the powerful mother, wretched Queen adieu! I lie with my head on the Queen's shoulder, my knee across her hips. "No more, sweet Hamlet . . ."

Gertrude was played by a very beautiful woman with long red hair, barely five years older than I. "Confess yourself to heaven . . ." I felt a strange and powerful longing as I wept on her shoulder. It was seen as a most Oedipal rendering.

"I must be cruel only to be kind."

JULIAN II

"WITH RATHER UNTHOUGHTFUL TIMING, QUEEN Victoria chose to die on January 22, 1901, six months before I was born, and on the eve of the January white sales . . ."

When dictating her memoirs to Julian, the one most interested in etiquette, costume, Edwardian style, Nada strives for an arresting opening. For a few seconds she and Julian give their silent laughs, heads bent down, shoulders shaking slightly.

"In the department stores of London and our provincial cities, thousands of citizens toiled all night to veil their window displays in black and purple. Throughout the British Isles mothers threaded their daughters' underwear with black ribbon, and within a few weeks the rigors of the Victorian Age were forgotten. . . . King Edward's hedonism was lavishly asserted, there was an avalanche of balls and dinners and country-house parties, more money was spent on clothes, more food consumed, more horses raced, more infidelities committed, more birds shot, more yachts commissioned, more late hours kept than ever before . . .''

"Oh this is so lovely," Julian whispered, writing.

'' . . . All of society modeled itself on the King's sumptuous tastes, even domestic pets were attired in lavish furs. There was a famous actress, Gaby Deslys, I once glimpsed her in the back of a daffodil-hued Daimler, she held on her lap a terrier wrapped in dark Russian sables and wore a rope of emeralds the length of her body given her by the King of Portugal. Of course the Portuguese people soon rebelled and deposed the man, as well they should, for Gaby Deslys was ruining the economy of a splendid little nation . . .''

"Let's get back to some of the evening events," said Julian, fearing that Nada was launching into one of her political asides.

"Oh, all right. First state ball given by King Edward after his coronation, Marchioness of Landsdowne in cream satin, trimmed with old lace and very wonderful diamonds, Countess of Dalkeith's *mousseline de soie* embroidered with aquamarines and topazes and hand-painted with forget-me-nots. The amount of clothes those women had to pack for even a two-day country weekend, several trunks the size of coffins! You put on a velvet dress for breakfast, and changed into tweed for the morning walk, still another velvet in order for lunch. Then full-length sealskin if motoring was scheduled, around four-thirty slip into a tea-gown, some diaphanous affair with low-cut bodice, and for dinner still another change into full evening dress with train, complete with ostrich feather fan . . .''

Julian is Nada's most docile and industrious scribe, so after an hour of dictation they take a tea break. She knows he enjoys silence and they drink their tea quietly, looking at the street below. She is our continuity, Julian often thinks during their rest, our rope to the past, an inheritance we must honor to keep ourselves whole . . .

But more frequently he thinks with longing about Paula. Seeing her off recently in the hall of their communal house, her bags packed to do a Shakespeare recital in Houston. She is having considerable critical success, has a way of looking playful, tragic, inscrutable in the span of five minutes. She wears capes in winter, swings them over her shoulder with the swagger of a diva. "You take such good care of us, my superb Julian . . ." One of his rare moments alone with Paula, her hands clutched about his shoulders. He's played the role to the hilt, modern man's most subtle and difficult part, that of the husband relishing his wife's success—he's rehearsed her lines, urged her to more demanding roles, cheered her in moments of discouragement, pretended not to care whether she's away for a weekend or a month, laughed the absences away, hung on to the serenity of a marriage with military loyalty—his faith in marriage has a quality of surrender that constitutes a state of belief, akin to one of those causes vastly larger and beyond him that he'd sought for as a failed priest . . .

After ten minutes or so of rest they might resume.

"You wanted to hear about the Orientalist movement. I was ten, I remember. Very exciting. It came from the hullaballoo created by Diaghilev's ballets, Bakst's Scheherazade costumes. The tornadoes of color he started! Invasions of scarlet, orange, purple, costume parties out of a sultan's dream, duchesses gave *tableaux vivants* dressed as Eastern slaves, with gold bangles on their hair, metal cymbals on their toes. . . . Poiret was the first couturier to turn Oriental. He created the century's first fashion revolution, discarded corsets, dictated high-waisted frocks that fell to narrow hobble skirts at the feet; look, Poiret used to say, I freed the bust but I shackled the legs! Women had to walk with steps even more mincing and minute, suffra-

gettes in hobble skirts had a dreadful time when charged
by policemen, at Mrs. Pankhurst's arrest . . .''

"You've always promised to tell me about your coming
out," Julian said.

"Ah, yes . . . when I was presented at Court, Mother
decided to play off my fair skin by dressing me in black
when all the other beauties wore the customary white. What
an eccentric she was! We did it all wrong, which means
we did it right. Mother dressed me in black velvet, and I
carried sheaves of black wheat in my arms instead of the
usual white roses. However, I was flustered by this curious
getup, and dropped my handkerchief before the Queen and
forgot to pick it up. . . .''

Julian was about to put down his pen and notebook for
another pause, but Nada wasn't ready to rest.

"Wait wait, Julian, another note on black . . . the Black
Ascot. Edward VII's end was obviously caused by his life-
long excesses in all matters of the flesh. On a May afternoon he suddenly collapsed of a heart attack after a few
hours in which he'd amused himself by talking to his pet
canaries. Two months later, at the first racing season after
the King's death, all of London appeared at Ascot dressed
from head to foot in black. As far as the eye could see
there were black dresses trimmed with long black fringe,
black lace parasols, two-foot-wide black hats piled with
black ostrich feathers, black ospreys amid mounds of black
tulle; all this was worn in mourning not only for a king but
for a glory that they thought had gone forever from the
world, whereas a new age of liberation was about to begin. . . .''

When Nada spoke the word "liberation" Julian's attention often swerved back to Paula or Georgia or some article
he was writing. A big commotion in the household the
previous fortnight, when Georgia and some classmates were
detained by police at a demonstration downtown protesting

prison conditions, Paula was playing a matinee, he'd had to handle it alone . . . he was secretly proud of his daughter, his Woman Warrior could continue the kind of service he'd begun in his youth and left unfinished, she might be the only one of them whose commitments were not dictated by any guilt or purgation.

"I wish everyone to know how degrading clothes were in those days," Nada was saying, "in a way they still are, but how much more degrading then. Those were the days when we merely saw ourselves as men's chattels. . . ."

Quite recently Julian had started taking notes on Saint Thérèse of Lisieux, whose brief life he'd begun to see as all the more remarkable because it was so modest, hidden, uneventful. Perhaps he was drawn to Thérèse, Julian reflected, because few lives were more contrary than hers to our current notions of achievement, to the world of spectacle and visible reward he'd been thrust into by his marriage . . .

"The main purpose of our finery" (Nada) "was to display the wealth of the men who supported us. . . ."

"The sole happiness on earth consists in being hidden." Julian would elaborate on that particular quote of Saint Thérèse; none of that drama and excess which had first drawn him to the subject of sainthood; coping with life's painful, sacred drudgery, which is what he'd often had trouble doing. He was beginning to think that Saint Thérèse, the Little Flower, might well be the subject of his next book, his first in twenty years.

"But will it sell, Julian dear?" Nada and Babs would have asked him ten years ago. As he put his notes away, promising Nada another session of note-taking soon, Julian dwelt on the following notion: For two decades he had been tyrannized by the fear that any work of his would disappoint this particular family if it weren't a great success.

PAULA II

ENTER ROSENCRANTZ AND GUILDENSTERN: "THESE tedious old fools. . . . Is it a free visitation? Come, come . . . there is a kind of confession in your looks . . ."

As I begin the second month of my Hamlet run I act that scene in a much calmer way. I buffet those traitors less, reserve most derision to my voice. My rage at Mother's world, at the shrinks, at the devious fops who'd polluted my childhood has abated. I redirect most anger to my former self, to all the false roles Paula had accepted, all the cowards who had lurked inside her. So as I wrestle with Rosencrantz or Gertrude, I throw the old Paula to the ground and stamp on her, I tear to shreds the docile smiling child curtsying in her mother's rooms, I'm killing the strumpet who let herself be groomed for the meatmarket of appearance and approval, I shed all the masks once imposed on me—dutiful daughter, punctilious student, compliant wife. I'd thought of myself much of my life as a gentle, submissive victim: that had been the falsest act of all. I've discovered that I can be a killer, as shrewd and ruthless as the Prince when he stabs Polonius, orders Rosencrantz's and Guildenstern's execution. I've never felt so joyous as in those months of playing Hamlet. Speaking out "I have of late lost all my mirth" is like pretending I'm an Eskimo or a fourteenth-century Russian serf . . . not a gram of melancholy left, I've finally given birth to myself, I've been no one's victim but my own.

"I AM BUT MAD NORTH-NORTH-WEST . . ." (A FLOURISH of my arm here, hand angled upwards).

Polonius: "Do you know me, my lord?" "Excellent well; you are a fishmonger." This I deliver with a finger playfully set to my lips, a mocking little smile.

Playing Hamlet I act out a central mystery of my own life: to what extent do we suffer from true madness, or only play its roles? Could I have gotten myself out of that closet twenty years back, could I not? We all carry a Hamlet in ourselves, and use our version as a mirror. I sense such madness is less than real and more than feigned. That it can be a pose and a pause which buys us time to plan our next tactic of survival. That Hamlet jockeys up and down the scale of sanity, experimenting with every method of the paranoid style to protect himself from adulthood.

The King, shortly before the Players enter: "How fares our cousin Hamlet?" "Excellent, i'faith; of the chameleon's dish." I lie down on the floor, opening my mouth, gaping like an insect. "I eat the air, promise-crammed." There is this frequent joy about the actor's trade: We are paid, in great seriousness, to recapture the liberties of childhood.

WHILE I REHEARSE THE PLAYERS' SCENE I KEEP REMEMbering the night I'd sung at dead Sala's door, planning my defiance, mad gypsy act that would lay bare the humbug of my mother's court. Having exposed those deceits I'm being redeemed by the most illusionistic vocation of all, I'm learning that roles and masks are the sharpest tools with which to dig for truth.

On the ramparts, Horatio seeing the ghost: "Behold! lo! where it comes again. . . ." He holds out his arm, striving to retain him, clutch him. "Stay, illusion!" It takes a phantom returned from the ethers of the afterlife to witness against the hollowness of flesh. It takes a ghost and the Players' mummery to disclose a murder, unveil the crassness of the King's self-righteous pomp. It takes a ghost and a play-within-the-play and Hamlet's half-feigned madness to bring the King to his knees, acknowledge the primal guilts of fratricide and incest. It took my madness—true or feigned, what's the difference—to discover the treachery of *Best*.

And come to think of it my mother's world was no more deceitful than most others. Sincerity is the consciousness of those totally caught up in their own acts. Babs Hollins and Nada Fitzsimmons had precisely that kind of self-absorption. I was the one at fault for failing in courage, postponing my adulthood, sweet and bitter, long-delayed adulthood.

HERE'S WHY I RELISH KILLING POLONIUS: I'M VERY ANGRY at my father's desertion, he's been absent most of my childhood fighting all those stupid wars, I want to retain my fantasies about him being still alive. By killing a weak father substitute like that dotard, I'm destroying the weak father who deserted me, waiting for the strong father to reappear.

Look at the swift impulsive way I pounce! One sound out of Polonius and I leap up from my mother's side, rend the curtain with my finest *passage d'armes*. "How now! a rat! Dead! for a ducat, dead!"

"Rash, intruding fool, farewell!" Watch the cool, matter-of-fact way in which I dispose of his body, dragging it behind me like a sack of grain. "I'll lug the guts into the neighbor room. Mother, good night."

I received a fine and total pleasure from killing Polonius. I decided not to think too much about it. I'd talked to enough shrinks in my time. *In a world of absent fathers children may fail to achieve spiritual autonomy. . . . It would have taken a lot of courage on Paula's part to take the risk of losing her mother's love by not being well behaved. . . .* I simply realized that I'd had a father all along. He'd been inside me, and I'd finally ferreted him out—his power, his authority, his control over others.

They said I died well, poetically, convincingly. "The rest is silence."

UNTIL I RETURNED TO NEW YORK TO DO HAMLET I'D lived in anguish and in solitude. I sat in grim hotel rooms studying scripts, walked the streets of unknown cities, rehearsing my lines. I played *Major Barbara* in Chicago, *Doll's House* in Minneapolis, *Streetcar* in Seattle. I rose at six in the morning. I refused all invitations. I dined with no one. I resisted all new bonds. I felt godforsaken. I forgot about meals. I forgot my body. I received moderately good notices. I lived in gratitude. I lived in fear of time. I walked forty blocks, forgetting time. I wanted to stop time. I castigated myself for wasting it. I kept to myself. I hated myself. I became. I became responsible. I told no one how lonely I was. I had to atone for my history. I overworked myself. I changed myself. I became someone else. I became responsible for my history. I was able to tell it. At home I was outgoing and cheerful. I became learned in specific rules. I'd learned to pretend. I became fit for society.

When I was home I spent all my time paying attention

to the family, playing those roles to the hilt—dutiful daughter, loving mother and wife, tender friend to Nicolas. Georgia—don't worry about Georgia, I'd cry out during those fancy family meals; I'd accompanied her on her rounds uptown, I'd sensed the danger, I urged her to keep to the wide brightly lit streets, come home earlier, go out less often. What more could I say, how devious for me to preach anything but perpetual defiance, perpetual questioning. How proud I was of her boldness, her independence, she was precisely what I would have been if I'd had the courage to defy the world properly, earlier, earlier. . . .

When I was home I ironed Julian's shirts, urged him to pursue new projects, typed out his notes. At times my gratitude to him was overwhelming, uncomfortable, I feared that he was perhaps the only thing I had; our child would leave us, all talents are fragile, he was the most enduring of life's gifts. . . . At times I resented my gratitude, at times I was confused.

I spent much time taking care of Mother, I took my turn helping her with her book, she was extremely demanding about her work. She would have wished to dictate to one of us every day for six-hour stretches, much tact was needed to curb her demand for attention. Our own Scheherazade! She seduced all of us into her text by offering those portions of her memory that interested each of us the most. When working with me, she concentrated on the years which had to do with Grandmother Fitzsimmons' days in Africa.

What magnificence, simplicity in that life!

While searching for her mother, Nada had visited a Sufi community where Georgia Fitzsimmons had once made a retreat. "He rose at dawn to meditate and study," she was told, "and until midnight he continued his meditations in the garden." He! I enjoyed the thought that Arabs elevated her to this gender, finding her freedom incomprehensible within her sex.

My heroine sitting hours at a time in some outpost village, watching the lumbering, groaning camels, the nomads striking camp in the pale green light of the desert sunset. Peach-gold of mosques, violet-deep of firmaments. Peace of Islam, etc.

That first year after her disappearance she'd traveled two thousand miles on her horse, a revolver at her belt, accompanied only by a native guide—She'd learned to live like a Bedouin on a handful of grain a day, sleeping anywhere, under the stars, in the shelter of a rock—she now carried all her earthly possessions in a bundle behind her saddle, she kept a cache of jewelry on which she survived, occasionally selling one of her famous amethysts or topazes in some large city of her wanderings to provide for herself, her guide, her horse.

MOTHERS
AND SONS

"FASHION," BABS WOULD SAY VERY SLOWLY. "All a question of what one adores for a moment. So for November, ultimate in drama . . ."

"A pivotal time," Nicolas would agree.

"Yes, startling message needed. Dazzling patterns glowingly in evidence."

Babs Hollins was very ill. She had been partially paralyzed by a stroke, a year after *Best* folded, and spoke with increasing difficulty. She lived in a rest home by the Hudson, a half hour from New York, where Nicolas went to see her frequently. She often imagined that she was still writing her seasonal notes for the magazine; Nicolas acted as her assistant, urging her to finish each statement, trying to help her speak more clearly.

"Immaculate, sublimely easy," Nicolas suggested.

"Yes, time to get timeless, no disturbing details."

"A simple, stunning sweep?"

"Minimal is the ticket. Ultimate uniform."

Babs' memory was failing, she occasionally mistook Nicolas for Saint-Laurent and Paula for different celebrities of the 1950s in Paris. But her nails were still done once a fortnight, she called the hairdresser in every month to keep her hair in style. Many mornings she asked for some papers and colors, a pot of glue and invented designs. During a recent visit Paula had made with Nicolas she'd called her Coco, and shown them a creation that was meant to be worn "to the last party ever in the black world out there." It was a birdlike construction glued with little bits of colored glass and bright-hued feathers, which Nicolas held up for Paula to see.

"New lines for an old favorite!" Paula exclaimed. "A very fresh feeling!"

"Moving freely," Babs said. "Needed immediately for evening—all that's very relaxed, very adult."

"Emphasis on clear shape?"

"Yes, darling, unexpected is the word. Might be fabulous fun. Always did like surprises."

And at such moments Nicolas conquered the reluctance Paula knew him to have, bent toward his mother and embraced her as a parent would a child, the two offering a perfect image of maternal-filial devotion.

Julian and Paula had persuaded Nicolas to visit his mother several months before the onset of her illness. Julian had talked about the difficulties of bringing up a child in the tyrannical frivolity of Babs' world. She's your only past, Julian said, you're lucky to still have one. When Babs fell ill Nicolas began to visit her regularly, found the visits essential and rewarding. He reported them frequently to the family, Babs still said wonderfully outlandish things about the Europe of decades ago. Bucharest in the thirties, the allure, the passion, the dash! Cavalry officers in pale blue jackets with mink cuffs and collars, good mink looks marvelous in the snow . . . the Bibescu palace, *une merveille,*

servants dressed in solid seed pearl, white lilac and burning
perfume, most fastidious, that Bibescu, had his shoelaces
ironed every day, a class act! There was much else in Babs'
talk about the Lebkowitzes' dinner for two thousand in the
grand ballroom of the Paris Opera House, collection clothes
photographed parachuting down from the Eiffel Tower for
an October issue of *Best*. Nicolas tried to report these fan-
cies to Nada but she sat by the window with an inscrutable
look, saying, "I've heard it all, I have heard it," brushing
the tale away, perhaps trying to hang on to whatever clarity
was left her.

She's been a good sailor, Nicolas often thought as he
returned from a visit with his mother, the only one who's
stayed with it, who's sinking with the ship. And just think
of all she's taught me, given me my dreams and my drives,
turned me into a fighter. Power doesn't have so much to
do with money anymore, it has to do with what she'd always excelled in, survival, flair, mystique. With knowing
how to startle and amuse, invent pithy sayings, controversial spectacles. Who has mystique these days? Not the
president of General Motors or the Secretary of State, not
on your life, no more. Robert Redford, Baryshnikov, Barbara Walters, they're the ones with mystique, that's the
crowd to go for when I finally open my own restaurant,
give them what they never knew they wanted, Mother always said. . . .

And just think of all the other men I could have been,
Nicolas mused as he took the train home from another visit.
Could have embarrassed her by joining the Mormon
Church, a pimply bank teller jacking off under his piles of
twenty-dollar bills in Salt Lake City. Could have joined
her gang and become vice-president of Revlon, group-sex-
ing at the San Juan Hilton. And if I'd had the kind of
mother I often wanted, a serious, understanding lady who

taught psychology at Iowa State . . . I might have become a fashion model and made my living with Hathaway shirts. Can't win.

NICOLAS III

W HILE PRETENDING TO BE FASCINATED BY NADA'S dictations, Nicolas often doodled birds or cats in the margin of his notebook. These sessions only interested him when they touched on details of Edwardian households—table settings, diets, menus. He always knew such a moment would come, Nada had an amazing way of telling every member of the family precisely what each of them wanted or needed to hear. Wanted to hear? Needed to hear? Interesting question. Moral question. More Julian's line. He continued to listen.

"Edward VII was a porcine, repellent man, a portrait of gross opulence. Heavy-lidded, protruding eyes, enormous cigars, and that overfed, superbly attired body . . . you can't imagine what he managed to stuff into himself in one day. Not satisfied with a breakfast of eggs, haddock, bacon, woodcock, he demanded snacks of lobster and cold chicken at eleven in the morning to appease his hunger, and even after a twelve-course dinner a plate of sandwiches was sent to the royal apartment, sometimes a quail or a ptarmigan . . .''

"Spelling?" Nicolas asked, writing furiously now.

"P-t-a-r-m, ptarmigan, water bird, no Edwardian day was complete without it, resurrect it at your restaurant, darling, it could sell smashingly. One particular dish worth noting, favorite of Edward—an ortolan stuffed into a quail, and a truffle within the ortolan, and pâté de foie gras within the truffle . . .''

All this Nicolas was recording most carefully. The recipe for ortolan within quail could be a show-stopper. He was at a point in his career when he needed novelty, bezzazz. He'd mastered the skills of his vocation so assiduously in the past years that he'd already refused secret offers to leave Le Pavillon for Lutèce, Caravell. He specialized in the central and most delicate art of his trade, the technique of concentrating and reducing sauces, the sorcery of producing a proper demi-glace, three different genres of mirepoix combined and simmered for six hours, deacidified, passed through sieves, tamed down to a consistency of honey or resin . . . yet could he spend his life continuing to make bordelaises by adding madeira to demi-glaces, sauces chasseur by the judicious addition of shallots and vinegar? Not on your life. The French tradition was becoming fossilized, he was ready to pioneer something irreverent and surprising, almost insulting in its surprises. . . .

"And on Edward's drawing room piano there was always a china bowl full of crystallized violets and angelica which he'd be constantly nibbling at between his enormous meals and snacks. . . .''

Nicolas noted the candied violets with interest. Startling effect—pulverize them into the base of a dessert soufflé. Plans for the opening of his own restaurant were beginning to take shape. He intended to serve food that would be international, eclectic, start *the* anti-French revolution, resurrect American regional cuisine, honor Creole, Cherokee Indian, Latin American influences, Hollins style. To hell with Point and his dumb little sauces, his staff would read Vietnamese, Caribbean cookbooks. Crabs in ginger sauce with a garnish of tofu fried in beer batter—such brainstorms came to him in the middle of the night, the way poems do. And to offset the effeteness of *nouvelle cuisine* he'd include some downhome American favorites—Virginia ham, bread pudding, Sala's sweet potato pie; play to current nostalgia, the back-to-family movement. Gastronomy was replacing couture as the prime status symbol, you had to watch every nuance. He wanted a talented clientele and an informal aura, famous actors could come to his place in blue jeans and turtlenecks, out with the asinine French folderol of coat and tie, who did you see in the passé, chichi joints with their bordello decor (Perigord, Côte Basque) but nouveau riche Texans with their painted molls. . . .

"Can't draw an accurate portrait of the Edwardian kitchen without touching on the desperate life of servants" (Nada). "There was a footman in my father's house who slept on a bed that folded into the wall of the pantry, a most unhappy man with no room of his own . . ."

Dear Nada, one must always allow her time for a few such digressions. Waiting for more Edwardian menus, Nicolas doodled table settings and flower arrangements on the margin of a page while thinking of his mother. He also took careful notes on all her conversations, sensing that someone who's studied style as well as Babs Hollins should be meticulously recorded. He'd begun to love her more when she'd become helpless and nearly senile. He should discuss that with Paula, who always understood such things, but Paula was away too much for heart-to-heart talks. Neither he nor Julian nor Georgia was enjoying Paula's company these days as much as each of them needed to, that was maddening, that was very unfair, one of these days she'd regret it. . . . Anyhow, he'd much looked forward to recording more series of Babs' Why Nots, but she never composed them anymore. They had been replaced by another pastime—making long lists of what was in and what was out in fashionable circles. Remarkable how she could keep up with the world in that little place up the Hudson, all he ever did to keep her *au courant* was to read aloud to her from recent copies of *Daily Wear*. On his last visit she had dictated to him a list of ins and outs which went something like this:

OUT	IN
truffles	oysters
Newport	fresh air
Yoko Ono	Bette Davis
hats	grey hair
Balmoral Castle	milkmen
Kennedy Center	King Juan Carlos
Woody Allen	golden retrievers
surfing	kindness

Kindness! That had thrown him. That had startled and moved him. Kindness—it sounded almost lucid. Whenever Babs came close to being lucid (for reasons, again, he couldn't understand) he grew a little scared.

"I'll tell you of a typical dinner at Buckingham Palace in 1908 or so: a Rudescheim 1893 might accompany the *soufflés de caille à la valencienne* . . ."

Nicolas was writing fast again—the quail soufflé was worth researching—and simultaneously thinking about what to name his future restaurant. He'd thought of Home Cooking and of Happiness III. Georgia had suggested Mother Love—trust a wise child's instinct, that would be very in. More French hot air bunk to rebel against, get rid of those asshole Gallic *maître d*'s in funereal black suits and obscene gold braiding who'd pushed him around in his childhood. Cooking had to do with love and community, Paris bye-bye his place would say. He'd have no sous-chef, no kitchen boys, all would be teamwork, egalitarian. He enjoyed the most humble aspects of his trade— slicing great mounds of onions, garlic, carrots into the stock base, grinding lobster shells for his famous bisques, which tasted, Paula said, "like crawling through superb rocks at the bottom of the sea," what talent for metaphor she'd always had . . .

"Of course if you weren't the Prince of Wales the carrying on of love affairs was quite impossible in London, seeing the hordes of servants you were surrounded with. The countryhouse party was by far the best solution, but it was easy to make mistakes in those dark corridors. . . . Lord Charles Beresford once picked the wrong room and dashed in with loud amorous noises, leaping into a bed where he found himself between the Bishop of Winchester and his Bishopess. . . ."

Well there Nada was quite wrong. Nicolas doodled again. There she's gone way off the track, thinking I'm still interested in that amorous fee-faw-fum. That had been a lot of braggadocio, another defense mechanism to fight off the fear of all those women who'd terrorized his childhood, not needed anymore, not at all. Since he'd settled in his vocation and found his true center—Paula's language— he'd discovered that at heart he was a gentle, domestic soul, made for loyalty, service, perhaps celibacy. Asexuals are in, as Babs might have said. He now had what he'd most ardently desired all his life—a real family, three generations of it, how many Americans could boast of that? Of course you had to continue being covert, secretive in life, otherwise the world would devour. You survived on many private little psychic drawers that were filled with life's most nourishing, seductive stuff. With friends you were dangerously open, with family you had to be secretive—he was better suited to family life. Leading an existence open to scrutiny, that had been out of the question after a year or two. He pretended that his only domicile was the shared house on 83rd Street but in fact he'd acquired a tiny studio apartment on the Lower East Side which had become his refuge. He went there to rehearse his most difficult sauces. He occasionally received pretty women there—cooking seemed to be very sublimating work. He sometimes spent the night in his secret haven, when he said he was going out of town to a chefs' convention, just to be alone and plan his life. . . . It was possible that eventually Paula might come to him there in a new way, a vision, an incestuous, utopian vision, she would always remain his ideal . . .

"Meanwhile, do you know what they were living on in the West End?" Nada was saying. "A woman . . ."

"I think we already put that down in the last chapter," Nicolas said gently.

"Well, perhaps I want to elaborate," Nada said defiantly, tapping her cane on the floor.

"It's time for your tea, Nada darling." When will you settle down, Nicolas, when will you stop dissipating your considerable talents. . . . Well I've settled down beyond anyone's wildest expectations, I'm presenting myself to Nada the way she's always wanted me to be, ever since she and Paula began saving my life at the age of eleven. How proud of me Babs might be, at last.

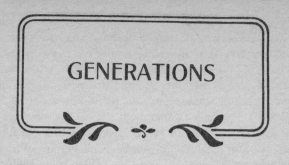

GENERATIONS

"**G**IVE ME A BREAK, GRANDMA, IT'S GOTTEN much worse since your time, take a swing around the city shelters some day . . ."

"But there were thousands of homeless sleeping in the streets in London in deepest winter," Nada said peevishly, "driving home from some ball, I was your age, I'd see every bench from Blackfriars to Westminster filled with citizens huddled against each other. . . ."

With Georgia, Nada was finally free to speak about the grimmer side of her memoirs; but to little avail, for Georgia constantly disrupted the dictation with her own comments.

"One hundred women and children shacked up in a Harlem gymnasium this week and the state is trying to evict them . . ."

"Most horrifying sight in London," Nada tried again. "Gentry out by the thousands parading their furs and diamonds on Sunday mornings, staring at the vagabonds stretched out on the grass . . ."

"Get this, Gram, the city offers the homeless shelter and the state is calling them uninvited guests. . . . Many children in your generation of vagrants?" Georgia asked. She'd noticed her grandmother's irritation, and started swiftly taking notes again.

"Oh, thousands . . ."

"Infant mortality in 1920 London?"

"One out of every four babies died before it was twelve months old. And what would you expect, with their dreadful diet?—I remember a sister of our scullery maid's, husband unemployed, twelve children in a row. Lived on bread and tea, a few times a year she'd manage to afford a sheep's head for sixpence—she earned the family pittance sewing shirtwaists from five in the morning until midnight . . ."

"The outrage of the sweatshop system," Georgia exclaimed. "Exploiting women and children . . ."

"Speaking of children," Nada interrupted firmly, "I particularly remember a boy who wandered about the park where Nanny took me for walks, Tommy. Walked with a bad limp, both parents alcoholics, served a two-year sentence for stealing a bag of apples when he was barely twelve . . ."

"But it's no different now, Granny, dig into the brains of Strom Thurmond or another Bozo Republican in the Senate and you'll find that they still think of the poor and unemployed as derelicts who refuse to help themselves, just as your mother's generation did. . . ."

"Let's have some tea, darling," Nada said. "Bozo," she wrote down carefully in her notebook, trying to keep up with the jargon of the young.

Georgia, having brought the tea, tried to pour it in the correct manner her grandmother had taught her, feeling too carefully observed, wishing her mother were there, her mother didn't give a hoot about such nonsense as tea strainers. It was so hard to remember which was supposed to go in first—sugar, water, milk or tea. This is so irrelevant, she thought, but for Grandmother I'll try to do it just right. So she poured them all at once rather sloppily.

"I ran fifteen miles yesterday," Georgia said, trying to hold her cup delicately in her right hand. "I'm down to seven minutes a mile, I think I might have a chance for the Junior Marathon if I pick up speed. I've got to increase distance, too, get myself up to the 20-K if I want to make it to the big race. Will you come along and cheer?"

" 'Come on, blue shorts, keep at it,' I'll be shouting."

Nada looked at Georgia with curiosity and tenderness as the young woman gulped down a cup of tea, rhythmically flexing her right fist to improve her forearm muscles. Dictation time was Nada's way of having each member of the family to herself, retaining her power over them, maintaining control. She particularly loved her tea breaks, when she questioned each of her scribes about their concerns, probing and giving counsel.

"How's Kelly this week?" Nada inquired.

"Off to visit Princeton, where I'm going with Dad next weekend."

"And Spencer?"

"Three months pregnant and she looks radiant."

"Is she going to keep the baby?"

"No way, scheduled for an abortion next Tuesday. What's the price of a young woman's passion?"

Nada calmly sipped her tea. Georgia burst out laughing.

"Hang in there, Grandma. I'm just pulling your leg."

"So," Nada said, pouring herself another cup of tea. "What other important thoughts have you had this week?"

"You know, I'm definitely thinking of doing premed in college, Grandma. Public health would be a terrific career. First year curriculum at Harvard Med: Pathology, Clinical Diagnosis, Abnormal Physiology. I look forward to having my own cadaver."

"Your own cadaver?"

"Every medical student has a corpse of his-her own to dissect, that's how you learn anatomy. Most expensive item in first year med, that cadaver."

"Ah, yes? How much?"

"Eight hundred dollars at least. Just think, you can give me a cadaver for Christmas."

"I shall stand by the tree, an incarnation of astonishment." Nada poured herself another cup of tea.

When Georgia grew impatient with Nada's stately tea ritual she'd make one of the hideous faces she'd practiced since childhood to frighten the family. She curled her lips over her teeth to disclose bare gums, rolled her eyes so only the whites showed. "Georgia, *please,*" Nada said firmly. When they resumed dictation Nada tried an issue that Georgia couldn't invade.

"Things weren't so bright on our side of the fence, darling, frightful to think how cold relations were between parents and children. For instance, it was interfering for a mother to visit the nursery more than once, in the evening for a goodnight kiss. I was unusually close to my mother, her friends considered it strange that I was allowed to come down and dine with her a few times a week . . ."

"You never talk about Great-grandfather," Georgia interrupted. "Where the hell are all the fathers, I mean I seem to be the first one in the family to have a father . . ."

"Yes darling, such a marvelous father. I wish he'd take more time off . . ."

"Let's talk about your father," Georgia ordered.

"Well. I don't know. Perhaps," Nada whispered, not prepared. "You see I barely knew Papa, at that time many of us hardly knew our fathers. What I remember best about him is the hall of his country house, which was hung with the antlers of stags and other animals he'd shot. Mother was a founder of the antivivisectionist league, she and I were fanatically opposed to hunting, the visits were not to our taste . . .''

"Well, all right, I can tell you're not comfortable with that material." Georgia blew out a large wad of purple bubble gum. She saw Nada frown and quickly retracted it. "No hassle, let's have some more golden oldies about Great-grandmother, we can always use much more about her."

Nada smiled, amused by the girl's instinct. "Mother had a generous and trusting nature, she never allowed the front door of her house to be closed. And imagine, she was never robbed!"

"Beautiful. Her party affiliations?"

"She joined the Liberals, upon which your great-grandfather cut her off without a penny, disowning me in the bargain. I'm not half the woman she was, and this has haunted me all my life . . .''

"Right before the war Great-grandma joined in some of the suffragettes' raids on Parliament, right? Fifty or a hundred women would march on Westminster, they'd be met by cops, and then what happened?"

"The women were knocked about, sometimes severely, often arrested. I remember Mother weeping about the case of Emily Davidon . . .''

"Spelling?"

"D-o-n. Davidon was a suffragette who threw herself under a race horse in the middle of the 1913 Derby and was trampled to death. Trampled by the King's own horse, Amner; that startled the nation, the world, the whole world knew that there were women in England willing to face death to gain their freedom. . . .''

"Gosh," Georgia said, writing like a whirlwind. "Do I have material for a great term paper."

Nada leaned back in her chair, closed her eyes. Her granddaughter was her most rebellious scribe, the only one who worked her to exhaustion, and she loved it. "How criminally ignorant we were," she whispered, "how indifferent . . . Mother learned in time, just in time. The disappearance. Looking back on it, I think it was quite the reasonable thing to do."

THE BATTLE

THE WAITING ROOM OF THE EMERGENCY WARD WAS pale green and crowded. A young man with a bloody foot limped on a relative's arm. Many persons were collapsed in chairs, clutching brown paper bags. Julian stood at the information desk, repeating Georgia's name. Every few minutes the doors of the emergency room swung open, bodies surmounted by bottles of pale liquids were wheeled in on stretchers. Nada sat by Nicolas, her hand trembling on his arm.

It had happened at an unexpected time and place, eight o'clock on a Friday night, very close to home. Nada, Julian and Nicolas had just begun dinner, Georgia was out for a ramble on her roller skates. Julian answered the phone. Georgia had been hit by a car as she was crossing West End Avenue and 86th Street. The driver was a white middle-aged man speeding through a red light. . . . In the middle of that sentence Julian hung up and turned toward Nicolas and Nada, who were slowly walking toward him from the dining room. He would always remember the pink dusk that had gathered at the window, the vase of crimson peonies set on the hall table.

"She'll be fine," Julian lied. "We must go."

"Should we call Paula at the theater," Nada asked as they rode in a cab to the hospital.

"Interrupting her 'To Be' soliloquy?" Nicolas said.

"Shut up, Nicolas," Julian answered. "No, what's the sense. She'll be through soon, I'll go home to meet her when she returns."

They sat in the waiting room and watched a thin woman with wild eyes and toes painted gold saying there there there to a screaming baby whose cheek was bleeding and lacerated, as if mauled by a cub tiger. They stared at a man in a baseball jacket who moaned softly, holding his bandaged arm. Finally, a young, dark-skinned doctor came through the swinging doors, calling them in a soft West Indian voice, "Fitzsimmons family."

Georgia's condition was critical but not hopeless. She was about to go into surgery and would not be out for several hours. There were multiple leg fractures and a contusion of the brain.

Is that like a concussion? Julian asked. A little worse, the young doctor said softly; a blood clot pressing on the brain.

"Possible loss of eyesight?" Nada had stood up and leaned on her cane, bending toward the doctor.

His eyes closed once, almost tenderly. Long-range effects of a brain injury were not known for days or weeks.

Nicolas asked about Georgia's leg. The doctor shrugged, looked a little vague. Multiple fractures of both femur and tibia. That was the least of their concerns.

But how was she when she was admitted? Julian asked. Was she conscious, was she suffering?

No, she had been in a deep coma. She would probably remain in coma for some days.

"What part of the brain . . ." Julian began. And then stopped in midsentence, thinking we are just passing the time, moving our mouths to delay pain, prisoners singing while waiting to hear sentence. He looked at his watch. It was ten o'clock. He went home to meet Paula, and an hour later they had both returned to the hospital.

THEY SAT IN THE WAITING ROOM, FOUR PERSONS IN MIDdle and advanced age who may never have loved anyone as they loved the girl whose life lay in balance a few rooms away. It's as if God had put His mouth to a trumpet, Paula thought, shouting you have dealt wretchedly with all I gave you. As if He had put His mouth to the ear of our lives, shouting what have you done to preserve my most precious gift. I wonder if they're sitting here asking some of my questions; have we been too busy redeeming the second, third, fourth of our trite lives with late-found truths, have we failed to contact the nation of the young, of the others?

She listened to the language of the green-robed medics crossing the room, I-C-U, E-E-G, A-E-S. Julian hasn't been in an emergency ward since he was a priest, twenty-three years ago. I haven't been in a hospital since you know when. And Mother has barely been out of the house for five years.

Here's one question they're not asking, will it go on like this until the end of time, will women be punished for their freedom, their choice of venture and of solitude? Am I being punished? Shall we always have to pay a price?

They stared at an aged Puerto Rican being wheeled in a chair, his gangrened foot missing two toes. His daughter shouted hysterically at the desk.

"Everyone here seems foreign or deformed," Nada said.

"New York," Julian said.

They kept waiting for the doctor to return with more news. Their thoughts, some silent, others spoken, often struck them as odd or outrageous. She will live, Paula said to herself. Thank God it happened near home, proving Nicolas wrong. And then she castigated herself; what a small, crass notion.

"I'm glad Vincent isn't with us," Nada said.

"Vincent?"

"He'd be in hysterics, a state I abhor."

" 'That they may obtain a corruptible crown,' " Nicolas quoted.

"First Corinthians 9," Julian said. "What's the relevance?"

"I don't know, just saw it on your desk," Nicolas said, and burst into tears.

"We're tired and *bouleversés*," Nada said.

Shortly after midnight the young doctor came to say that the blood clot had been evacuated, surgery was going well, cardiac monitors were giving good signals.

Their odd thoughts continued.

"The Somersets had such a lovely garden in Dorset," Nada whispered. "With marvelous fields of blue lupine. Only the English and the Russians got their blues right."

"We've always been terrific at suppressing our emotions," Paula said.

"The Duchess of S. lay in bed most of the day but she had a grand old time. She wasn't out of it, she'd pass out for a few minutes with tea bags on her eyes and she could conquer the world. More drivel for my book," she added, blowing her nose.

"This is the only way to survive it," Paula said.

Julian put his hand on Paula's shoulder. She brought it quickly to her lips.

"Paula, remember when we used to play reincarnation," Nicolas said.

"We were being dreamed by a magic white bull who lay on the seventh rim of the cosmos."

"The universe had already been dreamed by a tortoise, a lion, a boar, we argued about who the next dreamer might be."

" 'May you be reborn as a beetle, as a Turkish prime minister,' we used to say. This is the only way to survive," Paula repeated. She looked at her mother. The silver hair always hidden now in a neat turban. The trembling hand moving to the tired eyes.

Across from them a youth in an ankle-length coat and white tennis shoes pressed his hand to his bandaged ear. Through the window above their heads a neon light blinked Bud Bud.

"What is Bud," Nada asked.

"A popular beer."

Connais pas. I don't understand Puerto Ricans," Nada added, looking around the room. "They've seldom been successful."

She will live, Julian thought, and oh, the problems she'll have to face. Nineteen-nineties, what patience, what commitment will be needed.

"What people always lack is an attitude," Nada said. "They sat there waiting for Babs and me to give it to them."

It's the first time in months she'd mentioned Babs' name, Paula thought, and Babs might die any day now. "Give me a man who is not passion's slave," she began. And then it was her turn to cry.

"This might be serious," Nicolas said with agitation. "Paula can't get out of rehearsal, she can't get off-stage . . ."

"We'll think about Paula's breakdown later," Nada said sharply.

Paula was remembering the Christmas Georgia was nine and had asked for a toy called Fright Factory, from which she fashioned ghoulish masks and monstrous hands.

''Perhaps she should take up flying!'' she exclaimed. But no one knew what she was talking about.

They rose as one when the doctor returned a third time. The operation had gone successfully, Georgia's vital signs were good. For several days she'd be in intensive care, where it was preferable not to visit. He was the resident in charge of emergency services, he would stay in close touch.

Paula put her hand to Nada's face. A tear came down the wizened cheek. This is the first time in my thirty-eight years I've seen my mother cry.

THEY WENT HOME AND SLEPT A LITTLE. THEY SPENT THE next day at home pacing and pretending to read. Paula rehearsed her understudy. Nada carried *The Spoils of Poynton* about the living room. Julian leafed through his Book of Common Prayer, Nicolas through the *New York Times*. They phoned the doctor every few hours, and he never failed to call back. By the end of the fourth day Georgia left intensive care for a room of her own.

In the first week of their visits they simply came to watch Georgia sleep. They sat for an hour or two at a time, studying the still face swathed in bandages, talking at length about her paleness, a twitch they might have detected in her cheek. On the sixth day after leaving intensive care Georgia's face seemed flushed, her lips quivered. They interpreted this as a bad sign. They called in a doctor for the second time that morning. He reassured them to the contrary. This was an excellent sign. Georgia's eyes had opened a few times during the night, corneal blinks had been observed, she was coming out of coma.

They were learning many new medical terms. Nada often jotted them into the little notebook she always carried in her handbag.

As they came into her room on a morning of the second

week a nurse stood by Georgia's bed, smiling. "She's talking!" Paula exclaimed.

Four heads bent down toward Georgia.

"Can you hear what she's saying, Paula darling?"

"We might do better just watching her, lip-reading."

They all drew their heads back and studied Georgia's face.

"I think she's saying 'Jimmy Cliff,' " Nicolas said.

"Who is Jimmy Cliff?" Nada asked.

"Popular Caribbean singer."

"Le dernier cri," Julian added. "Favorite of the young."

Georgia's lips moved again. "She's not saying 'Jimmy Cliff,' " Paula reported. "She's saying 'Jimmy Carter.' "

"Well that makes more sense," Nada said. "Paternal authority and all that."

WITHIN A FEW WEEKS GEORGIA WAS TALKING SO FAST they had trouble keeping up with her. She'd managed to cut her hair herself so that it stood straight up and jagged, like the cartoon of a person terrified. She'd managed to walk on her crutches to the vending machines for bags of popcorn and Fritos.

"That Indian doctor is cute," Georgia said as the family came to her room one afternoon. "I just love the drugs. I could stay on Demerol for the rest of my life."

"Sweets, how about taking up downhill skiing this winter when you're out of rehab?" Julian suggested.

"Downhill *racing*—thrilling," Paula added.

"I'll be too busy cramming for Radcliffe," Georgia said. "It's either Radcliffe or City College, I'm applying nowhere else."

"A carefully chosen mélange," Nada said.

"City College on 135th Street?" Julian asked.

"How about including Penn in your applications," Nicolas suggested.

"Master Mind strikes again. No way."

"What's wrong with Harlem," Nada said, "so many people with style came out of there. Josephine Baker, Billie Holiday, they were *quelque chose.*"

"Where's Spencer applying to college?" Julian asked.

"Wherever she can get another ego transplant."

"Can't you choose a better fallback than City?"

"Give me another set of clichés to live by, Uncle Nick, our collection's shrinking fast." Georgia ripped open another bag of Fritos and munched contentedly, watching the expressions on the family's faces. "What's up in the big world out there, Grandma?"

"There's a large picket line outside the Museum of Natural History, protesting discrimination against women employees."

"And at the zoo the chimps are demanding co-ed housing," Nicolas added.

"Sexist *mierda,*" Georgia cried. "That's an important issue!"

"Profound apologies."

"Cut out the violins. You're a macho nerd, and you know it. What's with him today?"

"He's missed you," Julian said.

"I need everyone's help in thinking of a title for my memoirs," Nada added diplomatically.

"Why not *Redemption of an Edwardian,*" Julian suggested.

"Why not *The Glass of Fashion,*" Paula said.

"Why not buy a pied à terre in Leningrad for your winter vacations," Nicolas said.

"Why not fly to the People's Republic for a pedicure," Paula said, "it's the best in the East."

"Why not cover your walls in precious, nearly extinct alligator," Nada said.

"Why not call your book *Into Rags*, Grandma."

"Into Rags?"

"You got it. Here comes the nurse with my five o'clock fix. I'll see you all later."

THE FAMILY WAS EXULTING IN THE PROSPECT THAT GEORgia was coming home soon, that no permanent damage had been caused, that she would simply be on crutches for a few months. Only then did a confrontation occur.

"We have to face it, Paula," Julian said. "She's been rambling into parts of town where three out of four people are doing nose candy by the time they're twelve . . ."

"You're an innocent, Paula," Nicolas added. "I've worked up there, I've smelled the stuff and held it in my hand . . ."

"And as the head of the family," Julian ventured, "I . . ."

"Insofar as there's a family," Paula said.

"Insofar as there's a *head*," Nicolas said. "What do you mean, Paula, insofar as there's a family?"

"We're the illusion of a family."

"What do you mean, illusion? We're different in that most families are thrown together by genetic accident, and hate each other . . ."

"Tolstoi," Nada said. " 'Each unhappy family is unhappy in its own way.' "

". . . most families hate each other, whereas we've come together out of sympathy and . . ."

"Ah that's a most interesting difference," Nada interrupted again. "I'd never thought of it."

"We've come together out of fear," Paula said.

"Fear," Nada repeated.

"We're synthetic, we're not for real," Paula said. "Maybe no family's for real, but our kid feels it more than others. She sees that we've gathered together out of terror, or rather *you* have . . ."

"Terror of what?" Julian asked.

"Terror of solitude and change, terror of yourselves . . . like any solid kid she wants to stress her difference from us. And the most different thing she can do is to pretend that there isn't a thing in the world that frightens her. . . ."

"My whole career was particularly based on fear and illusion," Nada mused. "People's fear of being no one, illusion of being someone."

"Georgia's acting it out for us . . ." Paula tried again.

"Precisely, acting out," Julian picked up. "Another smashing bit of role-playing."

"It is *not* role-playing. She may be the only one who isn't playing roles, whose passion for the world outside our doors is genuine, anyone stuck in this pantry would welcome it."

"Someday I'm going to let you have it, Paula," Nicolas burst out. "Your way of manipulating us at long distance with three-thousand-mile-long strings . . ."

"Nicolas," Nada suggested, "why don't you return to your recent, more charming self."

"Have you thought of anyone or anything in the past seven years beyond improving your standing with Joseph Papp?"

"Quiet, Nicolas," Nada said. "Paula's been so marvelously well."

"Your way of shaping us like putty while doling out a phone call twice a week . . ."

"Who's doing the putty-shaping? Who thought of making up this loony family in the first place?"

"Stop it you two," Julian said. "You're carrying on as if you were still fifteen."

"This conversation has no style," Nada said. "It's rather rude, opening yourselves up like that."

* * *

THEY MANAGED TO SIT DOWN TO DINNER. NO ONE IN THE family had ever given much thought to drinking. But tonight Nicolas had opened some Pouilly-Fuissé to celebrate Georgia's impending return, and Paula was having a go at it.

"So there was an accident," she said. "It could have happened just as easily at Park Avenue and 60th Street, or on African Square in the heart of needle park. It's the skating rather than the neighborhood that's dangerous."

"Has it occurred to you that the only nights she doesn't go skating into Hell's Kitchen are the nights you're home?" Nicolas burst out again. "Don't you think she could use a role model once in a while?"

"The term role model should be restricted to the names of domestic pets."

"So should most of the psycho-babble you and Nada go touting, authenticity, supportive, search."

"What she's saying is who's going to pull the stops on the family junk, who's going to be the first to freak out of their role?"

"And who can go through life without roles?" Nada asked. "It's the essence of civilization, we'd be naked worms without them."

"You talk like my own poor dotty mother, Nada, and you're the one most at fault in this mess. You're the one who eggs Georgia on . . ."

"I have my reasons. Our little world is extremely withdrawn, I've contributed to its withdrawal."

"What a team the two of you make, one manipulating at long distance . . ."

"I've made a vow to teach this child that nothing is frightening or impure or impossible," Nada said. "I want her to . . . transcend the human condition."

"And so you babble nonsense about women being trampled by horses . . ."

"Nonsense! Women's struggle!"

"That's not the point, Nada dear. You only encourage Georgia's street act, you tell us it's part of her libidinal development . . ."

"Because if we exercise our repressive functions she might turn to something graver than the streets," Nada spoke firmly.

"Heavier stuff," Julian suddenly agreed. "We're risking misogyny, Nicolas, we'd never carry on like this if she were a boy, we're acting like patriarchs."

THIS FAMILY EXHAUSTS ME, PAULA THOUGHT, GET ME out of here. Maybe I'm only suited to live alone. Maybe I should take Georgia with me. Or she can stay with them for a while, I'll join her next year when she's in college.

Perhaps I should go back to college along with Georgia, I never had time to learn much of anything, I went straight from the loony bin to Julian's arms. I could major in social anthropology.

She looked out of the window. It was the most beautiful evening imaginable, and her daughter was coming home. The sky had been so tenderly blue it seemed that the day would never let it go. And now the night had gently laid its cheek upon the world.

"Look at those Magritte clouds up there," Nada was saying.

"I just fear that Georgia's tension states might be very high when she gets home," Julian spoke.

"No one's noticing what I did to the shad tonight," Nicolas complained. "I rescued it from ennui with a sorrel sauce."

MEN BORE ME, PAULA THOUGHT, LET ME OUT OF THIS hothouse. Are men ever holed in these days, are they ever stuck on their doodads, their Cuisinarts, their soufflés, their sensitivities, their art collections, protecting home like little sergeants, holed up as in a state of siege.

Perhaps a convent, she thought. A plain quiet room with pale blue curtains and no recriminations ever, not a guilt in sight.

Or the Moroccan desert. A small French hotel on the edge of the Sahara where I could read all day and keep a journal. No one to see save Berbers on the horizon, leading their camels to a new settlement. The desert, oh boy.

Most people in my trade remain a little daffy. I've never been good in crises or confrontations, maybe that's why I feel like splitting, I'm a selfish childish woman, I don't want to fall apart again.

"NEXT THING WE KNOW YOU'LL BE GOING FOR *King Lear* in drag," Julian was saying to Paula.

"Nicolas, will you understand that rebellion is the only way to sanity?" Nada was saying to Nicolas.

"Oh, I understand that very well."

THAT NICOLAS! PAULA THOUGHT. THE WAY HE CAN IN-sinuate himself into a family, it's brilliant. Nicolas was almost too thin these days, Nicolas had become very attractive. She'd lost interest in sex some years back—fairly early in life, like most people in her mother's world—but tonight she sensed again the seduction of Nicolas' broad lean back, that handsome blond head with the cleft chin.

We've taken the opposite ways out. He's kicked his mother's world in the ass and then picked up and stuck bits of it all over his psyche, only way he could keep whole. I've kicked *Best* clean and started all over again.

Well, maybe that's wrong, she corrected. Have I really kicked it. What's my recent life been but another scramble for approval, success. First step to sanity, bucking Mom's world. Step two, picking up its choice bits. If I don't watch out I might become just like the women who bullied me around, victim takes on the mask of the oppressor.

She suddenly realized that for years she'd had no one to whom she could speak the truth; no friend to whom she could admit how lonely and frightened she'd been on the road, how lonely and hassled she'd felt at home; that having no one to speak to she might become very dishonest with herself.

Well perhaps next year she could start talking out such things to her daughter, that was the loveliest and only hope in sight.

This family drives me up the wall, Paula thought. But I'm going to stay with it because any family would drive me nuts. And this one is mine. And unless we're saints or monsters there truly isn't that much else.

THE BEST

G EORGIA WAS WAITING TO HEAR FROM RADCLIFFE. Julian had begun another book. I was finishing my Hamlet run. And on a beautiful autumn evening in Manhattan Nicolas finally opened his own restaurant. He had decided to call it The Best, in honor of our mothers.

Babs had had another stroke and lay immobilized, almost silent at the rest home. So Nicolas called his venture after what had been her life, thinking it would have pleased her. We all pooled our funds to invest in the restaurant.

It was in South Soho, in a turn-of-the-century building that had once been a dress factory. There were to be only twelve tables, so the setting had to be all the more precisely planned. Nicolas had sought Mother's advice for his decor.

"I want it to keep its integrity as an American landmark, to be *itself* . . ."

"You're on the right track," Nada said.

"No fake Braques or photos of Mont Saint-Michel cluttering up the walls, perhaps just one Victorian mirror. What color do you suggest for the dining room, Nada dear?"

236

"I'd say a pale apricot," Mother said, "and keep the rest very stark."

So stark and apricot it was. Nicolas also settled on walnut chairs of Queen Anne style, thick, old-fashioned white linens, Victorian brass chandeliers for his lighting. A week before the official opening Nicolas had a dress rehearsal and held a family dinner at The Best in honor of two family birthdays—Mother's seventy-ninth, Georgia's seventeenth. While we sipped wine and admired Nicolas' decor, Georgia carefully studied the menu, frowning. Oh, God, I thought, there she goes, into one of her forays, the way I never dared to. Off she went.

"Your prices sure aren't understated, Uncle Nick. Twenty-one dollars for a piece of duck, eleven seventy-five for an hors d'oeuvre of quail eggs with nasturtium leaves and shiitaki mushrooms . . ."

"Don't fuss, sweetheart," Julian said. "It's still quite moderate compared to other gastronomic landmarks."

"Twenty-four fifty for sweetbreads with a crazy pear sauce," Georgia continued. "This menu makes me want to do public health in Nicaragua!"

"You are *not* going to Nicaragua," Nicolas said. "They've hung people for wet dreams in Nicaragua."

"I personally don't see *one* banality on the menu," Nada said, pretending the argument was over. "That's admirable."

"All I see for starters is nonsense like snails in garlic cream and scallops in cranberry sauce," Georgia persisted. "Any chance of a baked potato?"

"I've put together a special vegetarian meal for you," Nicolas said. "Cream of endive soup and a fiddle fern omelet."

"That's just fine," Georgia said. She must have caught a glance in her father's eyes. It may have been confusing to be brought up by four people. Her grandmother stood for memory, civility, tradition. I guess I was now stressing boldness, aggression. Julian was still hung up on tact. Nicolas just wanted us all to be happy, or so he said. At times Georgia had trouble keeping it all together.

"That's terribly thoughtful of you, Uncle Nick," she corrected herself. "Thanks for showing me the jerk I was in the past, and the nerd I'll be in the future. I can't wait to hear what everyone is going to have."

Georgia's critique was the only discord in a splendid evening. The dessert, in honor of Mother's and Georgia's birthdays, was a frozen Petite Sirah soufflé for which Nicolas asked every member of the family to find a metaphor.

"It's like Madame de Sévigné's breast," Nada said.

"Like supping on an angel's eyelid," Julian said.

"Like having an orgasm with a swan," Georgia said.

"Really, Georgia!" Mother exclaimed. She could still pretend to be very Victorian.

But Georgia didn't wince. She seemed to realize that Mother had helped to keep the family together by her keen sense of drama, which had to do with seducing us into listening to certain things at certain times.

"WHAT'S THE BEST TONIGHT?" BARBARA WALTERS ASKED a few weeks later at the nine-fifteen sitting of Nicolas' restaurant.

"I'd say the shad roe with rhubarb and leeks, and to start with, you might consider the lobster steamed in tea and cinnamon, Malaysian style. As a special tonight we also have calves' liver marinated in Maine cider . . ."

It was an evening off from my Hamlet. I was sitting at a corner table alone to see how Nicolas was getting on, pretending I was one of the food editors who were flocking to The Best to do their reviews. He seemed very pleased as he glanced about the room, waiting for the Walters party to put in their orders. In the past few weeks Lauren Bacall,

Walter Cronkite, Calvin Klein had already made an appearance. Barbra Streisand and John Irving had reserved tables for the weekend.

"Your veal is angelic!" a client called out as Nicolas passed one of the tables. "We love the chiaroscuro of the brains in fennel sauce!"

"I tried to make it epigrammatic," Nicolas said modestly. "It's a complication that works."

At another table a man and a woman were arguing about the state of gastronomy while waiting for two late guests.

"*Nouvelle* is one of the *genuine* trends of the future, it's to cuisine what Saint-Laurent is to couture . . ."

"Well I miss the Nantuas, the brioche doughs, the *sustenance* of the *ancienne* style," the dissenter said. He had a large, florid face and was sipping his second Bellini. "At least Hollins has the vision to include cassoulet and pot roast in his menu. Out with the itsy-bitsy vegetable abortions, they aren't going to sell through another season."

"You're missing the whole mystique: in for keeps, health!" The woman's black hair was cut into short zigzags and she kept a notebook by her plate.

"I'm all for freshness," the dissenter persisted, as they began to sample one of Nicolas' soups, "but the trout over there looks as if it had passed out right on the plate. And that grilled Long Island goat cheese smells like melted crayon."

"Your parsley soup transcends itself!" he called out to Nicolas. "Truly verdant! What aura!"

"Edible jade!" his colleague agreed. "Adele!" she exclaimed as one missing member of the party appeared at the door. "Where have you been for the last hour?"

"I am . . . just back . . . from L.A.!" the late guest announced slowly. She was a plump blond with a pale masklike face who had swept a fold of her black shawl dramatically over her shoulder, like a toreador. "Do you realize what happened yesterday in L.A.?"

"Calm down and order a drink," the *ancienne* fan grumbled.

"But you don't understand what happened!" the blond continued, still standing by the table. "Wolfgang Puck . . . has saved us! Our dear Los Angeles is saved!"

"Make yourself clear, Adele."

"Wolfgang Puck! *The* chef of our generation!" The traveler raised her arm in an oracular gesture. "Puck opened a new restaurant on Wilshire Boulevard last night . . . it is . . . sheer genius! The flair! The surprises!"

"How does he pull it off?"

"Is it the sauces?"

"Sauces!" the blond laughed derisively. "Out, out months ago! It's all in the grilling! Puck's variety of perfumed woods—grapevine, mesquite, peach! Pigeon breast and figs on a grill of apricot wood . . . pure charisma!"

"Served with what?" one of her friends inquired, scribbling.

"Guess! What would *you* do with chestnuts?"

"Stone Puck with them," the man grumbled.

"Chestnut gnocchi!" the blond exclaimed. "Wolfgang Puck! A boy of twenty-six. . . . The irony, the suspense he creates, the intermezzos of aquavit sherbet! What theater!"

NICOLAS WAS LEANING AGAINST THE WALL BY MY TABLE.

"Dear God, I think they're pros. I hope they make it back to New York. I hope they make it to one of my main courses."

"Are you sure you want to stay in this racket?" I asked him. "It sounds awfully familiar."

The blond had sat down and was swigging at a Tintoretto. "L.A.," she added, her voice trembling. "Nothing to eat for years beyond the limp pasta at Orsini's, the walking beef at the Wilshire . . . and now! My hometown . . . a gastronomic capital . . ."

"Basil!" the three diners exclaimed as a tall man with Colonel Blimp mustaches walked toward them from the door. "We're waiting! What's new abroad this week?"

"Nouvelle pauvre!" Basil lamented as he took off his cape. "Sweeping new fad for all manner of beans and legumes, rather odious. A Guided Missile, please," he waved to the waiter.

"Guided Missile," his companions scribbled in their little notebooks.

"Kumquat juice and Pernod," Basil said wearily, "no one's taking anything else in London. Is it the sign of a renaissance, the last gap of decadence? Virtually everything I've tasted this month is *round,* even the carré d'agneau at Lasserre."

"Isn't it ghastly," the California blond agreed. "You don't know if you're eating Chinese mice or the beads of an African necklace. At least at Wolfgang's . . ."

"And when will your compatriots cease to wear their pajamas out to supper," Basil interrupted. "This spot looks like the Who's Who of Who Hasn't. Good heavens, here comes one of your talkative American waiters. He'll tell us his social security number and his sexual preferences."

"Wait and see how I've trained the staff," Nicolas whispered.

"Good evening," said the young headwaiter of The Best. "As a special tonight we have roast pork."

"That does *not* give me a frisson," the brunette said.

"Moral Majority cuisine," the blond said. "Could be a trend."

"Original chap, that Hollins," the Londoner admitted.

"Basil!" the blond said. "How many stars did you give Chrysanthème?"

"Three. I was sticking to two over the gâteau de crabe, but I capitulated to his kidney beans with caviar sauce."

"Kidney beans and caviar! Now that is elegant!"

"Treat cheapies as if they're jewels, and precious stuff as if it's nothing. Very *Chanel* food."

"OH SHIT," NICOLAS SAID.

"SIMPLICITY, *simplicity* IS THE ONLY THING THAT'S REALLY happening," the dark-haired woman was saying.

"The newest trend is that there's no trend at all. Except for thousands more restaurants, right?"

"Ri-i-i-i-i—ight," the table agreed.

"Entertaining at home! What a monstrous thought!" the Londoner remarked.

"Haven't done it in a decade."

"Even if your flat does have room for a dining table, who has a family to sit around it anymore?"

"I understand that they still entertain at home in some regions of southwestern Texas."

"Only the kind of Fort Worth hostesses who buy the crowns of Nicholas and Alexandra at auction and use them as centerpieces for the buffets."

"A restaurant says everything about who you are these days," the *ancienne* fan said. "Show me where you eat, I'll tell you who you are. This place of Hollins' interests me. Bread so deftly herbed. Consummate eclecticism. Handsome young Wall Street crowd, minimum of punky Eurotwerps."

The waiter was walking back toward the four diners, who had begun to jot down items of Nicolas' menu into their notebooks. "Got to get this into my last October issue," one of them said. "I'm going to go for his lobster steamed in tea and cinnamon. You know so instantly whether a new chef will sell. You take a bite and it's history."

A FEW WEEKS AFTER THE FIRST TITI BARATON REVIEW came out (two stars, she was waiting for more consistent maturity in Nicolas' desserts before she gave him three) *Manhattan* magazine asked Nicolas for an interview. I decided I'd better be there, otherwise Nicolas might get outrageous again. The restaurant editor of *Manhattan* was tweedy and spectacled and had a doctorate from Columbia in Comparative Literature. He wanted to talk about psychosocial factors in the characters of the best chefs.

"You need inner tension, secretiveness, you need to get approval in a very immediate way," Nicolas said, sitting at his desk at The Best. "Many chefs have these drives because of some frustrated need for parental love. Yet paradoxically cooking tests your adulthood, it's a vocation for obsessed, highly motivated people, you're there from eight A.M. to midnight, a sixteen-hour stretch, a life in which there's very little time for sex . . ."

"That's all sublimated, since cooking is about seduction," I interjected.

Nicolas gave me an annoyed glance, I guess we were still trying to upstage each other. "It's really about entertainment," he said, "and entertainment is the only true necessity of life . . . *'L'inutile, ce luxe nécessaire,'* as Baudelaire put it."

He was leaning against the icebox of his kitchen, profiled for *Manhattan's* photographer, smoking out of a long black cigarette holder, much the way Babs or Nada had posed when they gave interviews. "We're rebelling against French culinary imperialism, ethnic pride is something that can't be curbed, can only spiral upward, so we're light years ahead of Lutèce or Grenouille . . ."

"We don't like Paris," I interrupted to soften Nicolas' tone.

"Oh boy do we ever hate Paris," Nicolas repeated.

"We were taken a lot to Paris as children," I explained.

"We sat through many a horror show," Nicolas said. "Getting rid of Paris is just one way of shedding the past. You want to grow up, you have to kill your mother first."

"He means that metaphorically." I always talked very slowly when I wanted to curb Nicolas' histrionics. "He means you have to reject all parental values and evolve your own."

"Maybe I mean it more tangibly than that," Nicolas said. *"Maman flambée* on a bed of sorrel." He'd teased me that way since we were twelve.

"Let's have some of our house wine," I suggested. "It's a Gewürztraminer from Litchfield County, Connecticut."

"Very substantial bouquet," the restaurant editor said.

I raised my glass. "What shall we drink to, Nicolas darling?"

"Let's drink 'To hell with Paris!' "

"To hell with Paris!" We all drank.

BABS DIED FAIRLY PEACEFULLY AFTER A FINAL STROKE, A few months after the restaurant had opened. Nicolas attended his mother's last hours. He kept his ear very close to her face to catch some last wish, some last saying. For some reason he couldn't define, he put a lot of importance on hearing her last words.

He thought that Babs' last words were "This is bad copy," but he wasn't sure. Her voice had been very slurred for months.

He came home after dinner, when it was all over. Julian was upstairs typing out notes on Saint Thérèse. Mother and I were waiting for Nicolas in the living room. "What did she say?" Mother wanted to know.

"I think she said 'This is bad copy,' " Nicolas reported. "But I'm not totally sure."

"Sounds right to me," Nada said.

THE FUNERAL WAS STRICTLY A FAMILY AFFAIR. NADA didn't remember the names of any of the people who had worked at *Best* with Babs. Or else she pretended not to remember, it was always hard to tell. Babs had given her life to the magazine and had made few friends outside of it. And since her friends in Paris and New York couture had abandoned her soon after *Best* folded there was no one to invite. Nada offered to go to the cemetery, but the family thought it too tiring and she did not insist. As they left the house Nada waved to them from her chair by the window; she'd given Georgia something to say at the grave site.

Julian was still a priest, officially, and had chosen a short appropriate rite. It was late fall, the sky was overcast and raw.

During Julian's brief service, members of the family each had different recollections of Babs. Nicolas remembered a time when he was eight years old, they were on the way to Gstaad to photograph skiwear and had stopped off in Vienna. "This city will teach you," Babs said, "to keep your demands for ravishment very high."

Julian recalled the day Babs had first taken him to La Grenouille to look him over, right after he and Paula had announced their engagement. "I've always been too hectically busy to think about God," she said. "God is so vague."

"I am a stranger with thee, and a sojourner," Julian was reading from his Book of Common Prayer, as he had read for Uncle Vincent. He was not sure whether Babs had been brought up in a Christian church and he didn't care, the service was intended for the happiness of Nicolas, who had asked for it.

"Edgar Allan Poe! 'Style is a symptom of our craving for the ideal,' " Paula recalled Babs saying to the baron on a Long Island afternoon. "Style, not sincerity, is the essential." There was some sense in that, Paula mused. She looked at Julian, his strong, grave face outlined against the November sky. It was one of those mornings when she loved him more than anyone else in the world along with Georgia and Nada. However, these feelings wavered a great deal. Nicolas had grown so gracious and powerful lately, so winsome, that on certain days she loved Nicolas equally, and wondered what the future would bring.

"Why not just decide to remain alluring forever," Nicolas remembered Babs saying. "Success is the only aphrodisiac." "In the end, we all get the waists we deserve."

"Saint-Laurent!" (Babs the year Nicolas went into the Peace Corps.) "The democracy of Yves! Anyone can wear his clothes, women in the street, people in Florida."

Everyone wondered why Julian had smiled throughout part of the service. They thought it was because he had finally started another book, but he was smiling for a different reason. He was recalling that when they were much younger, Paula and Nicolas had talked about *Best* as if there was much evil and corruption in it. The first time he'd heard them say that, Julian had laughed a great deal and said how can *Best* be evil, it's about dressing up dolly, it's only about kindergarten, there's not much evil in kindergarten.

"Seduction is the very point of life," Babs used to write in her fashion pages, Paula recalled. "Oversize is in," she'd exclaimed, as a way of approving Paula's maternity clothes, "clearly, it's a trend." Paula looked with pride at her daughter, who stood impassive at the grave site, holding a yellow rose. Contentious, fierce, a crusader. Always confronting. Perhaps even charmless. . . . She was a dream.

Paula and Nicolas, Julian was thinking back, had disliked the way he'd rubbed against the *Best* world, he was the one who'd dragged them home, reconciled them to their mothers and to each other. Doctors, statesmen, priests who use their power wrongly—that's where the genuine evil is, Julian had told them. Evil abides in places of true power, as it would have lurked in him if he'd remained in the ministry, miserable, inept. He'd come to *Best* exhausted, drained by years of scruples, self-scouring, dread. Watching its ephemeral spectacles he'd felt like an exhausted coal miner relaxing at some fabulous movie about Monte Carlo. Then after its glamour wore off *Best* simply became part of that fine unspiritual dust which is the human condition— as tedious and perilous and honorable and potentially beautiful as the drab parish he'd fled from as a child priest.

"For man walketh in a vain shadow," Julian read from the Book of Common Prayer, "and disquieteth himself in vain."

Paula had brought a bunch of yellow roses. They'd always been Babs' favorite flower. As the grave digger started to cover the coffin, Paula decided to place some of the flowers under the ground, unseen. She threw them in one by one. The family watched brown earth descend on the fresh yellow petals. As the last spadefuls were put in, young Georgia spoke. Her grandmother had taught her a Latin phrase to say at the grave site. She'd always thought that Latin was irrelevant, but she abided by her grandmother's wish.

"*Sic transit gloria mundi,*" she spoke for Nada.

"Death," Nicolas whispered.

"Needs pearls," Paula said.

About the Author

Francine du Plessix Gray is the distinguished author of WORLD WITHOUT END, LOVERS AND TYRANTS, DIVINE DISOBEDIENCE, and HAWAII: THE SUGAR-COATED FORTRESS. Her work has appeared in *The New Yorker*, *The New York Times Magazine*, *Vanity Fair*, *The New York Review of Books*, and other publications. Ms. Gray is most recently winner of a 1984 National Magazine Award for her two pieces on Klaus Barbie in *Vanity Fair*.